1 2 3 4 5 6 7 8 9 10

OAKBRIDGE
K27923
ISBN 9781838053598 (paperback)
ISBN 9781739549602 (eBook)
A CIP catalogue record for this book is available from the British Library

Black, Peter Jay
Murder on the Ocean Odyssey / Peter Jay Black

London

RUTH MORGAN INVESTIGATES...

MURDER
on the Ocean
Odyssey

PETER JAY BLACK

1

A mile up the coastline from England's third southernmost town, on the west side of the country, lies the inconsequential seaside village of Bonmouth.

It's sandwiched between the only two hills in the British Isles famous for not being adorned by ruined castles, nor the remains of Iron Age forts, nor for having anyone significant dying on them in spectacular fashion.

Now, on this particularly overcast morning—even by Bonmouth standards, with drizzle so fine the locals described it as the type that *soaks yer through to the bone and keeps goin' till yer dead*—an American-sized motorhome, far too grand in scale for the dainty British roads, wound its way along narrow lanes.

Behind the wheel sat Ruth Morgan, a kind-faced woman in her mid-sixties, dressed all in black. She winced as low-hanging branches clawed at the motorhome's roof and scraped along its sides, while its brakes screeched at every corner, attracting disapproving scowls from the residents.

"I really should get those seen to." Ruth waved at a man with a stoop and gnarled features as she trundled past.

He gawped back at her and almost toppled over. In fact, if it hadn't been for his chunky shoes with nonslip soles and his sturdy four-wheel rollator, he would have.

Ruth yanked the steering wheel hard and somehow missed a postbox, but subsequently struggled to navigate the next corner without decimating a historic stone wall and a well-established oak tree that looked like it predated the village.

However, whether by luck or actual driving prowess, Ruth guided the gigantic land yacht to the seafront—a compact quay of old buildings battered by salt and wind, wooden fishing boats in various states of disrepair, and walkways littered with piles of broken nets and crab pots.

She squeezed into the only spot large enough to accommodate the motorhome's bulk—a raised concrete platform once used to launch ships—and the engine came to a rattling stop.

Wasting no time, Greg Shaw, Ruth's grandson, a gangly lad in his late teens, tumbled down the steps behind her and threw open the door. No sooner had his trainer-clad feet touched terra firma than he clapped a hand over his mouth.

His head snapped from left to right.

Spotting somewhere he must have deemed suitable for his immediate requirements, Greg hurried to the edge of the nearest dock, dropped to his knees, and let go of his lunch.

"Oh, come on." Ruth unbuckled her seat belt, snatched a black coat from a hook, and climbed from the motorhome. "My driving is not that bad, Greg. You're being absurd."

Greg heaved.

"Well, granted, maybe I was a little aggressive on a few of those last corners, but how was I to know the roads would be so narrow and winding?" Ruth sniffed salty air and then squinted up at the grey sky as she pulled on a matching pink woollen hat, scarf, and gloves. "Hmm." She shielded her face from the worst of the drizzle. "Perhaps I should fetch an umbrella. What do you think, Greg? Umbrella?"

"Won't do yer no good 'ere." A man with a bushy grey beard stained yellow around the mouth leaned against a wall, puffing on a pipe held together with duct tape. He wore wellies and a tattered fisherman's coat. "On account of the wind, yer see?"

Ruth lowered her hand and glanced about. "Wind?"

Although overcast and damp, the air seemed quite still.

"It's sudden like," the man said in a sage tone. "It senses yer about to fetch an umbrella and then . . . *whoosh*. Strikes. No warning." He nodded. "My advice: don't bother. Pointless, see?" He resumed puffing on his pipe and studied her.

"Right." Ruth smiled. "Thank you." Her teenage travelling companion got to his feet, wobbled, and then bent over as if he was going to be sick again. "All better now?" Ruth asked him.

Greg muttered something suspiciously like several swear words strung together in a new and inventive way, and then he regained his senses and straightened for a second time.

"Good, good." Ruth glanced about and rubbed her gloved hands together. "I assume this is the right place, Greg?"

"It is," Pipe Man replied.

Ruth inclined her head at him.

He plucked the pipe from his mouth and used its stem to point across the road to a brown brick building with pillars, tall windows, and an archway over a set of double doors. "The others are huddled in there."

Greg joined Ruth at the motorhome. "Others?" He wiped his mouth with the back of his hand.

"You're 'ere fer the *Odyssey*, right?"

"We are," Ruth said. "How very astute of you."

"If yer mean I'm observant," Pipe Man said, "then it don't take much of a genius to spot strangers, especially when they arrive in one of them things." He eyed the motorhome with disgust.

"Indeed." Ruth cleared her throat.

"Better wait 'ere." The man slipped his smouldering pipe into his coat pocket and made his way toward the building.

Greg leaned in to Ruth. "I've got a bad feeling about this, Grandma. I think we should turn around and get out of here."

"Not likely," Ruth said. "These people have paid me three times my normal rate. I want to know how come, and why they've gone to all the trouble to hire me specifically."

For the last six years, Ruth had travelled the country as a freelance food consultant, advising restaurants, hotels, cafes, and bistros on their recipes, menu engineering, health and safety, nutrition, and general culinary standards.

However, she had to admit, there were plenty of other consultants equally—if not more—qualified. Ruth suspected nothing made her stand out over any of them.

On top of her overwhelming curiosity was the fact that if she made a good impression, a glowing recommendation from these people would look fantastic on her résumé.

Greg shuffled from foot to foot. "I still say we shouldn't be here. Something feels off."

"You'll have my back," Ruth said. "You spot anything you don't like, we'll leave." Even though he was being paranoid —after all, Ruth was a food consultant, not a spy—the high level of pay and the demand for secrecy *was* rather odd.

Greg looked as though he was about to argue some more when the doors to the brown brick building opened and five people wheeling suitcases and carrying overnight bags trudged out.

A man an inch or two over six feet led the group. He appeared to be in his early seventies, white hair slicked back, his dimpled chin held high, a military bearing.

"Ex-army," Ruth murmured to herself. "Major, I shouldn't wonder." It was the way he marched with heel-to-toe precision, back straight and chest puffed out as if to inflate his self-importance.

The other four were a little harder to gauge but far from impossible for Ruth to figure. Well, at least she'd have a good stab at a guess. She couldn't help herself.

Second out the door was a striking woman with wavy red hair past her shoulders, dressed in a long dark blue overcoat and high heels, early forties, sharp cheekbones. *A model?*

A much younger woman tottered after her, twenties, black hair cut into a messy pixie crop, wearing a puffy white jacket and bleached jeans. She reminded Ruth of one of those internet influencers Greg so often talked about with such reverence and exuberance. Each time it came round to that topic of conversation, Greg's anecdotes sailed over Ruth's head. At least she pretended they did. Some of it went in by pure chance and osmosis, unfortunately.

Next strode out a well-groomed man with a dark complexion; he wore a fine tailored suit with a black polo-neck, or turtleneck as the Americans called them. Ruth found it trickier to estimate his age, but she placed him at around mid to late thirties. A gentleman who took care of himself. Pride in his appearance. *A lawyer?*

After him stumbled a guy in his late forties or early fifties, wearing thick-rimmed glasses, long messy brown hair to his hunched shoulders, bushy salt-and-pepper beard.

He struggled with his oversized suitcase, and despite the mild temperature, his forehead glistened with sweat, which mingled with the drizzle and affixed strands of hair to his skin.

A computer geek? Ruth guessed. *Programmer?* Someone not used to being outdoors, with an acquired stoop from years spent in an office chair, huddled over a keyboard.

As he adjusted his grip on the suitcase, Ruth focussed on his hands: they did seem rather soft and callus-free. *Definitely a desk job,* she mused. However, Ruth couldn't get a good read on the fellow, which she found odd.

Her eyes narrowed as she concentrated, searching out what seemed off about the guy. She couldn't put her finger on it: something in the way he didn't make eye contact with anyone else.

Ruth turned to Greg to ask his opinion, but her grandson now gawped at the influencer girl with the black hair and white jacket.

"Close your mouth, darling," Ruth breathed. "You'll drown." She smiled as the others approached.

"Good afternoon, madam," Army Guy said with a tip of an imaginary cap. "You're our host, I presume?"

"I'm afraid you presume incorrectly," Ruth said. "I'm—"

"One of yer lot. This way." Pipe Man gestured. "And be quick about it. Not got all day." He traipsed past a small marina with ten forlorn boats huddled together as if frightened of the open ocean.

Greg hinged up a panel in the motorhome's side, clicked it into place, and removed a couple of prepacked, bulging suitcases.

Ruth went inside for a moment, fetched her handbag, and carefully lifted a plain oak box—sixteen inches wide and tall, twenty-two long—by its brass handle, from a table.

The box had slits down each side, clasps, and several grated vents.

As she turned to leave, Ruth's gaze rested on an umbrella hanging from its designated hook, but, on balance, she opted to leave it there. After all, she didn't fancy the inconvenience of having to buy a new one should the local wind decide to get all "*sudden*" on her.

As the eight of them trooped along the quay, several seagulls sat on a low wall, appearing as downcast as the weather.

Ruth looked askance at her grandson. "They have wheels."

"Huh?"

"Those suitcases." Ruth adjusted her grip on the oak box. "They do have wheels, you know? Extendable handles too. They're utterly twenty-first century. If you used them, it would save you all that huffing and puffing."

"Oh, right." Greg continued waddling along with the cases, and with every step his arms seemed to get an inch longer.

Ruth chuckled. Despite his lack of common sense, Greg was a bright lad and had secured both archaeology and history placements at Oxford University. He was now on a gap year, taking the opportunity to travel the country with his dear old grandmother and gather some firsthand experience with their country's history.

And, Ruth mused, true to his word, Greg had been studying hard during their time, all to give him a head start.

The merry band of misfits reached the end of the quay, rounded a run-down RNLI building with half its roof missing and boarded-up windows, and then trooped along a jetty.

At the end, they stopped alongside a twenty-eight-foot-long modern motorboat out of place compared to its surroundings. It had a sleek, aerodynamic hull made of impossible angles and advanced mathematics.

Greg moaned. "We don't have to go on that, do we?"

"How else do you expect us to get there?" Ruth asked. "Eat some ginger."

"Don't have any left."

Ruth's eyebrows lifted. "You got through the entire jar?"

A young deckhand, dressed all in white, sprang from nowhere and saluted.

Pipe Man gestured to a gangplank that led to the aft deck of the futuristic taxi boat. "All aboard."

Greg's eyes widened. "You're the captain of this?"

"Fer now." A sneer cracked Pipe Man's dry lips, and he lowered his voice. "If it sinks, though, don't expect me to go down with it. I'll be the first one to jump ship and swim ashore."

Influencer Girl stumbled along the gangplank with her suitcase and asked in a shaky voice, "Do we get life jackets?"

Pipe Man eyed her puffy coat. "Don't look like yer need one, luv."

She glared at him, almost tripped over her own chunky shoes, but somehow got the suitcase and herself aboard with no serious drama or incidents. The deckhand helped stow her case, and then the other guests followed.

Ruth made a mental note to change Pipe Man's name to *Captain Pipe* from now on. It rolled off the mental tongue better.

As soon as everyone was aboard and seated, Ruth wedged the oak box safely between her feet and placed her handbag by her side.

Greg gave her an uneasy look.

Or it could have been a queasy look, she wasn't sure.

Maybe a bit of both.

He had strategically placed himself opposite the model and the influencer girl. *Where else would he be?* He kept trying to make eye contact and hit them with one of his patented crooked smiles, but they paid him no mind.

"There, there." Ruth patted his leg. "This is a three-day excursion. You'll have plenty more chances to charm them with your dry wit and winning personality."

Greg mumbled something about dying alone.

A slender young man with slicked-back hair stepped from the cabin. He wore a deep-blue suit, and a pair of glistening gold cuff links, each engraved with the letters *DD*.

Ruth squinted at his name tag, which simply read:

SHIP MANAGER

The ship manager held a clipboard and studied a list. "We appear to have one extra." He looked over at Greg. "Who are you?"

"He's with me," Ruth said. "My assistant."

"I'm sorry," the ship manager said, "but we were very clear in our correspondence—only *your* services are required. No one else. That's vitally important."

Ruth blinked at him. "We go everywhere together. Peas in a pod."

Greg nudged her. "Grandma."

"Grandma?" Captain Pipe's bushy eyebrows lifted to his cap. "I thought he was yer boyfriend."

This resulted in a few stifled laughs, and Greg's cheeks flushed scarlet.

"Can you make an exception?" Ruth asked the ship manager. "He's no bother." She couldn't believe how strict they were being over something so trivial.

The ship manager shook his head.

Greg looked over at the model and then at the influencer girl, but still neither paid him any attention. In fact, the influencer now only had eyes for the ship manager. "Come on," Greg murmured to Ruth, and stood. "Let's get out of here." He grabbed his suitcase and headed back across the gangplank.

Ruth went to follow but stopped short. She had to know why they'd chosen her for this job. *Did someone recommend my services? If so, who? And why are they paying me three times my standard rate? Why all the secrecy?* These questions gnawed at her insides.

When he reached the jetty, Greg turned back.

Ruth didn't move.

Perhaps she could argue with the owner of the ship once she was aboard and convince them to let Greg come too.

"This is ridiculous." The model had an American accent. "Are you leaving or not? You're holding everyone up."

"If it 'elps any, my grandson Steven can keep 'im company when he returns to Bonmouth." Captain Pipe waved toward the deckhand.

Ruth let out a slow breath and gave Greg an apologetic look. "It's only a few days." Despite her words, she tried to also convey to him that she wouldn't give up so easily. The fight wasn't over.

He stared at her for several seconds, and then his shoulders slumped, and he traipsed off with his suitcase, head bowed.

At the sad sight of her forlorn grandson walking away, Ruth called after him. "There's plenty of food in the motorhome. See if someone local will let you have some of their whiffy."

Greg didn't look back. "It's pronounced *Wi-Fi*, Grandma."

Despite the situation, Ruth chuckled.

The boat's engines roared to life. Steven the deckhand retracted the gangplank, untied the ropes fore and aft, and then leapt back onto the taxi boat like a sure-footed mountain goat. A second later they were off: heading across the harbour at an increasing rate of knots.

Ruth sighed.

"The young lad will be a'right, Mrs Morgan," Captain Pipe said from the wheel. "Steven can take 'im clubbing. He'll enjoy that."

Ruth cringed at the imagined sight of her long-limbed grandson laying down some awkward shapes on a dance floor.

She yanked off her scarf and unbuttoned her coat to reveal a black blouse and a silver cat pendant on a fine chain.

Influencer girl stared at it for a second, and then looked away.

Ruth's attention moved to the model. She fingered a set of emerald green worry beads. Ruth nodded to them. "Frightened of boats?"

The model offered her half a smile in return. "Frightened of drowning."

"Understandable."

"I like your outfit," the model said. "It's minimalistic."

"Thank you. I'll take that as a compliment." Ruth closed her eyes and pulled in deep breaths of the sea air.

It had been almost four decades since she was last on the water rather than in it—like during one of her daily bubble baths or that time she'd fallen into her sister's ornamental koi pond—and it certainly had been a long while since she'd found herself on the open ocean.

Ruth had grown up loving boats because of her father's fascination with sailing. There wasn't a time during her childhood that he hadn't owned a sailboat. They'd spent most summers on the ocean, and those had been the happiest times of her life.

However, the last time she recalled being on a boat was not at sea but on the river Thames with her late husband— bike fishing, a pastime Ruth had never heard of until he'd suggested it.

It essentially involved throwing a metal hook attached to a rope into the murky waters, and then dragging it slowly back on board. They hoped to snag bicycles—and if they turned out to be stolen, then return them to their rightful owners; but if there were no identifying marks, then John would refurbish them and give the bikes away to whoever needed them.

Ruth loved it. Including the restoration part. However, most of the time they only caught rusty shopping trolleys, garden chairs, and traffic cones. On a bad day, some satisfaction came from the fact they helped clean the river, so win-win.

John had always insisted on the most unusual holidays too: camping in Madagascar; hiking across rural China; exploring temples and tombs in exotic locations. Never a dull moment, and never stuck on some Spanish beach, or at a chateau in the south of France.

Although Ruth had nothing against those types of sun-soaked holidays, not in the slightest—after all, she'd gone on a few such excursions since John's untimely death—but she missed his sense of adventure, and she longed for the excitement of those days.

2

Thirty minutes later, Bonmouth was nothing more than a vague sliver of land on the horizon behind them, and the taxi motorboat was well and truly up on the plane.

As it sped across the ocean, Army Guy dropped onto the bench, almost launching Ruth off the other end. "Weather's brightened," he said to no one in particular.

He was sharp-eyed, seeing as how the drizzle had indeed stopped, and at least some of the clouds had parted to reveal blue sky in odd patches.

Army Guy gazed at the horizon for a few seconds before leaning in to Ruth, hushed. "I say, madam, what do you know about the owner of the ship? I assume it's a company or an organization?"

"I don't, but I want to talk to them." In fact, when Ruth had asked Greg to do some of his internet sleuthing, the only records he'd uncovered were that of a firm listed in the name of Axiom. Apart from that, most filings were anonymous, and the ones that weren't had restricted employee and financial data, which wasn't uncommon for large businesses in competitive markets.

"I searched for the name of the ship," Army Guy said.

Ruth's eyebrows lifted. "What did you discover?"

"Only that it must be new. I found at least two others with the same designation, but neither seemed likely candidates." He stared out to sea and mumbled, "Damned bizarre if you ask me." He looked back at Ruth. "What do you suppose—"

She stiffened. "There it is." Ruth pointed in the direction of the bow, off the port side, as a cruise ship came into view: a white hull, sleek and as modern as the motor yacht they travelled in, eight decks high, and more than four hundred feet in length.

Army Guy gaped at it. "That is an impressive vessel."

Ten more minutes, and the name came into focus:

OCEAN ODYSSEY

The motorboat slowed and pulled alongside.

Ruth was eager to get on board and convince the owners to allow her grandson to accompany her.

The model and the influencer girl took a break from their gossiping to stare up at the ship towering high above them, with its angled hull and dark, tinted windows.

"How on earth do we get all the way up there?" Army Guy asked. "Grappling hook and climb?"

"Perhaps they'll fire us from a cannon," Ruth suggested.

However, a door in the ship's side opened, and a gangplank extended automatically to the foredeck of the motor yacht, where the teenage deckhand eagerly received it and locked it into place.

Then, single file with their suitcases, everyone shuffled

on board the *Ocean Odyssey*, with Ruth nearly last, carrying her oak box, and Captain Pipe bringing up the rear with her suitcase.

After passing through a set of doors, the group found themselves in a grand atrium that stretched the full height of the ship. Balconies ran around each deck, connected by a glass elevator and a golden spiral staircase.

Ruth set the box down.

Chairs, tables, and lush sofas filled the lower floor, giving it a comfortable feel, inviting repose and relaxation.

However, what drew all eyes was the focus of the space: a gigantic crystal sculpture, shaped like a whirlwind, forty feet tall, illuminated from within, glowing in various shades of blue, purple, and green.

Army Guy whistled. "Impressive stuff."

A row of twenty staff members were ready to greet them: porters, a chef and his kitchen workers, security personnel, plus a cleaner and a maintenance guy.

"Is this the entire crew?" the lawyer asked.

"We're currently operating with the minimum number of staff," the ship manager said. "Another team will be along shortly. Our job is to get you settled."

"Where's the owner?" Ruth asked, eager to bend their ear.

The model's Botox-infused brows struggled to pull together. "Only six guests?"

"If it turns out to be a success," the ship manager said, "then the next batch will be fifty guests, and we'll move on to full capacity after that."

The model walked over to a cylindrical aquarium filled with marine life. She leaned in and stared at an oval fish with bright orange and white vertical bands as it darted among the rocks.

"Peppermint angelfish," the ship manager said. "One of the rarest and most expensive specimens in the world."

This got the influencer girl's attention. "How expensive?"

"If you have to ask," the lawyer said, "you can't afford it." He was well spoken and a strong hint of a Yorkshire accent shone through.

"I'll go check on the bridge." Captain Pipe tipped his cap, saying, "'Ope yer all 'ave a good stay," although his tone didn't seem sincere, and he strode off.

Several porters came forward and assisted everyone with their luggage.

One of them reached for Ruth's oak box.

She picked it up and pulled away from him. "I'll take this." She offered a smile in the way of an apology.

He bowed and backed away.

Three trips in the elevator saw the rest of the group safely up to the top deck, but Ruth stayed put. When the ship manager returned for her and held open the doors, beads of sweat formed on her forehead at the mere thought of stepping into the enclosed space.

"Claustrophobia?" The ship manager motioned to the stairs. "May I escort you?"

Ruth let out a breath. "Thank you."

In fact, she wasn't claustrophobic, as people often assumed, but Ruth rarely corrected them. She had an anxiety disorder called cleithrophobia: the fear of being trapped. The smaller the space, the more intense it became.

In her mid-thirties, misfortune had forced Ruth to endure her phobia in all its horrific glory: a moment during her last year as a police officer.

She and a fellow constable received a call about a tripped alarm. They arrived at a dingy pawnshop a few minutes later. Someone had used a mechanical car jack to lift the shutter barring the front door by several inches. Shattered glass lay on the other side.

Peering underneath, a quick search with her torch disclosed a compact showroom and no sign of the perp. Ruth, being the junior officer, petite and of slight build, reluctantly volunteered to go in.

That was her first mistake.

She removed her radio, vest, and belt, and then lay on the pavement. Ruth slid under the shutter with only half an inch to spare, almost cut herself on the broken glass, and made it to the other side without injury.

The robber had smashed several display cases, leaving behind empty stands, and Ruth was about to return to the door when a dark figure leapt up from behind a counter, knife raised. Ruth scrambled back as they vaulted the counter. However, the figure dove for the gap under the door. Ruth reacted fast, grabbed their boot and pulled.

That was her second mistake.

The robber's arms flailed about, and in their panic, they grabbed the car jack, yanked it free, and the shutter dropped, sealing them in.

They were trapped.

Ruth stood her ground as the robber got to their feet and rounded on her. What Ruth wanted to do was kick the knife from the robber's hand in a feat of selfless heroism, but what she actually did was drop to the floor, press her back against the wall, and pull her knees to her chest.

This caught the robber by surprise. He was only a lad—in his late teens, shaven head—and Ruth would never forget his expression: a mixture of surprise and confusion. He asked what was wrong with her, and when Ruth explained through a clenched jaw, his face turned to pity.

Then, in a weird, surreal twist of fate, the kid robber

spent the next hour keeping her calm while her colleagues and the fire brigade freed them.

After that, Ruth had put in a good word during the lad's subsequent trial, but he'd turned out to be a prolific thief and hadn't managed to avoid jail time.

That was only one of several incidents Ruth had endured in her life, all of which she'd rather forget.

On the top landing of the atrium, Ruth, the ship manager, and the other guests strode through a set of golden doors into a hexagonal room with sofas. Screens displayed relaxing images of dolphins, whales, and coral reefs.

Anyone would think they were on a submarine.

"Please, take a seat." The ship manager consulted his clipboard and then looked over at Ruth as her bottom touched a cushion. "Madam?"

She leapt up. "Yes?"

"This way." He opened a door.

Carrying the oak box, Ruth followed him down a long hallway with numbered doors while a porter wheeled her suitcase behind them.

When they reached 810, the ship manager stepped to one side of the door and indicated a panel to the right. "Place your palm to the screen and hold it there."

Ruth hesitated—tech was *not* her thing—and then did as he asked. The light above turned from red to green and then back to red.

"Hold." The ship manager removed a gold card from his pocket and pressed it to the side of the display. "Hold . . ." The light pulsed and then snapped to green again. "You can let go."

Ruth pulled her hand away, and the lock clicked.

"It's now encoded to your palm print," the ship manager

said as he pocketed the gold card.

Ruth's eyebrows lifted. "Clever."

The ship manager pushed the door open and ushered her inside.

Ruth hesitated on the threshold. "Could I have a word with the owners, please?" She still wasn't happy to have left her grandson behind.

"I'll see what I can do."

"Thank you." Ruth stepped through, and her jaw hit the floor. She'd expected a single room with a bed, TV, and, if she was very, very lucky, some strong internet so she could email Greg and check that he was okay.

What she got, however, was the biggest suite she'd ever laid eyes on. The sitting room stood thirty feet wide by twenty deep, filled with plush furnishings: an L-shaped sofa bigger than Ruth's bed back at the motorhome, an armchair that demanded immediate repose, and more scatter cushions than should legally be allowed to gather in one place.

Mounted to one wall at one end of the room, above what appeared to be a real fireplace, was a television bigger than most cinema screens, and at the opposite end of the room sat a bar. Not a mini bar but a full-sized one with a granite top and more bottles of wine than a rich alcoholic's cellar.

A basket of fruit sat on a coffee table next to a hamper of snacks and a giant bouquet.

"All this is for me?" Tears formed in Ruth's eyes as she shuffled into the suite and set down the oak box. She loved her motorhome and felt a little unfaithful gawping at all the luxury, but this was ultra-extravagance dipped in generous amounts of indulgence, topped with sprinkles of opulence.

The ship manager hit a button on the wall, and drapes retracted to reveal glass doors spanning the entire width of the room. They led to a generous balcony and a glorious panoramic view of the Atlantic Ocean beyond.

Ruth clapped a hand over her mouth, and her voice broke. "It—It's beautiful," she breathed through her fingers.

The ship manager opened a door to the right, and the porter wheeled the suitcase through the master bedroom with a modern four-poster bed and into a walk-in closet.

Ruth felt dizzy.

As the porter returned to the door, the ship manager said, "We'll serve dinner at eight."

Ruth reached into her handbag and hunted for her purse.

The ship manager held up a hand. "No need."

"Please remember to tell the owner I'd like to speak to them."

He bowed, and they left.

Ruth let out an excited squeak, threw her handbag aside, and danced around the sitting room. Then she opened another door off the bedroom to find a bathroom with a shower cubicle, toilet, and bidet, and a double sink with gold fixings. And then, as if in a dream, Ruth gazed lovingly at a—she could hardly breathe—gigantic corner bath.

Ruth punched the air with unrestrained exuberance. She danced around the sitting room again and then dropped to the sofa, lay on her back, and kicked her legs in the air.

A minute later, a little out of breath and a tad warm, she threw off her coat, scarf, and hat and sat back in the corner of the sofa, buried in scatter cushions. She grinned from ear to ear. "Merlin will love this."

Speaking of which . . .

Ruth leapt to her feet again, hurried to the door, and picked up the oak box. She carried it into the bedroom and set it on the floor by the French doors. Kneeling, Ruth undid two metal clasps and hinged the front of the box aside.

Nothing happened.

"Oh, Merlin?" she called in a singsong voice.

There came a low, raspy *meow* in reply.

Ruth peered into the box.

Merlin, her eight-year-old Burmese cat, lay curled on his handcrafted faux-fur cushion. For his comfort and safety, the customised box also included padded sides, plenty of air vents with built-in battery-driven fans, and more space than he needed—Merlin was a petite cat for his breed, standing a little shy of seven inches.

"Are you coming out of there?" Ruth asked.

Merlin opened one eye, gave her an icy stare, and then promptly closed it again.

Like most cats, Merlin had a fascination with impossibly tight spaces. However, he took it to a whole new level of obsession. Ruth always struggled to get him to leave his comfortable and familiar domain.

Merlin had started by claiming a drawer in Ruth's bedside cabinet that had been far too small for him, even by his standards. So, she had spared no expense and had this custom box made for his fussy and exacting needs.

"You want to come and explore?" Ruth slid a litter tray from the bottom of the box, set it aside, and removed bowls from a hidden compartment in the back.

She took a bottle of filtered water from her suitcase and filled one bowl, and then broke open a sachet of cat food and emptied its contents into the other.

Ruth deliberately set the bowls a couple of feet away from Merlin's box. "Come on, then. Din dins."

With obvious reluctance and an annoyed growl, he climbed out, stretched—showing off his deep chocolate coat

—and glanced around his new surroundings with disinterest. Merlin sauntered over to his bowls.

"Now, you be quiet while we're here, and no wandering off," she warned him. "Or you'll get us both in trouble." Ruth hadn't asked permission to bring a cat on board and was now certain the owner would have refused if she'd asked. A wave of guilt washed over her as she thought about Greg again. The sooner she convinced them to let him aboard, the better.

Ruth opened the French doors a crack and retrieved a mug from her suitcase—one at least four sizes bigger than a standard coffee mug, handcrafted, deep green with a gold filigree pattern—and returned to the sitting room.

She made herself tea with two tea bags, five sugars, and plenty of milk, and then dropped into an armchair. Merlin purred and hopped onto her lap.

As Ruth sipped her tea, her gaze fell on an envelope poking out the top of the fruit basket. Someone had written her name on it in fancy curly writing.

She set her mug on a large black glass coaster and opened the envelope. Inside was a card with the *Ocean Odyssey* logo embossed in silver letters across the top.

Written underneath in neat calligraphy, it read:

Dear Mrs Morgan,
We hope you enjoy your visit.
At your earliest convenience, please power on the tablet and press play to watch a personalised video message.
Forever at your service,
The Ocean Odyssey Team

Ruth frowned and looked about. "Tablet?" Her gaze fell on the glass coaster beneath her mug. She cringed—"Oops"

—and lifted her mug. Ruth examined the tablet computer, found the power button on the side, and the screen sprang to life. She propped it up in the fruit basket. Then, mug of tea back in hand, Ruth hit play and sat back.

Soft pipe music played.

White letters appeared on black:

IT'S TIME TO GET AWAY

A vibrant blue sea filled the display. The view glided over waves, soaring high until the *Ocean Odyssey* came into view.

WITH THE ONES YOU LOVE

The image changed to a handsome young couple standing on a balcony, toasting one another with champagne flutes and wistfully gazing across the ocean. Wind danced through their perfect hair as the sun set on the horizon.

A new image appeared, now inside the ship's atrium with its twisting glass sculpture.

A woman in a dark blue suit stepped into view, mousy-blonde hair tied back, her smile painted on. She spread her arms wide. "Welcome to the *Ocean Odyssey*." She interlaced her fingers. "A major overhaul and refurbishment carried out over the last few years has seen this already world-class vessel elevated to a league all its own." She strode off-screen and appeared an instant later on a balcony above.

Ruth muttered, "Magician," and sipped her bucket-sized brew.

As she walked, the woman said, "Every guest suite has been meticulously designed and furnished with comfort in mind, sparing no expense, ensuring the absolute pinnacle of comfort and luxury."

Ruth raised her mug. "Amen, sister."

Again, the image changed, and the young woman now sauntered along the upper deck of the ship, smile still in place. "With all new facilities, the *Ocean Odyssey* will leave you wanting for nothing. You're invited to experience a world-class gym . . ."

"Not likely." Ruth cleared her throat.

". . . a top-notch health spa—"

"Okay, you twisted my arm."

". . . and first-rate dining."

"That's a definite *yes* from me, dear." Ruth took a gulp of tea.

Now the young lady stood on the aft deck of the ship as it left a wide foaming wake in the ocean.

"As far as this vessel is concerned, no expense has been spared with its modern, state-of-the-art engines, and high-tech security features."

Ruth cocked an eyebrow.

"All together this makes an already wonderful ship with its timeless, elegant design, a modern powerhouse of engineering for the twenty-first century." She cupped a hand around her mouth, leaned in to the camera, and whispered, "Not to mention its lower carbon footprint, for the planet-conscious among you."

The image on the tablet vanished.

Ruth sat up. "Hey, small lady, where did you go?"

As if she'd heard Ruth's call, the woman returned, now against a plain black backdrop, and the smile had vanished. "Good afternoon, Mrs Morgan."

Startled, Ruth glanced about. "Hello?" When the lady didn't react, she let out a breath.

Definitely a recording.

"Thank you for agreeing to work with us," the woman on the tablet said. "It's an honour to have you on board. As per our correspondence, we've hired you for your unparalleled expertise and professionalism in your chosen field. We'd also like to remind you to please not discuss your line of work or any personal details with your fellow guests. We want to maintain an overarching, impartial, and independent evaluation, with no internal or external influences. First names only. Failure to maintain anonymity will result in the termination of your contract and forfeiture of the fifty percent balance payment due on completion of your work."

Ruth stared at the screen. "They're taking this really seriously." She couldn't understand why knowing people's last names and line of work mattered, not to mention the fact they'd banned Greg. *Why would he upset their evaluation?*

The woman's smile returned. "Thank you for your service. We look forward to reading your report."

The screen went black.

Ruth finished off her tea, lifted Merlin from her lap, and grabbed her phone from her handbag, ready to call Greg and make sure he hadn't eaten the cupboards bare already.

Her brow furrowed.

No signal.

Ruth hurried across the room, slid one of the French doors open, and stepped onto the balcony.

Still no bars.

She held her phone high and swung it from side to side, hoping to catch some elusive microwaves.

Nope.

She assumed they were too far from land to get a signal from there, but Greg had explained a lot of cruise ships had an at-sea provider. "Don't they have that here?" Or maybe it wasn't activated yet. Ruth hunted for internet too, but nothing came up.

She huffed and stormed back into the suite. Ruth looked about for a telephone to call for the owner, but there wasn't one of those either. "This is ridiculous."

Ruth eyed the tablet. *Does that have internet?* She screwed up her face, trying to remember her email login details, and that was when her attention moved to the time: 7:50 p.m.

Ruth gasped, almost dropped her phone, and raced off to the bedroom to get dressed for dinner.

3

Determined to talk to the ship's owners and ask for Greg's inclusion, Ruth marched into the dining room of the *Ocean Odyssey*. It spanned three floors, with various seating areas on each, including balconies, all filled with large tables and high-backed chairs. A central column, twenty feet across, dominated the middle of the space, and above that a gigantic glass dome spanned the entire room, showing the night sky, albeit a mostly cloudy one.

The ship manager stood by a cart, arranging cutlery.

Ruth hurried over to him.

He held up a hand. "I have passed on your request. Can you please wait until tomorrow?"

Ruth let out a slow breath. "I guess so." Greg would be fine, she was sure of that, but she'd feel better once he was on board.

The ship manager waved toward a sectioned-off waiting area where three of the guests mingled. Everyone save for the lawyer and the computer geek.

Soft classical music played from hidden speakers as Ruth dropped into a curved seat.

In front of them stood a table of hors d'oeuvre, a jug of water, glasses, and a vase of tulips that looked so perfect Ruth had thought they were fake. They weren't. She touched them to find out. Several times.

Ruth sampled each of the hors d'oeuvre—an impressive selection of canapés, some with crab meat, shrimp, and salmon; others with cucumber, goat cheese, and avocado—and gave them a mental star rating in order of preference. To be fair, they all tasted great, including the crudités and garlic dip.

Army Guy looked about the otherwise empty dining room. "A snifter of whiskey wouldn't go amiss." He tumbled a coin across the back of his clenched fist. It glided over each finger and disappeared into his palm, only to reappear a second later and start again. "Damn slow service, if you ask me."

"I guess being a retired major, you're used to being waited on at your gentlemen's club?" Ruth cringed inside, but she couldn't help herself—sometimes words tumbled past her lips without any prior consent.

"A major?" Army Guy bristled. "I'll have you know, madam, I'm a—" He stopped himself and waggled a finger at her. "Now, now. You almost had me there. Are you trying to get me fired?"

"Not at all," Ruth said. And that was the truth. Anyway, from what Army Guy had almost spilled, he was more likely a retired colonel.

What is a former high-ranking officer in the British army doing on this ship? A rush of excitement coursed through her. *This really is an odd situation.*

"I think it's silly we can't share personal details," the influencer said. "I mean, why does it matter if we know about each other or why we're here?"

"Those are the rules," the colonel said with a hard look, "and we must abide by them."

Ruth leaned forward and smiled at her. "I'm glad we don't know—makes us all very mysterious and intriguing, don't you think?"

"Speak for yourself," the model said before the influencer could answer, and she helped herself to an hors d'oeuvre. She gave it a tentative sniff, shuddered, and returned it to the plate. "We can share first names though. At least that's what the video said."

The influencer thrust out a hand to Ruth. "I'm Laura."

She shook it. "Ruth." Then she held her hand out to the colonel.

"I'm Thomas. You may call me Tom." Colonel Tom looked over at the model. "And you are?"

"Gabriella."

Ruth was about to ask where the computer geek and the lawyer had gotten to when the ship manager walked over to them.

"Although usually reserved for lunch," he said to the group, "we felt you'd enjoy your first dinner as a more relaxed buffet type of affair." He smiled, but it didn't reach his eyes. "It is our marvelous dining focus, after all." The ship manager motioned toward the middle of the room with a flourish.

A staff member standing at the far end pressed a button on the wall, and the central column lifted to reveal a circular serving area with a multilevel buffet carousel.

Ruth leapt to her feet in amazement.

"By jove." Colonel Tom gawped at it.

The ship manager led the guests across the dining room. He then motioned Ruth to step forward, and he demonstrated how to order.

Instead of staff serving guests, you selected what you desired from screens, and then a corresponding level of the buffet carousel would rotate, presenting your choice.

Ruth lifted a glass lid and helped herself to mixed salad and then chose other delicacies, scooping one of everything onto her plate.

The ship manager watched her stack items several inches high. "Would you care for another plate?" A hint of sarcasm underlaid his tone.

"This is fine." Ruth heaped more food onto her plate and worked her way round the carousel, sampling each dish on every level, apart from the desserts. She smacked her lips. "Don't go anywhere, I'll be seeing you later."

The computer geek arrived, head bowed, gaze averted. He worked the buffet controls with ease, his fingers a blur of movement.

Ruth frowned. *Has he been here before?*

The geek whispered something to the ship manager.

The ship manager shook his head. "Fear not, sir. No nuts in any of these selections. Chef was careful to take your allergies into consideration." He pointed to one of the containers. "Vegetarian sausages, made specially for you."

Once they were served, the ship manager led the guests to a table big enough to seat twelve. An oil painting hung on the wall. It depicted a seaside village busy with fishermen unloading boats of their catch.

Ruth recognised the brown brick building from earlier. "Bonmouth?"

"In its heyday," the ship manager said.

"Must have been ages ago," Laura said.

Gabriella chuckled.

"You've both visited Bonmouth before then?" Ruth

asked. When this didn't get a response from either of them, she murmured, "Right. No personal information."

Ruth could believe the buildings were once well-maintained, and the village lively during its peak, but what made the image more fantasy-based rather than reality was the vibrant blue sky.

That never happened, she said to herself.

"Who's this?" Laura pointed at a man with dark brown eyes and black hair. He stood on a pontoon in the middle of the scene, staring back at them. He appeared to be in his twenties, although the beard made it difficult to pinpoint an exact age.

"A descendant of Bonmouth's founding family," the ship manager said in a low voice.

Ruth squinted at the man in the painting. There was something familiar about him, but she couldn't quite put her finger on it.

Computer Geek dropped into a chair at the far end of the dining table, away from the group. As he reached for a saltcellar, his shirtsleeve rode up, revealing a cobweb tattoo on his elbow.

Colonel Tom looked over at him. "I say."

The geek didn't respond.

Colonel Tom cleared his throat and raised his voice. "I say, are you not joining us?" When he still didn't get a response, he muttered, "How rude."

"Leave him be." The lawyer strode past the table and stood at the carousel. Under the ship manager's tutelage, he selected his food and then joined the others.

"Nice of you to turn up," the colonel said with a wry smile. "Did you fall asleep?"

"Something like that." The lawyer glanced over at the

computer geek and then sat opposite Gabriella and helped himself to the jug of ice water.

"I'm Ruth." She leaned across the table and extended a hand.

The lawyer didn't take it. "Logan."

Ruth looked over at the geek. "And you are?"

"He's Jeremy," Logan said. "And he likes to keep himself to himself." He gave Ruth a hard look.

Taking the obvious hint, she sat back.

"Is this all we've got?" Colonel Tom eyed the jug with disgust. He then looked about. "Or can we expect androids to serve us drinks?" He chuckled to himself. "Daleks with trays? That little pedal-bin robot from Star Wars beep-booping about the place?"

"Only me, I'm afraid, sir." The ship manager appeared at the head of the table.

Colonel Tom waved to Ruth. "After you, madam."

"Can I have a glass of dry white wine, please?"

"Certainly."

"I only drink real lemonade," Laura said.

"Ah, of course, miss." The ship manager bowed his head. "We brought some on board especially for you. The fridge behind the bar has several bottles. I will fetch one."

"I'll have a bottle of red," Gabriella the model said. "Your finest Bordeaux."

Logan winked at her. "I'll join you."

"And you, sir?" the ship manager asked Jeremy.

He shook his head, swept strands of long hair from his face, and still didn't make eye contact with anyone else.

Colonel Tom ordered a whisky, and then the ship manager left.

As Ruth tucked into the first quarter section of her heaped plate, which consisted of lean turkey, carrot sticks, and celery, combined with sausage rolls and mini pork pies, her thoughts returned to Greg. "Have any of you been able to access the internet?"

"No," Laura snapped. "It's ridiculous. I'm going out of my mind. Can't live a second more without my socials."

"I asked the ship manager about that," Logan said, his Yorkshire accent slipping through again. "Their system is down. A glitch. Says they're working on it. Phones too."

"They need to hurry up," Laura said. "My followers must be so worried about me."

Logan rolled his eyes and muttered, "I bet."

Ruth continued to tuck in, albeit with a twinge of guilt. Greg had missed out. He was like a dog: food was his one true love. Ruth vowed that when this was over, she would make it up to her grandson. She'd treat him to one of those junk food MacDoogle's, or JFC, or whatever those places were called.

An hour later, and after two more essential visits to the magical buffet-go-round, both consisting of dessert selections—a gigantic slab of chocolate cake, followed by cheesecake topped with lashes of cream and an enormous strawberry—Ruth sat back, rubbing her tummy, ready to burst, and sipped an espresso. It didn't ease her overburdened belly. She considered surreptitiously unfastening her belt, and asking if someone wouldn't mind rolling her back to her room.

A server cleared the table of dead plates and cutlery. No sooner had he finished than Jeremy left the dining room without a backward glance.

"I've got things to do." Logan gulped his wine, winked at Gabriella, and left too.

Colonel Tom watched them go, and a slight crease furrowed his brow. "Something entirely odd about those fellows. They seem to know one another."

Ruth downed the rest of her wine to hide a smirk. The colonel reminded her of a soufflé: all bluster and little substance. This was going to be a long three days.

The model sat back and sipped her drink. She'd only eaten one teaspoon of potato salad, a handful of lettuce, and a slice of chicken, but had also helped herself to an oversized jam tart when she thought no one was looking. Now she played with her worry beads.

Laura leaned in to Ruth and whispered, "What's the deal with the cat?"

Ruth stiffened. "Cat? What cat?"

Laura pointed to her silver pendant.

"Oh." Ruth let out a breath. "In honour of my late husband."

"He was a cat?"

"A breeder. Very successful. Won lots of awards. A clever man." Ruth glanced over at the colonel to make sure he hadn't heard her giving away any high-level secrets about her personal life to a fellow guest.

"I'm sorry for your loss," Laura said in a low voice. "I miss my grandad. He died last year." She paused for a second and then whispered, "Do you mind if I ask what got him? Was it a heart attack? A stroke?"

Ruth stared forward. "Kitchen knife to the chest."

Laura gasped and pulled away from her.

The other two looked over at them.

"Something the matter?" Colonel Tom asked.

Ruth winced and hoped he hadn't overheard any of that.

After all, he seemed the type to grass her up, and she didn't want to lose out on this well-paying gig.

Me and my stupid mouth running off.

Laura stood. "I'm— I'm going to bed," she said in a rush.

"Already?" Colonel Tom said. "The night is still young."

As Laura went to leave, Ruth said, "The knife wasn't from *my* kitchen, if that's what you're thinking." Despite making light of it, which Ruth tended to do at inappropriate times, the trauma and grief still tightened her stomach into knots.

However, Laura didn't look like she believed her and whispered in Gabriella's ear as they left the dining room.

That night, in a bed so comfortable and warm she wondered how she'd ever leave, Ruth read from a 1901 copy of *Mrs Beeton's Book of Household Management*. She had reached the midway point of a recipe for *Brain Fritters*—which, as the horrific name suggested, consisted of marinating and then frying pigs' brains in batter—when a soft click drew Ruth's attention.

Her bedroom door stood open, and shuffling came from outside in the hall.

Ruth swung her legs out of bed and tiptoed to the main door. She held her breath and peered through the peephole. The fish-eye lens gave her a view of the lawyer leaving the suite next to hers. However, she couldn't make out more than ten feet on either side of her door, and after he passed Ruth's suite, she lost sight of him.

Her eyes narrowed. "And where are you sneaking off to?" As quietly as she could, Ruth opened her door and peered out.

The lawyer knocked on another suite door at the far end of the hallway. It opened, and he slinked through.

Ruth stared for almost a full minute, fighting her overriding curiosity, resisting the urge to knock on the door too, but finally forced herself to mind her own business.

For the time being, at least.

The next morning, Ruth enjoyed a good soak in a bath filled with so many bubbles and bath bombs she had expected to dissolve in the resulting chemical soup. Ruth then read a set of instructions next to the open fireplace, twice, and followed them with unrivalled accuracy. "Press this, hold, listen for the beeps, wait five more seconds, and release." Ruth squealed when flames flickered to life among faux logs.

With a toasty-warm bathrobe wrapped around her, a pair of fluffy complimentary slippers hugging her feet—*heaven*—Ruth sat at the bar in her suite, a bucket of tea close by, with a notepad and pen.

When it came to food, Ruth considered she had a photographic memory. Well, sort of. Not only could she picture the presentation with crystal clarity, but when Ruth closed her eyes, the texture and taste of each canapé played on her tongue, and their scents filled her nostrils. Ruth separated ingredients in her mind's eye, and then gauged the quantity of each used, plus the presentation.

Eager to do well with this job—after all, if the *Ocean Odyssey* owners gave her a good recommendation, it could open the door to other cruise ships—Ruth took her time jotting down every item she'd sampled, from the canapés to the chocolate cake. She described the good and the bad points, scoring them for various aspects, and then she figured out what elements complemented each other, which balanced, what needed more work.

Of course, a buffet was the safest bet for the *Ocean Odyssey* galley team to start with—simple ingredients separated out for the most part, and classic recipes. Ruth assumed that had been the chef's conscious decision for their first night.

Quite clever, really.

"You can't go far wrong with a mixed salad and a few Scotch eggs." Although, the chef had also added a few subtle spices to enhance the flavour.

Ruth set her pen down, stretched, finished her tea, and looked at her phone. Still no bars and zero sign of any internet either. She sighed. Influencer Girl would be fit to burst. Ruth slipped her notepad and pen into her handbag and padded off to the bedroom.

Pairs of black trousers, black shirts, black pullovers, black cardigans, and black skirts lined both sides of the walk-in wardrobe. Underneath, in neat rows, sat several pairs of identical black shoes. In striking contrast, on the far wall hung a selection of bright pink belts.

Ruth picked out an outfit—trousers, blouse, walking shoes with pink laces—and got changed.

Ten minutes later, once she'd done her hair and makeup, Ruth gave Merlin his breakfast, put down fresh water, and cleaned his tray. Once he had settled down, Ruth headed for the door, not yet convinced she wanted her own breakfast after yesterday's overindulgence, but willing to give it a darn good try.

As she stepped from her suite, the door at the end of the row opened and Gabriella stormed out.

"Ridiculous." Despite every hair being in place, her

makeup perfect, Gabriella's face twisted with anger, and her cheeks were flushed.

"Something wrong?" Ruth asked.

Startled, Gabriella turned to her. "Oh, it's you." She lifted her chin. "I know I brought it with me."

"Brought what?"

"My blue Dior dress." Gabriella shook her head. "Someone has stolen it from my room. The nerve. I mean, seriously?"

Ruth's brow creased. "Are you sure?" It didn't seem like the kind of place where petty crime would be rampant, especially with only six guests on board.

"Of course I'm sure," Gabriella snapped. Her American accent had a Southern drawl to it when she was angry. "I distinctly remember hanging the dress up before I went down to dinner last night."

Ruth let out a slow breath. "Well, I'm sure there's a rational explanation." She gestured. "Let's go to breakfast, and we can bring the matter up with the ship manager. Perhaps a maid removed it for dry cleaning." Although, she couldn't see why they would.

Gabriella harrumphed, spun on her heel, and marched away.

Head bowed, Ruth followed.

When they reached the dining room, the other guests, apart from the lawyer, were already seated in the waiting area, dressed in casual attire. Colonel Tom wore a sports jacket and what appeared to be golfing trousers.

Ruth smiled, said, "Good morning," and sat.

A furrow marred Laura's brow. "Hmm."

"Don't worry," Ruth said, guessing what the issue with her was. "I'm sure they'll sort out the internet connection today. You'll be tick-tocking in no time."

"It's not that." She glanced uneasily at the others.

Ruth's heart sank, and for one terrifying moment she assumed Laura had told them about the fact she'd shared some private information.

However, Colonel Tom said, "We can't find anyone."

Ruth blinked. "Excuse me?"

"It's crazy," Laura said, her expression intense. "They've literally vanished."

Jeremy the computer geek scratched his beard and stared at the floor.

"Who's vanished?" Ruth asked, not comprehending.

Colonel Tom leaned forward and whispered, "The crew. Everyone on board, apart from us, is missing."

4

In the dining room with the other guests, Ruth took a few seconds to gather her thoughts. "The entire staff can't have vanished." The mere thought of it was insane. "Besides, the ship manager told us they're running on a skeleton crew."

"Well," Logan said as he marched into the dining room, "those skeletons are now ghosts." He dropped into a chair with a heavy sigh. "I've searched half the boat. There's no one about."

"Then do you think someone should search the other half?" Ruth glanced at his hand—the tip of his right index finger had remnants of black paint, and she wondered exactly where the guy had looked. She addressed the other guests. "Perhaps they're dealing with an emergency somewhere." Ruth could not believe this was happening. There were at least twenty other people on board, and they couldn't all have simply disappeared.

Laura wrung her hands. "We don't have a way to call for help."

"Is there no chance we can get the Wi-Fi working?" Of

course, Ruth had known all along how it was really pronounced, but she enjoyed winding Greg up. Kept the boy on his toes and gave him a sense of purpose when he had to correct her. She really could use his technological smarts right about now.

"We can't get a phone signal or internet," Colonel Tom said. "We're too far from land, but this ship will have a radio."

Ruth shrugged. "If my grandson doesn't hear from me in the next couple of days, he'll realise something's up." At least, she hoped he would. Ruth forced a smile at the group. "We'll be fine." Then, trying to act casual, she stood, sauntered over to a placard next to the door, and examined a plan of the ship. "Now, where could they have gone?"

Logan joined her and motioned to Jeremy. "He suggested someone should check out the bridge."

Ruth's eyebrows lifted. She hadn't heard Jeremy utter a single word yet. She then traced her finger over the layout. "It's not marked on this map, but if I were to guess, I'd say the bridge must be toward the bow of the ship, upper deck . . . here."

"Yes." Colonel Tom cleared his throat and stepped beside her. "That's generally where they put them."

Ruth beamed at him. "Great. Let us know how you get on." She dropped into a chair.

"Well, don't look at me," Logan said, sitting too. "I've already been all over this ship."

Colonel Tom eyed everyone else, but they avoided his gaze. "Very well. Stay put. I'll be back as quick as I can."

"Hold on." Ruth let out a breath. "I don't think we should go wandering off on our own until we figure out what's happened."

"I'm staying right here." Gabriella folded her arms.

"That manager guy will expect us to be waiting for breakfast, and I've got a bone to pick with him. A two-thousand-dollar bone in the shape of a missing dress."

"I'm staying too," Laura said. "That's survival 101."

Ruth checked the clock on her phone. It was a little after eight in the morning. She wasn't sure what time they officially started breakfast on the *Ocean Odyssey*, but most land-based hotels served from around 5:30 a.m.

Colonel Tom stepped over to her. "Will you be so kind as to escort me, madam? We'll get to the bottom of this together."

Ruth hesitated, reluctant to get involved. She wasn't an investigator, a finder of lost people. Those sorts of shenanigans were in the past where they belonged, and she'd vowed never to get caught up with nonsense like this ever again. She was a food consultant, not a detective.

Colonel Tom looked down at her with what he probably assumed were his best puppy-dog eyes.

If he thought that would work, then he . . . well, he was right. *Damn it*. Annoyed with herself for relenting so easily, Ruth stood. Besides, it really wasn't wise to go roving off on their own.

Logan went to stand too, but Colonel Tom motioned for him to remain seated.

"I think it prudent the rest of you stay behind." Colonel Tom zipped up his jacket. "At least for the time being. You understand?" He glanced toward Jeremy, who still stared at the floor, and then he motioned Ruth to the hallway. "Shall we, madam?"

"If we're going outside, I'll need my coat," she said before she changed her mind.

The Colonel escorted her to the suites' hallway, and

Ruth grabbed her hat and coat. She hunted for her scarf but couldn't find it. Ruth vaguely remembered tossing it aside when she'd danced around the room like a lunatic the evening before. *It must have gone behind one of the million scatter cushions.* She'd hunt for it later.

Ruth met Colonel Tom back in the hallway and they hurried to the upper floor of the atrium and into another corridor, where they faced an elevator. Ruth cringed. "Can we take the stairs?"

Colonel Tom hit the call button. "I don't think there are any."

Ruth took a step back as the doors opened. "There have to be." She spotted a nearby rack filled with deck plans. She snatched one and held it up.

"Good thinking," Colonel Tom said. "We may forget where the bridge is."

Ruth shot him a look and studied the blueprints inside.

The elevator doors opened.

"Madam?"

"I think the stairs are that way." She pointed to a door farther down the corridor.

Colonel Tom nodded. "Very well. If you insist."

Ruth let out a juddering breath. "Thank you."

On the other side of the door, they found the stairs, and as they started their ascent, Ruth reminded herself they were on a ship, and of another water-related activity she'd endured with her husband decades ago.

John had bought a rickety ancient sailboat from a place called *Christchurch*, on the south coast of England. He hadn't owned a trailer, so he'd chosen to sail it to Cobbs Quay Marina in Poole Harbour, some twenty miles away.

Somehow, John had convinced Ruth to go with him,

based on the fact her father had owned boats for most of her life and taken the family out often. However, as a kid, Ruth hadn't paid attention on how to sail a boat. She had no idea what to do, and had always left the technical parts to her father and sister. So, to this day she couldn't understand why she'd agreed to John's insane idea.

They'd started out with calm water and clear skies, but halfway through their trip a storm had rolled in. When the waves reached several feet tall, John had opted to drop the keel and stabilise the boat.

Ruth remembered him disappearing into the cabin right at the moment a wave larger than the mini yacht had appeared from nowhere. Before she'd had time to react, or scream, the wave had slammed into the fragile hull, and the boat rolled over.

After Ruth had spent more than enough time underwater, the boat had sprung back, and a bewildered John stumbled from the cabin to find her draped over the boom.

"Ru-ru," he'd said, face pale. "Are you okay?"

All Ruth could manage was a groan.

"What do you think happened?"

Ruth snapped out of her memory of John and looked back at Colonel Tom. "Sorry?"

"The crew, madam." He gazed up at the stairs. "Where do you think they are? What happened to them?"

"Oh." Ruth shrugged. "I have no idea. It's very odd." She continued to climb. "Maybe they had a little too much to drink last night and slept in." She glanced back again.

Colonel Tom didn't look convinced by this possible explanation, and Ruth couldn't blame him.

They reached the top floor, strode down another hallway, and on through a set of double doors, which led to the promenade deck. Outside, with the wind's current level at "*stiff*" and "*decidedly bracing,*" the two of them strolled along the port side of the ship.

Colonel Tom paused at the railing and looked down. "No sign that we're sinking." He smiled at Ruth. "That has to be good news. Haven't struck an iceberg."

Ruth frowned, trying to remember if there was some mention of an "*ice-class hull*" in the welcome video, but forced herself to relax. They couldn't be that far north of Bonmouth.

She then considered whether there was not supposed to be breakfast on offer, but Ruth quickly dismissed that idea as absurd. She couldn't remember ever visiting a hotel that didn't serve breakfast, let alone on board a luxury cruise ship.

Ruth stiffened as another thought struck her: "Food poisoning?"

"I beg your pardon?" Colonel Tom said.

Ruth shook herself. "Doesn't matter." Besides, if illness had struck down the crew, then the guests would have likely suffered the same fate. Unless the crew had eaten something earlier in the day, before the guests had arrived, which could have made sense. *Bad fish?*

As they walked along the upper deck, Ruth said, "We're still not moving. I thought we would be. Maybe that explains where the crew is? Lower decks? Engine trouble?"

"Perhaps they've run out of fire lighters for the boilers."

Ruth chuckled. "So, you do have a sense of humour?"

"And you sound surprised?" He stopped at the base of a set of metal stairs, opened the gate, and bowed. "After you."

Ruth headed on up. She reached a landing with a window, and cupped her hands around her face to peer through. "Can't see anyone."

Colonel Tom opened a door and stepped onto the bridge.

Ruth followed.

Windows spanned the room and curved round the sides, giving a perfect wide-angled panorama of the ocean.

Consoles set out in a horseshoe shape dominated the middle of the space, with more screens, dials, and readouts than Ruth could fathom. Two chairs sat side by side on a raised plinth, with yet more controls between them.

A shudder ran down her spine as she glanced about. It was so quiet and creepy. "Where are they?"

"I'm ex-army, not navy," Colonel Tom said, "but I can't imagine the bridge of any ship, military or no, should ever be left unattended." He pointed at a black device mounted in the console. "Here we are. Radio." He hurried over to it and grabbed a microphone and tapped a few buttons. "Damn."

"Let me guess," Ruth said. "It's dead?"

"No power."

Ruth tensed and faced the door in the back wall. "What do you suppose is through here?" Before she knew what she was doing, she opened it to reveal a narrow grey utility corridor.

"Might as well check it out now we're here," Colonel Tom said. "Given the unusual circumstances."

After a furtive glance at him, Ruth stepped on through. She read the labels on the doors to the left and right as she passed them: "Storage, Captain's Ready Room, Electrical." She checked each, finding them empty. "Oh, looky here." She opened a door marked CCTV and stepped into a room six feet by ten.

Screens dominated an entire wall, with a control desk and a chair underneath.

Colonel Tom waved. "After you."

Ruth shook her head. "Technology and I don't mix. We have a mutual understanding to stay out of each other's way and never speak of the incident again."

"Incident?"

"Let's just say a television once exploded and almost set fire to my lounge curtains." She nodded at the console. "I'll keep my distance."

"Noted." Colonel Tom sat and examined a track pad and keyboard. "Seems simple enough."

"What is your area of expertise?" Ruth asked. "When you were in the army, that is."

Colonel Tom remained tight-lipped.

"Oh, sorry," Ruth said. "No personal details, right?"

He gave a firm nod.

"Need the money?" Ruth winced. There she went again, letting her mouth get ahead of any rational thinking. "I mean—you don't want to break the rules and lose the—" She clenched her fists and closed her eyes. "Sorry. Stupid."

"It's fine," Colonel Tom said. "You're right."

Ruth opened one eye and peered at him. "I am?"

Colonel Tom lifted his head. "The truth is, I don't want to lose that second payment. No, I . . . *need* it."

"Gotcha." Ruth offered him a sympathetic smile. "Say no more." She pulled up another chair and sat next to him. "It's a lot of money. It will keep my grandson supplied with cheeseburgers for months." Ruth nodded at the screens. "Now, let's see if we can figure out where the crew are hiding."

~

"Can someone please tell me what the hell is going on?" Gabriella said as she crammed into the CCTV room with the others. "I don't have time for this nonsense."

Influencer Laura and Logan the lawyer had puzzled expressions too, but Jeremy remained by the door, not making eye contact with anyone.

"Now that everyone is here." The ashen-faced colonel swallowed and sat. "Let's show them what we've found, madam."

With trembling fingers, Ruth gestured to the bank of monitors. "These are the camera views of both the inside and outside of the ship." Eight smaller displays divided each monitor.

Colonel Tom worked the controls, bringing them up to full screen in turn and scrolling through.

"We looked everywhere," Ruth said.

Images of the lower decks came up first; the engine room, galley, storage rooms, and various other parts of the ship off-limits to guests cycled through.

"Couldn't find a single crew member."

"And?" Logan scowled. "Where are they, then? They can't vanish."

Ruth let out a slow, juddering breath. "We had a look through the recordings to see if there were any clues to what has happened."

Colonel Tom brought up an image of the dining room— a view of the night before—with the six of them seated at the table, chatting and eating.

Gabriella leaned in and squinted at the screen. "I'm never wearing that blouse again. It's ghastly."

"It looked lovely on you." Laura smiled.

Colonel Tom sped the recording on.

At the dining table, Ruth and Colonel Tom stood, along with Gabriella and Laura. Jeremy snuck out while no one was looking, and then Logan left too.

Once the rest of the guests had departed, a server and the ship manager cleared the table.

"What's so damned important about this?" Logan folded his arms.

Ruth nodded at the screen. "Watch."

Logan shook his head. "This is a waste of time. We should search the ship, not be in here messing about." He turned to leave, but Ruth stepped in front of him.

"Stay," Colonel Tom said. "You'll like this part."

Logan scowled and turned back.

On the screen, Logan burst into the dining room, stormed over to the ship manager, and waved his hands about in an aggressive manner.

The ship manager raised his own hands, but palms out, placating, and said something. This appeared to anger Logan further.

"Is there no audio?" Gabriella squinted at the screen. "I can't make out what they're saying."

Colonel Tom shook his head. "Unfortunately not."

After a minute or two of this one-sided argument, Logan stormed off.

"We tried to follow the ship manager, but he leaves through a door not covered by cameras." Colonel Tom hit pause, and all eyes moved to Logan.

"What?" Logan looked between them. "I was angry."

"Clearly," Ruth said in a level tone. "What about?"

Logan snarled. "If you're suggesting I had anything to do with—"

"We're not suggesting anything," Ruth interrupted,

trying to ease the tension. "We only want to figure out where everyone has gone. That's all." The sooner they got this nonsense over with, the quicker she could return to her job.

"It seems you were the last person to see the ship manager," Colonel Tom said to Logan, his eyes narrowed. "Care to explain?"

Logan glared back at him, and then when his gaze met Ruth's, his shoulders relaxed. "I can't tell you why the owners asked me to come here. Obviously." He looked round at them all. "None of you can. But I can tell you they annoyed me when I learned David Franks isn't here."

"Who's David Franks?" Gabriella asked.

"A health and safety inspector," Logan said. "I need his report."

If he was meeting a health and safety inspector, Ruth mused, it wasn't very likely Logan was a lawyer after all. "How did you find out he's not here?" she asked.

Logan tugged at his cuffs and spoke through a tight jaw. "When I got back to my suite after dinner, I discovered an anonymous note slipped under my door."

Laura inclined her head. "What did it say?"

Logan frowned at her. "I told you: the health and safety inspector isn't here to meet with me, as we'd arranged." He looked between Ruth and Colonel Tom. "David and I were supposed to discuss a few . . . things. It makes my job a lot harder with him not being here."

Ruth studied Logan. As far as she could tell, he was telling the truth, and she resisted the urge to ask exactly what his job entailed and why it was vital he met with the health and safety guy.

Gabriella worked her worry beads. "I still don't understand what this has to do with the crew."

"We're getting to that part." Ruth nodded at Colonel Tom.

He brought up a new camera recording. This one showed a view of the bow of the ship from high above, looking down at an acute angle. Colonel Tom sped the video forward.

In the recording, Colonel Tom, Gabriella, Laura, and Ruth came into view, their gestures animated and comical, like an early 1900s Charlie Chaplin film.

No one in the room laughed.

They all remained transfixed and stony faced.

After a few minutes on the footage counter, the four of them left the bow of the ship and rounded the corner, out of sight, but Colonel Tom kept his finger pressed on the button.

An hour ticked by, then two, three, four . . . A little after five hours—gone three o'clock in the morning—Captain Pipe sauntered into view, plumes of smoke billowing behind him.

"Guess he had insomnia," Laura murmured. "I know what that's like."

"Or he was working a late shift," Gabriella said.

Laura's brow furrowed. "Doing what?"

Captain Pipe stopped at the bow of the cruise ship, and as Colonel Tom and Gabriella had done hours before, he leaned over the railing and peered down at the ocean.

"Is he the captain of this ship?" Gabriella asked with a look of incredulity.

"I think so," Ruth said.

A dark, hooded figure appeared, hesitated for a beat, and then snuck over to the captain. Creeping. Menacing.

Everyone in the security room held their breath, and

although Ruth knew what was about to happen, her pulse quickened.

The dark figure lunged, grabbed the captain, and heaved him over the railing.

Gabriella and the influencer both gasped as Captain Pipe's feet disappeared over the edge and into darkness.

5

A s soon as Captain Pipe fell from view, as if they knew the position of the camera and the fact it watched them, the hooded figure kept their face turned away in shadow and rushed off.

"We tried to follow that person on the other cameras," Ruth said, "but lost them when they went back inside."

Colonel Tom brought up a few seconds of another recording that showed the hooded figure dart through a service door. Once again, the camera looked almost directly down on them, which made it impossible to gauge their height and build.

Ruth faced the room. She looked between the other guests, studying everyone's reactions. "They seem to know where the cameras are. They did their homework."

Laura clapped a hand over her mouth. "Is he dead?" she whispered through her fingers. "The captain?"

"Undoubtedly," Colonel Tom said.

"You're suggesting one of us pushed him?" Logan looked at Jeremy the mute geek and then back to Ruth. "Well? Are you pointing your finger at one of us or not?"

"We don't have enough evidence to know who that was," Ruth said. However, as far as she was concerned, she was the only person she could rule out entirely. Unless she'd sleep-walked without knowing.

"I can't believe it." Laura shook her head. "This has to be a nightmare." She moved from one foot to another and started to hyperventilate.

"It's okay." Gabriella rubbed her back. "You'll be fine." She then addressed the others. "He could have survived. I mean, seriously, couldn't he? It's possible, at least, isn't it?"

"Right." Laura panted. "He said he could swim."

"That's a fair old drop into cold water," Colonel Tom said. "If the captain survived the fall, he wouldn't have been able to swim ashore, and there's no way back onto the ship without help."

"Maybe a crew member saw what happened," Laura said, now with a sparkle of hope in her eyes.

"Not according to the CCTV recordings," Colonel Tom said. "He was alone."

"Has anyone checked for a body?" Logan asked in a subdued tone.

"I had a quick look on my way to fetch you," Ruth said. "No signs of him. And there's more," she added with a heavy heart.

Colonel Tom turned back to the security console and brought up another view. This one showed an image of the starboard side of the ship.

Everyone leaned in for a better look.

A door opened, and the ship manager strode onto the deck, shortly followed by the entire crew, all twenty of them.

"What are they doing?" Laura said, aghast.

"Escaping from the killer," Gabriella murmured.

Laura clutched her chest.

The ship manager opened a box on the wall and operated a set of controls. A lifeboat swung from its mounts, suspended from davits, up and over the side of the ship.

Logan gaped. "You have got to be kidding me."

Sure enough, the crew climbed into the lifeboat in an orderly manner and carried on down the side of the ship until they dropped out of sight.

Everyone inside the security room, apart from Ruth and Colonel Tom—because they'd already watched these scenes unfold—gaped at the screen.

Ruth attempted to speculate what had caused them to leave, and why they hadn't informed the guests, but her mind drew a blank. It was a crazy situation with no obvious and logical solution.

"They left us with the killer." Laura wrung her hands. "We need to get off this ship."

"Agreed," Colonel Tom said. "With no phone signal, internet, and the radio out, I don't see any alternative."

"Someone broke the radio?" Gabriella asked with a shocked expression.

"I'm afraid so." Colonel Tom stared at Logan. "Bit of a coincidence, wouldn't you say?"

"Why didn't the crew come and get us?" Laura asked in a shrill voice. "Why leave us here?"

"Because they thought one of us was the killer," Logan said, glaring back at Colonel Tom. "They got spooked and ran."

Ruth took a few deep breaths, trying to get a grip of the situation and think it through. The fact was, like the crew, they would be safer in a lifeboat rather than on board a ship with a potential killer on the loose. She glanced around at them all. "I think everyone should return to their suites, grab your belongings, and meet us in the dining room."

Ruth indicated Colonel Tom. "We'll get a lifeboat ready." She'd already decided to ditch her own suitcase and only take Merlin.

"We could hunt for some life jackets," Logan said, nodding at Jeremy. "He can help me."

Jeremy shrugged.

Ruth had almost forgotten he was there.

"Then it's settled." Colonel Tom lifted his chin. "I suggest we stay in our pairs," Colonel Tom said.

"Pairs?" Logan laughed. "Wouldn't sticking in threes make more sense? What if one of us is the killer?" Logan glared at the colonel as he asked the question.

"Then the rest of us will know who they are when they don't return with their partner," Colonel Tom said.

Ruth winced. Although that was true, it was rather harsh.

Colonel Tom moved close to her. "Leave no one's side. Watch your backs. Understood?"

This received half-hearted nods in reply.

Logan muttered as they filed out, "Who died and made that guy boss?"

"The captain," Laura said.

On the bridge, Colonel Tom checked the radio again. "Still out of operation." Then he followed Ruth through the side door.

When she reached the bottom of the metal steps, Ruth hesitated, turned back to Colonel Tom, and then changed her mind and kept walking.

"Is there something wrong?" he asked.

Ruth stopped again, bit her lip, weighing whether to trust him or not, and then faced the colonel. It wasn't something she could keep to herself. Ruth took a breath and kept her voice low. "I heard a noise last night." She glanced about to make sure they were alone. "I climbed out of bed and had a look through my door's peephole thing."

Colonel Tom cocked an eyebrow. "And what did you see?"

"Logan," Ruth breathed. "Sneaking off." She watched his reaction.

Colonel Tom nodded, and then his brow furrowed. "Why didn't you say something just now? We've got the fellow. Caught him red-handed." He went to turn back, but Ruth stopped him.

She shook her head. "It can't have been much beyond midnight when I saw him go to someone else's suite. I'm not sure whose. That killer pushed the captain overboard at around three, right?"

"Indeed, but Logan could have stayed out," Colonel Tom said. "Bided his time before murdering the poor captain."

"I'm not sure." Ruth frowned as she thought it through. "We can't be positive Logan had anything to do with it. We need evidence."

"Did you hear him return?"

"No, but when we reach shore, we could tell the police to look at all those CCTV recordings. They would have caught him sneaking about too."

Colonel Tom hesitated. He looked unsure if he should tell Ruth something or not.

Her blood turned cold. "What is it?"

"I—" He cleared his throat. "Well, I looked at the rest of those recordings when you went to fetch the others."

Ruth nodded. "Okay. What did you discover?" She braced herself.

Colonel Tom took a breath. "There are no more of them."

Ruth stared at him. "No more of what?"

"Recordings," he said. "Someone wiped them."

Ruth stared at him. She couldn't believe what she was hearing. "Deleted files? Someone did that on purpose?"

"And they did a poor job because they didn't delete all the files, did they?" The colonel gave a sage nod. "Thank goodness. Otherwise, we wouldn't know as much as we do. Those recordings we do have are merely the leftovers."

Ruth continued to stare at him. *Had the killer known what we were doing and deliberately left the recording of Captain Pipe's murder for us to find?* A shiver ran down her spine.

"What's more," Colonel Tom said, keeping his voice low, "I think the CCTV software is now corrupted. I tried pressing record, but it didn't work. Whoever did this was in a hurry but determined to cover their tracks."

Ruth leaned against the railing and caught her breath. "Maybe it's not such a good idea to climb on board a lifeboat with a potential killer."

"No one can do a lot with all of us in a confined space," Colonel Tom said. "Fear not, we'll keep an eye on one another."

The blood drained from Ruth's cheeks. "Confined space? Trapped?" She hadn't thought of that. However, modern lifeboats were designed to take at least a hundred people. There were only six of them. Plenty of space to move about. Besides, she could always stick her head out of the door. "We'll report what we know to the police, and they can deal with this mess." After all, she had come to sample the food, not get caught up in a murder investigation.

Colonel Tom pursed his lips and nodded. "Let's move."

They hurried along the deck and found a lifeboat. Sure enough, it looked big enough, with a large door, so as not to trigger her cleithrophobia.

Ruth reached for the control box. "Have you ever used one of these before?"

"Can't be difficult," Colonel Tom said. "They need to be operated during an emergency, after all."

Ruth swung the door of the control box open and stiffened. "Oh, I think it might be difficult."

Someone had torn away the buttons and all, leaving nothing but bare wires.

Ruth and Colonel Tom checked the remaining lifeboats on both sides of the ship, but that same someone had gone to a lot of trouble to sabotage each control panel.

Colonel Tom also examined the mechanisms to see if they could manually crank the lifeboats over the side, but they'd also removed several gears from the davits, making it impossible.

"They certainly went to great pains to keep us here," Colonel Tom muttered.

Ruth tensed at that. "Why, though?" They'd only arrived the day before and were strangers to one another.

After looking over the last lifeboat, Colonel Tom stepped back and shook his head. "It would definitely appear someone would like us to remain on board this vessel for the foreseeable future." He glanced about. "I believe there should be a few inflatable rafts, but what's the betting we don't have any?"

Ruth cringed at the idea of having to do any physical exercise. "Didn't fancy rowing anyway." She peered across the ocean to the horizon and squinted at the sliver of land. "Do you think we could try signalling?" She'd seen a few black-and-white war movies where they used lanterns.

"I do happen to know Morse code," Colonel Tom said in a proud tone as he followed her gaze. "However, on this occasion, we'd need a powerful light. We're quite a way offshore."

"Let me guess," Ruth said, already knowing the answer. "We don't have a powerful light, do we?"

Colonel Tom gave her a sympathetic look. "Not that I have seen thus far. There could be something on board we could use. We'll be on the lookout, but I don't hold much hope."

Besides, if someone did spot the light from land, they'd have to know Morse code too, or at the very least realise it was a distress call.

Colonel Tom scratched his chin. "We could do with some flares."

Ruth's eyebrows arched. "Planning on a seventies fancy dress party?" She couldn't quite picture him as the John Travolta type. "You want to strut your stuff under a disco ball? Point at random things on the ceiling?"

"Very funny, madam." Colonel Tom smirked. "Not trousers. Emergency flares." His frown returned. "We can keep an eye out for any of those too, but my guess would be our captor has already taken all these things into consideration."

"Captor?" That was an interesting way to phrase it, and Colonel Tom certainly made a lot of assumptions, unless he knew something and wasn't letting on. Ruth's gaze then scanned the ocean. "Whoever planned this has picked a quiet spot. I've not seen another boat since we arrived."

"Far from any shipping lanes." Colonel Tom nodded in agreement. "But the sea is still a busy place, so perhaps we should keep watch." He waved to a door. "For now, I suggest we return to the others and break the bad news to them. What do you say?"

Ruth nodded, and as they trudged back to the stairs, she

thought about her husband. If John were alive and with her right now, he'd consider this another grand adventure.

Back in the dining room, Ruth and Colonel Tom explained their findings, and that there was no apparent way to leave the ship or signal for help.

Laura gaped at them. "Wait." Her voice turned shrill, and she looked between Ruth and Colonel Tom as though she couldn't believe what they were saying. "We're trapped? So, what do we do now?"

"We stay here." Colonel Tom glanced around at all their gathered luggage. "We don't have a choice. Stick together and wait it out."

Ruth dropped into a chair with a heavy sigh and thought about grabbing the mug from her room and making an extra milky, extra gigantic bucket of tea with a kilogram of sugar. Plus, she'd have to check in on Merlin soon. "My grandson will realise something is up when I don't return." She looked at the clock on her phone. "It's morning on the first day. Which means we have fifty-eight hours to go until we're expected back at Bonmouth. Then Greg will come looking." At least she hoped he would. Greg could be a bit hit and miss when it came to cottoning on to things, but he got there in the end. Mostly.

"Might as well be forever." Gabriella scowled. "If you think I'm sitting here, waiting to be picked off by a deranged killer and—"

"Who says the killer wants to pick us off?" Colonel Tom asked with an inquiring look.

He made a good point.

"Oh, come on." Gabriella threw her hands up. "We're trapped here. Together. The crew abandoned ship." She tilted her head. "You're saying someone has done that deliberately, right? That's what you're getting at?"

"We don't know their motive," Ruth said. Although, she tended to agree with Gabriella's hypothesis. If someone had gone to all the trouble of trapping them here, the killer's next move could hardly be benign.

"Right." Logan clapped his hands and stood. "We should turn the tables." He clenched his fists. "We outnumber him six to one."

"Or her," Ruth muttered. After all, the hooded figure on the CCTV camera could have been either male or female. She leaned toward it being a man, given the strength needed to hoist the captain over the railing, but supposed a woman could still have done it, given the element of surprise.

"Or them," Laura said in a small voice. "Could be more than one person doing this." She shrank into her chair.

Everyone stared at each other in sober silence.

Finally, Gabriella spoke up again. "Do you think this might be some kind of joke?" Her face lifted as she looked around at everyone. "I mean, come on, could it be an elaborate prank? Someone's having a laugh?" She then looked over at Jeremy, but he sat a little way away and stared at the floor, long hair flopped forward, as was his modus operandi.

"Of course," Laura said, brightening too. "We're paid to be here, right? This is all part of it. We're supposed to evaluate things, as though there were a real emergency going on. It's a test. It has to be."

"Question is," Logan said, "who are they testing?"

"Not who, but what," Gabriella played with her worry beads and looked about. "This ship. Its safety."

Colonel Tom scanned the dining room, his brow furrowed. "Doesn't explain why someone heaved the poor captain overboard."

Ruth pursed her lips. She was fairly positive this wasn't a test or a prank. That wouldn't make much sense. *Why sabo-*

tage the lifeboats? That was a risky move. No, someone had murdered Captain Pipe. That same someone had spooked the crew and was most likely still on board, although she had no way to be sure unless they made themselves known or left an obvious clue somewhere. And, given the fact Ruth had sworn off any type of investigating three decades ago, it would have to be up to someone else.

The others seemed to realise the gravity of their situation too because all their faces had turned downcast.

Laura hugged herself. "I don't think we should stay here either. It's too open. I don't feel safe."

6

Ruth's gaze moved around the various windows in the dining room and then up at the glass dome way above their heads. She had to agree with Laura about not feeling safe here. "Why don't we grab supplies: some food, toiletries, anything and everything that'll help us last the next few days?"

"More alcohol," Logan muttered.

Gabriella pocketed her worry beads and cracked a rare smile.

"And then what?" Laura asked.

Ruth looked at Colonel Tom. "Fortress?"

"Excuse me, madam?"

"We all return to our suites," Ruth said. "It's where we'll all feel most comfortable, but we can barricade the end of the hallway. Make it like a fortress."

"A good idea," Colonel Tom said. "A fortress indeed."

"Sounds like a prison," Gabriella said with an exaggerated shudder.

"I agree," Logan said. "That's a terrible plan. What if the

killer really is one of us? You expect us to stay in a confined space with no escape from them?"

"We'll lock ourselves in our own suites and hunker down," Ruth said. "To be extra safe." Although that wasn't the best solution, it was a compromise. She'd rather stay in her suite with Merlin than wander the ship.

Gabriella and Laura bobbed their heads in agreement.

Logan paused for a second, and then muttered, "Whatever."

Ruth took that as the nearest to a positive reply she'd likely get from him, and she glanced over at Jeremy. "Do you also agree?"

He shrugged, which was the biggest reaction she'd seen out of him thus far, so Ruth also took it as confirmation he was on board, so to speak.

"This'll be fun," she said, attempting to lighten the mood in an otherwise dire situation. "It'll be like a camping holiday. Even better—glamping?" When this received several scowls, Ruth murmured, "Or perhaps not." She cleared her throat. "I think you were right earlier," Ruth said to Colonel Tom. "Whenever we get the chance, we should keep an eye out for other ships, just in case."

"Why?" Logan interjected before the colonel could respond. "If we spot one, how can we signal to it? What are you going to do? Flap your arms about? Jump up and down? Do the Macarena?"

"Ooh." Gabriella smiled at him. "Flashback."

Ruth blinked because that *was* actually what she had in mind. Well, the jumping up and down and flapping her arms.

"How about you"—Colonel Tom nodded at Logan— "and the mute over there"—he waved a hand in Jeremy's direction—"hunt for torches and flares, plus anything else you think might be useful."

"We need furniture to barricade ourselves in," Ruth said. "Block the end of the hallway. Look for anything not tied down."

Logan stood. "There's plenty of chairs in the atrium." He glanced at Jeremy. "We'll get the job done, won't we, *mate?*" He emphasised that last word in such a way that it was clear they'd remain far from friends.

Jeremy hesitated and then joined him.

Ruth rubbed her hands together. "Great. We'll gather food." She pointed at a side door, one the ship manager and the server had used the night before.

"What do you want us to do?" Laura asked, indicating herself and Gabriella.

"Could you two please return everyone's belongings to their suites?" Ruth said. "Leave them outside each door. Then gather any other supplies you think might be useful. Don't stray too far, though. We'll meet back in the hallway outside our suites in an hour."

With everyone partnered up, and with jobs to do, they went their separate ways.

Ruth watched them go, finding it hard to believe any of them could be a killer, and then nodded to the side door. "Shall we?"

"After you, madam," Colonel Tom said.

They headed on through, and, sure enough, a vast galley lay beyond, with stainless steel worktops, numerous stoves and ovens, plus pots and pans hanging from the rails.

At the far end of the galley, Ruth pushed open a heavy door and stepped into storage room, at least forty feet long, crammed full of racks filled with food.

"Over here. I've found a megalarder." She stepped

inside, grabbed a cart next to the door, and started loading it. "Incidentally, do you know why a place to store food is called a larder?"

Colonel Tom joined her. "No. Why's that?"

"It comes from a mediaeval Latin word, *lardarium*, meaning *a room for meats*. The French for bacon is *lardon*."

Colonel Tom cocked an eyebrow. "Is that true?"

"No idea." Ruth shrugged. "But makes me sound intelligent, right?"

Colonel Tom grabbed a can of beans and read the label. "What do you make of our silent friend?"

"Jeremy?" Ruth shovelled bags of pasta into the cart, realised they had no way to cook it, and returned them to the rack. "I don't know. He's quiet. Hard to get a read on him."

"A little too quiet, if you ask me." Colonel Tom placed cans of spaghetti hoops and beans into the cart. "And the other fellow, Logan?"

"I'm not sure what to make of him yet." Truth was, Ruth wasn't sure what to think about any of the others, including present company.

"I think we should confront him with what you saw last night," Colonel Tom said, clearly oblivious to her concern. "The fact he snuck off somewhere doesn't sit right with me."

"It doesn't mean he's a killer," Ruth said.

"True." Colonel Tom picked up a can of baby carrots, screwed up his face, and returned it to the shelf. "But it doesn't mean he's *not* a killer either."

A logical conclusion. Flawed, but undeniably logical.

"Without that CCTV evidence," Ruth said as she perused the other shelves, "we have no way to prove where Logan went last night. He could lie to us, and we'd never know."

"Then I suggest we keep a close eye on him."

Ruth vowed to keep a close eye on everyone, not only Logan. A yellow tool bag sat at the end of the shelves. Inside were various pliers, wrenches, and screwdrivers with yellow handles, plus electrical test equipment.

Deciding none of that was useful to their current situation, she faced a door to a walk-in freezer. Ruth grabbed the handle and was about to open it when Colonel Tom called, "Madam?"

She turned back.

Colonel Tom waved at a nearby rack with packets of crisps and snacks, and then to shelves loaded with bread and buns. "Shouldn't we go for room-temperature items? Things we don't need to cook? Anything we take from in there will defrost."

"Good point." Ruth had a fridge in her suite but not a freezer. She hurried over to him, and together they loaded the cart. Ruth grabbed extra boxes of tea bags, and bags of sugar, plus coffee for those who wanted it. Then she opened a fridge and pulled out cartons of milk. "Lemonade." She glanced at Colonel Tom. "For the influencer girl? Laura?"

He threw boxes of cereal into the cart. "Influencer?" Then he smirked. "Ah, I see."

Ruth smiled back at him, surprised he knew what one of those was. After all, she'd learned of their existence from her grandson. She tossed a few more loaves of bread into the cart and hunted for cutlery, plates, and a can opener.

"Very well," Colonel Tom said, grabbing tins of tuna. "We'll make a detour via the bar. I believe that's where the ship manager said he stored the lemonade."

"No need." Laura stood in the doorway with Gabriella. She grasped two bottles of lemonade, whereas Gabriella held up a large bottle of vodka. They giggled and hurried off.

Colonel Tom snatched up more cans of beans, throwing them into the cart.

After several trips back and forth with the cart—with Ruth taking the stairs each time, while Colonel Tom escorted the cart into the elevator—they had managed to stack various items of food along the corridor outside their suites.

There were eight doors in the hallway, and although there were only six guests, the other two suites were locked with the electronic palm scanners, with no way to open them, otherwise they would have used those rooms as makeshift store cupboards.

"I think that will do." Ruth set down bags of apples, bananas, and grapes, and then leaned against the wall, breathing hard. "No more stairs. I'm so done with them."

"Do you think this is wise?" Colonel Tom said as he appraised their haul.

Puzzled, Ruth turned to him. "What do you mean?"

"I've been thinking that our decision to barricade ourselves in here may not be the most well-thought-out plan after all." He scanned the hallway.

"Because Logan mentioned one of us could be the killer?" Ruth asked. "I know what you're saying, but I'd rather—"

"Keep your enemies close?" Colonel Tom said with a wry smile.

"Well, I wouldn't quite put it that way, but sure. Why not?" If someone was determined to murder her, Ruth would rather have a chance at seeing them coming at least. Granted, she wouldn't be able to do much if they wanted to finish her off, but at least she'd go out kicking and screaming.

Having said that, they'd not seen another soul on board the ship. The killer could very well be among them, that was true. With the CCTV recordings deleted, they had no way to be sure. However, Ruth wasn't taking any chances from now on. They'd sit out the next three days, and then they'd let the police take care of it.

Should the Colonel and I return to the CCTV room, find the computers, and remove the hard drive thingies? Perhaps it was a good idea to preserve what little evidence remained, but given her history with tech, she'd likely break them.

Ruth's eyes widened. "Hold on." With a rush of excitement, she pulled a map from her pocket.

Colonel Tom stared over her shoulder. "What are you hunting for?"

"The ship manager's office."

"Oh." Colonel Tom stepped back. "I know where that is."

Ruth looked at him in surprise. "You do?"

"Yes, indeed. Would you like me to take you there?"

"Lead the way." Ruth followed Colonel Tom down a couple of corridors, her little legs having to move several times faster than his to match his long stride.

As they strode along the top landing of the atrium, Ruth peered over the railing and froze.

Colonel Tom turned back. "What's wrong?"

She pressed a finger to her lips and beckoned him over.

Below, Logan had Jeremy shoved against a pillar, with an arm across his throat.

"I say." Colonel Tom went to hurry to the stairs, but Ruth grabbed his arm.

"Wait." She strained to hear.

"Why did he give it to you?" Logan snarled. "What

makes you so special? Have you got something to do with what happened?" He leaned in, eyes intense. "Let me have it instead. Then we don't have to do all this."

Jeremy looked away and muttered something.

After a few seconds, Logan grunted his annoyance and released him. "Fine. Keep it. See if I care." He waved a finger in his face. "But the others are bound to find out eventually, and when they do . . ." Logan pointed to one end of a sofa. "Lift."

Ruth backed away.

Colonel Tom's eyes narrowed. "What was that about?"

Ruth shook her head. "No idea."

"We'll have to confront him." Colonel Tom tugged at his cuffs. "I can't abide a bully."

"I agree," Ruth said. "But we're about to spend the next few days in very close quarters with these people. We don't want to aggravate the situation." She'd once travelled to Switzerland with her sister, and the coach had broken down on a mountain road. They'd spent the next six hours with Margaret winding up the fellow passengers, as was her way, and with Ruth doing everything she could to ease the tension. It had been hell. How someone hadn't thrown Margaret off that mountain was still a wonder to this day.

Colonel Tom considered Ruth for a moment. "If our friend Logan makes another wrong move, I'll have to act." He motioned to a door. "Through here."

As Ruth followed him, she felt bad for lying, because she had every intention of confronting Logan about his actions, but she wanted to do it alone. They'd only recently met, but the colonel came across as a little overbearing at times, a bit like Margaret, and Ruth hadn't figured out his agenda.

She would do her best to reason with Logan and get to

the truth, if that was what needed to happen, but for now Ruth would do everything she could to avoid confrontation.

After a couple more minutes of walking, they entered the ship manager's office: a room six feet by ten, with a desk, a chair, a filing cabinet, and a blank notice board.

Ruth checked the drawers on the left-hand side of the desk and signalled for Colonel Tom to look through the ones on the right.

"What are we searching for?" he asked.

"The ship manager had this magical card thing," Ruth said. "When we got here, he used it to set up the security on my suite door. I'm hoping he left it behind."

"Ah, yes." Colonel Tom nodded. "You think that's some kind of master key?"

Ruth let out a breath. "I hope so." If they could find that, she'd feel a lot safer, plus they'd have access to extra rooms for storage.

They checked the drawers.

"Nothing." Colonel Tom waved a hand at the filing cabinet. "Maybe there's an emergency radio in there. The ship manager should have one."

Ruth tried the filing cabinet drawers, but the ship manager had locked them. "No use."

"It was a nice idea. Perhaps we should try to break them open again later." Colonel Tom nodded back to the hall. "For now, shall we see how the others have gotten on?"

They returned to the suite hallway. Logan and Jeremy had hauled up four large armchairs and two sofas from the atrium to use as a barricade once they were all in, plus several small tables to push together as a makeshift dining table.

The pair of them now leaned against the wall at the far end of the corridor.

"Never. Doing. That. Again." Logan panted, and his face was so red it looked like he might explode.

Probably the most exercise he'd done in years. However, Jeremy hadn't broken a sweat, and he kept his usual distance, gaze averted.

Clearly the fitter of the two.

"Did you find any flares or lanterns?" Colonel Tom asked them.

Logan stared. "What? From the atrium?" He shook his head and pointed at a first aid kit. "Got that, though."

Gabriella and Laura returned with bags, boxes, and armfuls of supplies.

To Ruth's surprise, they had done extremely well on their sorties. Not only had the pair of them gathered ample toiletries, including loo rolls, sanitary products, shower gel, shampoos, conditioner, six different varieties of scented soap, and a giant selection of towels in various sizes, thicknesses, and shades, but they'd also found a stack of board games.

This elicited a groan from Logan, but Colonel Tom looked eager.

"Do you have Scrabble?" he asked like a bright-eyed kid.

Laura shook her head.

However, the biggest surprise was the fact they'd also stumbled across an office with an open door. From there they'd snatched several notepads, pens, and markers. But, most importantly of all, they had secured a gold key card.

"We found it on the floor outside." Gabriella thrust a thumb over her shoulder. "The ship manager must have dropped it."

Ruth gaped, and muttered, "What are the odds?"

7

Colonel Tom examined the ship manager's gold key card with an expression of incredulity. "Exactly what we were looking for. A grand find. Well done, ladies."

Laura beamed. "Thanks."

Colonel Tom handed the key card to Ruth.

She strode to the end of the hall and leaned down to the door's lock. She pressed the key card to the side of it, and it locked then unlocked. Ruth smiled. "Bingo."

Logan let out a groan, slid down the wall, and sat on the floor. He glared at Jeremy.

"Don't worry," Colonel Tom said. "All your furniture moving wasn't in vain. We can still use it as an extra layer of security, should the need arise."

Ruth nodded. Although, now they had a way to secure the door, she felt better that should an emergency arise they'd not have their only exit blocked by masses of heavy furniture. That is, as long as the killer didn't have a key card. If that was the case, then a barricade wasn't such a terrible idea.

Ruth put her hands on her hips and surveyed everyone's work. "This is fantastic. We have enough here to weather any storm, for a few weeks at least, should we need to."

"Weeks?" Laura's eyes went wide.

"Don't mention storms." Gabriella thumbed through her worry beads with swift dexterity. "You'll jinx us."

Ruth recoiled at a brief mental image of a hurricane, the ship drifting toward land, and it being dashed against the rocks. She frowned. "Hold on." Ruth turned an ear but couldn't make out any rumble of engines running. In fact, now she came to think of it, she didn't recall hearing any since they'd arrived. "How are we stationary? Don't the ship's engines need to be running?"

"Long-chained anchors." Colonel Tom leaned against the wall. "We have them at both port and starboard. Saw them yesterday. Most cruise ships have those, coupled with dynamic positioning technology. We have power." Colonel Tom looked up at the ceiling lights. "Would explain why we don't appear to have drifted. Main engines have no need to come alive yet."

Logan's eyes narrowed. "You seem to know a lot about cruise ships. Why's that?"

Colonel Tom made a zipping motion across his lips.

"Haven't we moved past the need for secrecy?" Gabriella said in an exasperated tone. "I mean, come on." She looked between everyone. "Privacy is pointless now, don't you think?"

Logan's lip curled. "There's no chance of that second payment. Not after all this."

Laura gasped. "Someone died, and all you can think about is money?"

He shrugged.

Laura crossed her arms and scowled at him. "In that

case, you go first. Who are you and what are you doing here?"

Logan glanced at Jeremy, and then looked away. "Mind your own business."

"Why do you have those?" Colonel Tom gestured to the beads in Gabriella's hand. "What are they?"

"They're called, kombolói." Gabriella sighed. "They help with the stress of being here." Her eyes narrowed. "Or they're supposed to."

"You have a phobia?" Ruth asked, knowing first-hand how debilitating they could be.

Gabriella stared down at the beads. "When I was seven, I fell off the back of a riverboat. I would have drowned if I hadn't got caught up in some kids' fishing lines. They dragged me onto the bank. Saved my life."

Logan smirked. "If you've got a phobia of drowning, agreeing to board a cruise ship probably wasn't the best idea."

Laura opened her mouth, but Ruth cut across her before things got too heated. "Why don't we have lunch?" She checked the time on her phone—a little after twelve. She waved a hand at the tables and chairs. "I'm sure we can set something up."

And so, they did: two tables pushed together at the far end of the corridor with the sofas and chairs around it. People had to climb over the arms and walk across the cushions to sit, but it was better than nothing.

As Ruth laid out some sausage rolls, she thought back to thirty years prior, when circumstances had forced a career change. That was when she'd turned her passion into a revenue stream.

That stream had started out as a trickle: travelling round local industrial estates in her van, selling homemade sausage rolls, cakes, and sandwiches to the workers. Then came the shop, then more shops, and over the years the stream had the good fortune of becoming a river. Toward the end, Ruth had a mini empire, catering for a wide range of places and events, everything from weddings to wakes, plus supplying hotels and restaurants when they were short-staffed.

Then more luck: an offer to buy the business she couldn't refuse; enough money to retire at the ripe old age of fifty-five. That, coupled with the steady income from John's old business—now taken care of by their daughter, Sara—kept Ruth more than comfortable and meant she could put aside money to pay for Greg's tuition and lodging.

However, after a year of pottering about, Ruth had gone out of her mind with boredom. So, that was when she turned her attention to a degree in food management, plus hospitality, nutrition, and general culinary arts.

The guests spent the afternoon and early evening eating, playing games, and making small talk that avoided anything to do with their private lives, which was quite hard given Ruth's natural predilection to be nosey.

Ordinarily, she would have thought it silly they stuck to their privacy, especially given the circumstances, but she wasn't ready to share her life story with them either.

Throughout the afternoon and evening, Ruth excused herself several times for bathroom breaks but also used the time to check up on Merlin, making sure he had plenty of food and water, and anything else he might need. Truth was, Merlin really wasn't bothered as long as he had access to his padded box and a litter tray.

Back in the hallway, Jeremy made himself a cheese sandwich.

Ruth eyed the slices of white bread. "In the novel *The Expedition of Humphry Clinker*, there's mention of bread containing 'a poisonous compound of chalk, alum, and bone ash.'" She winked at Jeremy. "Perhaps that's where the line from 'Jack and the Beanstalk' comes from: 'I'll crush his bones to make my bread.'"

Jeremy screwed up his face and set the sandwich aside.

Having busted open a packet of peanuts, Logan offered them around.

Jeremy recoiled.

"Allergic?" Logan grinned, grabbed a handful, and stuffed them into his mouth. "Yum. You're missing out."

Jeremy looked away in disgust.

Colonel Tom fanned a card deck and held it out to Ruth. "Pick one."

Ruth selected a card at random—seven of diamonds—and showed it to the others.

"Now put it back," Colonel Tom said with an air of confidence.

Ruth did as he asked and slid the card somewhere near the middle.

Colonel Tom handed her the deck. "Shuffle them."

Ruth did, thoroughly, and returned the cards to him.

Colonel Tom waved his hand over the deck, clicked his fingers, and then smiled. "Hold very still." He reached over Ruth's shoulder and threw the deck down the hallway. The cards hit the wall and tumbled to the floor. Colonel Tom sat back. "Check the top pocket of your blouse."

Ruth reached in and pulled out the seven of diamonds.

Laura clapped and laughed. "How did you do that?"

"Sleight of hand and misdirection," the colonel said. "All quite elementary once you grasp the basics."

Although it was only a little after nine, Ruth yawned. "Time for my bed."

The others agreed, climbed from the chairs, and headed to their suites.

Ruth locked the door at the end of the hallway.

"No one leaves their rooms until morning," Colonel Tom warned them. "And don't let anyone into your suites. Understood?" He received half-hearted acknowledgements, and he nodded at Ruth. "Good night."

"Hold on," Logan said. "Who gets that key card?"

Ruth held it up. "I do." She hesitated at her door and stared at the lock. "I wonder if these connect to a computer somewhere?" she said half to herself. "They'd have logs, wouldn't they?"

"Seriously, why you?" Gabriella asked, ignoring her question. "Why do you get that key card?"

Ruth snapped out of her daze. "Oh, because I'm the only one who can trust me. In me, I trust, and I trust alone." She stepped into her suite before they could question her logic, and as Ruth closed her door, she let out a slow breath. "I don't know about three days, Merlin," she said as he sauntered from the bedroom. "I have a feeling this is going to be a long night."

She dropped the key card onto a side table, gave the silly cat precisely three strokes—any more than three would warrant a swat of his paw—and then she padded off to the bathroom.

Ruth spent way too long in a hot bath, watched recorded TV programmes with Merlin curled on her lap on the sofa, fireplace lit and flames in full effect, and had just about decided to go to bed when something thumped in the hallway.

With a strong feeling of déjà vu, Ruth rushed to her door and peered through the peephole.

As on the previous night, Logan had snuck out of his suite and now tiptoed past her door, slinking down the hallway.

"And there he goes again." Ruth pulled back, shaking her head. "These youngsters have way too much energy." She stepped toward her bedroom and hesitated. On the other hand, perhaps she should say something to him. After all, it wasn't wise to sneak about. However, by the time Ruth opened her suite door again, Logan had gone. Ruth yawned and shuffled to her bedroom. She climbed into bed and opened *Mrs Beeton's Book of Household Management*, ready to be dazzled.

There came a soft knock.

Ruth rolled on her side and pulled the bedsheet over her head.

The knocking came again, more insistent.

"All right." With her eyes still closed, Ruth swung her legs out of bed and sat up. She considered lying down again and seeing how fast she could get back to sleep, but instead her treacherous feet searched the surrounding floor for her slippers. Finding them, Ruth blinked herself awake and grabbed her phone from the bedside table: 4:16 a.m.

She groaned, and there came more knocking, unrelenting, annoying. "All right. Keep your hair on."

Ruth grumbled about, feeling like she'd only just laid

her head on the pillows, but dutifully obeyed the summons, although she didn't want to, and stood.

She snatched a bathrobe from the back of a chair, wrapped it round her, and walked from the bedroom. "This had better be good." Ruth tensed and stopped short of the suite door. "Or bad?" That was a point. For a moment Ruth had forgotten where she was. Now fully awake as though someone had thrown a bucket of ice water in her face, she held her breath and peered through the peephole.

Laura stood in the hallway, wringing her hands, looking left and right, bouncing on the balls of her feet. She went to knock again, but Ruth opened the door an inch. "What do you want?" she asked in a level tone. "It's late."

Laura barged into the room, almost barreling Ruth over. She closed the door behind her and pressed her back against it, breathing hard, her chest rising and falling, a manic stare fixed on Ruth.

Ruth staggered a few steps and raised her fists. "I warn you; I know king fu."

Laura frowned. "Don't you mean kung fu?"

Ruth waved her off. "Whatever. I'm tired. What do you want?" She kept her fists high in case Laura got any funny ideas.

"I heard a noise."

"Great," Ruth said. "Me too. Someone knocking incessantly at my door. Seems to have stopped now. Go back to bed."

Laura took a step toward her, eyes intense. "I mean outside." She nodded at the French doors to the balcony.

"Oh." Ruth lowered her fists and scanned Laura for weapons. The girl was slight of build, but those types of people were so often the ones you had to watch out for: the wiry, snakelike creatures who could strike in an instant, with ferocious rage and zero warning.

Laura rushed past Ruth, making her flinch.

Can you order tranquilizers off the internet? Scratch that, we still don't have any blinkin' internet. Besides, Ruth wasn't sure the postman would appreciate having to row halfway across the ocean to deliver a parcel.

Laura pulled back the curtains and peered out. "I had one of my doors open." She frowned. "I don't remember opening it." She shrugged. "But my air-conditioning has stopped working, so guess I must have done it in my sleep."

Ah, sleep. Wouldn't that be a fine thing?

Ruth glanced at the floor-level vent. Come to think of it, her heating had stopped too, while she was in bed. Ruth's brow furrowed. She had her thermostat set to volcanic.

Laura seemed to notice her confusion. "I can't sleep unless my bedroom is icy cool. I like to wrap up nice and snug in a duvet."

"To each their own." Ruth studied her unwanted guest. "So, this noise you heard?" Hopefully they could solve the riddle in swift fashion so she could get back to sleep.

Laura beckoned her over. "Come see." She threw open one of the French doors, and Ruth followed her onto the balcony. "My room is this one," Laura whispered, and pointed to the next balcony along. "I heard a scrape." She raised her eyebrows and then stepped to the balustrade and pointed over it. "Down there."

Keeping a wary distance, Ruth edged her way to the railing and peered at the promenade below. "What am I looking for?"

All seemed quiet. As it well should.

"There." Laura glanced at Ruth and jabbed a finger. "Right there. That door. I saw someone go through it."

Ruth squinted. "What did they look like?"

"I don't know," Laura said. "I only glimpsed them for a second."

"Man or woman?"

"Man, I think. I'm not sure." She glanced over her shoulder, as if afraid someone might overhear, and lowered her voice further. "If we're all locked in here together, that means there definitely is someone else on board this ship, right?"

"If you had to guess, who do you think it was?" Ruth asked, trying not to let any tone of dubiousness slip through.

Laura shrugged, and then her eyes narrowed. "That guy with black hair. It might have been him. Actually, now I think about it, I'm sure it was."

Ruth's eyebrows lifted. "Jeremy?" She'd expected Laura to say Logan. After all, he seemed to have a habit of sneaking about. "Why do you think it was Jeremy?" Ruth asked, still not sure she believed a word.

"He's shifty. Something's not right about that guy." Laura shuddered. "He's too quiet. Odd. Creepy."

Ruth yawned. "You can't suspect someone is bad only because they don't say much." Come to think of it, she wasn't sure she'd heard him talk at all yet.

Laura took another step closer, so they now only stood a foot apart. "Lean over here." She waved a hand. "You'll see the door I mean." Her eyes returned to their previous wide and manic state.

"That's okay. I believe you." Ruth hesitated for a couple of seconds as Laura gave her a look as if to say there was no way she'd drop it unless Ruth took a peek, and then, tense, ready to lash out should the girl make any sudden moves, Ruth leaned over the railing and peered down.

Sure enough, a door farther along the promenade stood

ajar. Ruth was about to pull back when she spotted a duffle bag ten feet away, by the wall. It had not been there the previous night, otherwise they would have found it during their stroll.

For a few seconds, Ruth wondered why Laura hadn't mentioned the bag, but perhaps it wasn't visible from the other balcony's vantage point.

"Where does that door go?" Laura asked, wringing her hands.

"I don't know," Ruth murmured. "Erm. Look, do you know which suite the Colonel's staying in?" She thought about calling him to see what he made of the situation. Besides, she was awake now and might as well spread the misery.

Laura shook her head. "I went to bed right after you. I didn't see which door he went through."

"Right." Ruth pursed her lips. She didn't see the point in waking everyone, especially as she didn't know who to trust other than Colonel Tom. They all needed a good night's sleep, and Ruth included herself in that.

Laura bounced from one foot to another again, and sweat glistened on her forehead. "My brother warned me not to take this job. He said it sounded fishy."

Ruth chose to ignore the pun. She was far too tired for jokes. Instead, she yawned. "What do you mean?"

"My brother said something was off. That it's weird we're not allowed to share our histories, and the amount they're paying me is too good to be true." Her expression intensified. "I need that money though. I'm overdrawn." She huffed. "Now I wish I'd listened to him. He told me not to come back."

Ruth's brow furrowed. "You've been here before?"

"Well, not the ship, obviously. I'm talking about

Bonmouth. They paid for my honest opinion then too. Didn't pay me as much though." Laura clapped a hand over her mouth, realising she'd said too much.

Ruth rested a hand on her shoulder. "It's okay."

Thirty-five years ago, she vowed not to get caught up with situations like this again. Doing so before had almost wrecked her life and certainly had ended her chosen career at the time.

She should stay away. That's what she should do—keep her nose out and let the police deal with it in a few days. After all, that was their job, but now Ruth had seen the duffle bag . . . She swore. "Fine. Wait here." She'd get down there and back in a few minutes, and then they could go back to sleep. She was being nosey, *not* investigating. No harm in that.

Ruth rushed through the sitting room, into her bedroom, and closed the door. Inside the walk-in closet, she threw on a pair of comfortable shoes, plus her hat and coat. She checked Merlin and studied herself in the mirror. Am I being overly reckless? *Well, yes*, but overriding curiosity still got the better of her, *so nuts to it*.

8

Back in her suite's sitting room, Ruth snatched up the key card and waved Laura over. "I'm going to check it out," she whispered.

"The door on the promenade? On your own?"

Ruth couldn't tell if Laura looked impressed or like she thought Ruth was crazy. Probably a bit of both. Ruth held up the key card. "I'll be quick. Lock the suites' hallway door when I'm gone and don't open it for anyone else. Wait for me to come back."

"How will I know it's you?"

Ruth blinked. "Oh. That's a good point." She clicked her fingers. "How about a secret knock?" Ruth rapped her knuckle on the table: *two fast, one slow, two fast.* "Got it?"

Laura scratched her head. "I think so."

"Good girl." Ruth put a finger to her lips and then opened the door and snuck through.

The pair of them crept down the hallway. At the end, Ruth unlocked the door. She handed the key card to Laura and winked.

Laura winked back and mouthed, *"Be careful."*

Fat chance. Ruth took a breath, opened the door, and stepped through.

Ruth stood on the other side for a moment, heart racing, and when the door locked behind her, her pulse sped up to a few notches past *ludicrous speed*.

Ruth took a deep breath and, before she chickened out, hurried down the next corridor. She kept glancing over her shoulder as her imagination played tricks. Every shadow, every tiny creak was the killer coming to get her. She hung a left and jogged to the stairs.

"Grab the bag and go. No hanging about. Got it?" Ruth murmured under her breath as she raced down two flights. "Got it." Ruth then said through tight lips, "Are you sure? You promise? Seriously—grab and go, grab and go. Nothing else." After all, she knew how easily distracted she could sometimes become.

At the bottom of the stairs, Ruth peered into a dimly lit hallway. She eyed the elevator, and then her gaze moved to the right. A vase of flowers sat on a table. Ruth jogged over to them, set the vase on the floor, and then she walked the table over to the elevator and hit the call button.

After a minute, the doors opened. Ruth slid the table between the doors, and then stepped back, hands raised. Ten seconds later, the doors closed onto the table. "That should hold you," she murmured.

Now anyone following her couldn't use the elevator, which would buy her a few more seconds and hopefully increase her chances of hearing them coming.

Ruth glanced about, shuddered, and then jogged along the corridor, staying close to the wall, and stopped at a door with a sign above it that read:

Promenade Deck

It stood ajar. This had to be the same door they could make out from their balconies.

Ruth took a moment longer to compose herself and then opened it. All was quiet outside, and the duffle bag sat several feet away.

Ruth glanced up at the suite balconies, and stepped to the bag. She knelt. "Please don't be a bomb," she said, unzipping it and peering inside. She stared for several seconds, her eyebrows knitted. "What the—?" Ruth reached into the bag, but a muffled scream startled her. Her head snapped up. It had come from one of the suites. Ruth grabbed the bag's handles and raced back inside.

She jogged along the hallway but stopped dead in her tracks and gasped. The table was back in its original position, with the vase of flowers on top, elevator doors closed.

Eyes wide, body stiff, she stared into the darkened hallway, ears straining.

After a few seconds' hesitation, Ruth edged over to the stairs, and then hurried up them two at a time.

On the floor above, she raced along the corridor, and peered into the duffle bag again. Folded neatly inside lay an army officer's uniform, complete with medals.

Back at the door to the suites, Ruth knocked: *two fast, one slow, two fast.*

No answer.

Ruth frowned. "Have I remembered the secret knock correctly?"

She tried again: *two fast, one slow, two fast.*

Nothing.

Ruth's blood pounded in her ears.

Now she came to think of it, the scream had sounded like Laura.

With her heart in her throat, Ruth dropped the duffle bag to one side, and with both fists clenched, she banged on the door as hard as she could and shouted, "What's going on? Let me in."

A click from the lock forced Ruth back a step, and then the door swung open to reveal Colonel Tom in the hallway, ashen-faced. "Why are you out there?"

"I was checking something." Ruth blinked. "Why, what's happened?"

"A murder, madam."

Dazed, Ruth shuffled into the suites' hallway and closed the door behind her.

Laura sat in a chair by the wall, head buried in her hands, sobbing, while Logan comforted her. Jeremy stood away from them, with his usual blank expression, hands clasped, staring at the floor.

Ruth's heart sank. "Gabriella," she murmured. "Oh no. What's happened?"

Colonel Tom pointed to the last suite door at the end of the hallway. It stood ajar.

Ruth shook her head. No way was she going in there.

Logan jumped to his feet and stepped up to her, his face twisted with anger. "Where were you?"

Ruth stared at him. "Sorry?"

He stepped close, so their noses were only a few inches apart. "Just now," he shouted, "where were you?"

"I say," Colonel Tom interjected.

Ruth held up a hand, set her jaw, and glared at Logan. "Back off."

He motioned over Ruth's shoulder. "You were out there. What were you up to?" He edged even closer, face red, fists clenched.

Ruth placed a hand on Logan's chest and pushed him a

couple of steps away from her. "Shouting will do none of us any good."

"Then explain what you were doing," Logan snarled.

Ruth took a breath to compose herself. "I heard a noise on the promenade deck." She didn't make eye contact with Laura, deciding to keep the girl out of it for now. "I went to check it out. A door stood open. Probably left that way by the crew when they abandoned ship, and it banged in the wind."

"You expect us to believe that?" Logan shouted. "Do you think we're idiots?"

"I suggest you calm yourself, sir," Colonel Tom said.

"I've got this," Ruth said to him, keeping her focus on the bully.

"Might have known you'd be on her side," Logan snapped at Colonel Tom. "You two have been like peas in a pod since we first got here." His eyes narrowed, and he looked between them. "You already knew each other, didn't you? You're working together."

"Don't be absurd," Colonel Tom said in a low tone. "I will not warn you again, sir. Get a grip of yourself, or I—"

"Who the hell do you think you're talking to?" Logan waved a fist at him. "Don't expect for one moment we haven't noticed you sneaking off together and talking behind our backs."

Ruth kept her voice calm and measured like Colonel Tom's. "Why were you in her room?"

Logan's face fell. "What?"

"Earlier," Ruth said. "I saw you sneak out of your suite and into . . ." She pointed at the door that stood ajar. "You left your room the night before too. What was going on?"

All eyes moved to Logan.

Laura sniffed. "What's she talking about?"

Colonel Tom glowered at Logan. "Yes, I think we would all like some clarity. What were you up to, sir?"

Logan glared at Ruth, and then shook his head and stormed off.

"Where are you going?" Colonel Tom called after him.

"Mind your own damn business." Logan entered his suite and slammed the door behind him.

Ruth let out a slow breath.

"I don't trust him," Colonel Tom said.

Ruth had to agree, but now was not the time to elevate tempers further. In spite of herself, she turned to Gabriella's suite and wrestled with her conscience.

On the one hand, Ruth should close the door and stay away, but on the other, if there was a clue as to who had murdered Gabriella, she needed to find it. They all did. Any hint at all could solve the mystery and keep them safe until help arrived.

She took a deep breath, trying to calm her racing heart and not think about the fact she was going to break a promise she'd made to herself a long time ago. However, after a glance at Laura, she lifted her head and walked on through.

The colonel went to follow, but Ruth stopped. "Give me a minute alone, please?"

He hesitated and then backed off.

"Wait, I have a question." Ruth kept her voice low. "Who found the body?"

Colonel Tom tipped his head toward Laura.

Ruth winced. "Poor girl." She faced the sitting room again.

Someone had dimmed the lights, but it looked identical to Ruth's with its L-shaped sofa, TV, fireplace, bar, armchair, and a billion scatter cushions.

A basket of fruit, a bouquet, a snacks hamper, and a tablet sat on the coffee table.

Tensed, Ruth faced the bedroom door and nudged it open with her foot. The bathroom door stood ajar, and a pair of feet were visible inside. Ruth's vision tunnelled, and she held her breath as she approached.

Gabriella lay in the foetal position on the bathroom floor: knees pulled to her chest, face pale, fingers curled. She wore silk pyjamas, and air from a floor vent played with her hair, tossing red strands across her doll-like face.

Ruth stared. "You poor, poor thing." A mixture of sadness and horror washed through her.

She muttered a prayer, and then curiosity got the better of her. "What's happened here?" Careful not to disturb evidence, Ruth edged past the body and scanned the bathroom.

Items around the sink lay on their sides, some fallen to the floor: perfume, hairspray, makeup . . . Ruth glanced in the sink and spun away. Gabriella had been sick. The bin nearby had a few makeup wipes in the bottom, covered in smeared foundation and eyeliner.

Steeling herself, Ruth knelt by the body. Around Gabriella's mouth was more evidence she'd felt under the weather in her final moments, and her makeup-free skin had a blueish-green tinge, with blotches of red.

Ruth leaned in close to her mouth and sniffed. Apart from an acidic scent, she caught a hint of bitter almonds and maybe garlic too. She tried to think back to what Gabriella had eaten earlier but was sure she'd not sampled any of the nuts, and Colonel Tom had brought nothing back that contained garlic. Ruth would be sure to check later.

Going slow and careful not to touch her, Ruth examined Gabriella's hands: pain had curled the woman's fingers, but her fingernails were clean and manicured. Ruth moved along the arms, searching for any needle marks, then over the hair, scalp, neck, and all areas of exposed skin. Nothing stood out, apart from bright red hypostasis.

Having had enough of this tragedy, Ruth got to her feet and backed out of the bathroom. She kept close to the walls and scanned the bedroom, along with the walk-in closet, but nothing looked disturbed or out of place.

Back in the sitting room, she walked to the bar. An open bottle of Laura's lemonade sat on the marble top, along with vodka. Ruth leaned in and gave both bottles a tentative sniff. From the lemonade, she got the powerful scent of— surprise, surprise—*lemon*, but it masked faint hints of the almonds and garlic.

Ruth's gaze drifted to a half-empty glass next to the bottles.

Poisoned lemonade? Does that mean the killer tried to murder Laura but got Gabriella instead?

Without knowing when the killer slipped the poison into the lemonade, they had no way to figure a timeline. Even so, it meant someone had poisoned the lemonade earlier in the day. *But when? And who? Logan? Laura?*

Ruth's attention then moved to Gabriella's worry beads lying on the counter, and another wave of sadness washed over her.

"Are you okay?" Colonel Tom entered the suite.

Ruth stepped back. "Laura has a bottle of lemonade too. Please get it."

Colonel Tom marched off.

While he was gone, Ruth turned on the spot and scanned the rest of the room, but nothing seemed out of the ordinary.

Staying close to the wall, she made her way over to the

curtains, pulled them back, and peered out before using them to open the door without leaving fingerprints. She stepped onto the balcony.

Ruth peered over the railing but could not make out the door on the promenade deck from this vantage point.

"Madam?"

Ruth jumped, spun back, and clutched her chest. "Don't do that." She never was any good with jump scares, which was why she'd always avoided horror movies and surprise parties.

Colonel Tom held up Laura's bottle of lemonade. It was half-empty.

"That answers that particular question." Ruth took it from him, removed the cap, and gave it a sniff anyway. "Smells normal." She handed it back. "Best she not drink it, in case." They stepped back into the sitting area. "Try not to touch anything." Ruth sat on the edge of the sofa and stared at the tablet. Then a thought struck her. Ruth leapt to her feet again. "Wait here." She dashed past Colonel Tom. "Don't move."

In the hallway, Ruth hunted through the mountain of food and found a slice of cake wrapped in aluminium foil. She tore off a piece of the foil and raced into her suite.

Ruth opened a pack of cotton swabs, removed one, wetted the tip, and returned to the sitting room. There she snatched up a ballpoint pen, slid out the ink reservoir, and shoved the cotton bud into the pen's opening. Next, Ruth wrapped the foil around the pen shaft, making sure it was tight and touching the wet Q-tip.

Then, improvised device in hand, she strode back into the hallway.

Laura frowned as Ruth raced past her. "What's going on?"

"Checking something." Back in Gabriella's suite, Ruth sat on the sofa. Then, using her makeshift stylus, she pressed the power button on the tablet and navigated to the video. If it was like her welcome message, it wouldn't contain much information about Gabriella, but Ruth had to be sure to leave no stone unturned.

"What's that device you've made?" Colonel Tom said. "I thought you weren't tech savvy."

"I'm not," Ruth muttered. "I learned this somewhere else."

"Where?"

She glanced at him. "A documentary on forensics."

Colonel Tom's eyebrows lifted. "Ah. You've made that so you can use the screen without leaving fingerprints? Impressive. How come you're interested in such things?"

"I'll explain later." Truth was, Ruth didn't understand the science or mechanics of why it worked, but she'd always kept an interest in the subject of forensics and investigations. She couldn't help herself.

Old habits die hard, as the saying goes. Literally.

Ruth pressed play, skipped the video's introduction, and got to the part with the personalised message, while Colonel Tom sat beside her.

As with Ruth's video, the woman in the blue suit stepped into view, with her mousy-blonde hair, standing against a plain black backdrop. "Good afternoon, Miss Roberts," she said. "Thank you for agreeing to work with us. It's an honour to have you on board."

"That precious woman said the same thing to me." Colonel Tom shifted his weight. "I thought I was special."

Despite the dire situation, Ruth smirked.

"As per our correspondence," the woman said, "we've hired you for your unparalleled expertise and professionalism. You came highly recommended. And, as you can see, we have followed your design and furnishing suggestions, and like with the rest of the *Ocean Odyssey*, have spared no expense." She half smiled. "We hope to have satisfied your high standards." The lady's face turned serious again. "Please do not discuss your line of work or any personal details with your fellow guests. We want to maintain an overarching, impartial, and independent evaluation, with no internal or external influences."

Ruth frowned at the screen. "Why, though?" She hit the pause button and let out a breath. "Interior designer, not a model."

"Ex-model." Laura stood in the doorway.

9

Laura stepped into Gabriella's suite, her expression full of intense sadness. Her eyes darted to the closed bedroom door and back again. "Should you be in here?" She sniffed.

"None of us should be in here," Ruth said. "This is a crime scene. How do you know she was an ex-model?"

Laura hesitated and then said in a small voice, "She might have mentioned it to me yesterday."

Colonel Tom clucked his tongue.

Ruth looked around the sitting room again, hunting for anything she might have overlooked.

The interior designer was here to inspect the ship builders' work? That meant the owners had also likely instructed her to compile a report and hand it in at the end of her stay, as they'd asked of Ruth. *And what about the others? Why are they here?*

Ruth composed herself and stood. "Let's get out of here before we contaminate the scene more than we already have." Now was not the moment to let Laura know something added to Gabriella's lemonade had poisoned her.

Besides, Ruth didn't know whether that same poison was originally intended for Laura and the killer had simply messed up and got the wrong person.

As they left the suite and closed the door, Ruth stopped dead in her tracks. She had to tell her. It was only fair.

Laura and the colonel turned back.

Ruth steered the former to a chair. "You might want to sit down for this." Jeremy was not about. Clearly, he'd returned to his suite. A wise move given the circumstances, and Ruth couldn't blame him.

Laura's brow furrowed, but she did as Ruth asked and sat.

Ruth dropped into a chair opposite, and her face softened. "I—" She sighed. "There's no easy way to tell you this —I'm sorry—but Gabriella was poisoned."

Laura clapped a hand over her mouth.

"There's more." Ruth glanced up at Colonel Tom and back again. "It was the lemonade."

Laura stared at her for several seconds, eyes as large as dinner plates, and then realisation dawned on her face. She gasped. "The killer meant to kill me?"

"We don't know that for sure," Colonel Tom said.

Laura's chest rose and fell as she started to hyperventilate. "No." She shook her head, and tears streamed down her face. "No. That can't be."

Ruth slipped from her chair and knelt in front of the girl. "It's okay." She rested a hand on Laura's leg. "It's not your fault. Some twisted piece of—"

Laura let out a high-pitched cry and leapt to her feet, almost toppling Ruth. She ran down the hall and into her suite, sobbing and wailing as she went.

"Let me speak to her," Colonel Tom said as Ruth clambered to her feet to go after her. "Leave it to me. I'll see if I can calm her down." He followed Laura inside but left the door open.

Ruth stood in the hallway, staring after them. Laura's continued howls reached her ears, along with Colonel Tom's muffled words, but she didn't try to make sense of them.

Then she swore under her breath. "I forgot." Ruth hurried to the end of the hallway, threw open the door, and went to grab the duffle bag, but it was gone.

Stunned, she closed the door again and turned back around. She stared into space, confused as to who might have taken the duffle bag—and why.

She searched among the supplies and furniture, but it wasn't there either.

When I was in the suite with Gabriella's body, where was everyone else?

Ruth tried to remember the moment she'd made it back clearly in her mind's eye: Logan had stormed off to his room like a scorned two-year-old; Jeremy kept his usual distance; Laura sat in one of those chairs, sobbing her poor little heart out; and as for Colonel Tom . . . Ruth had assumed he'd stayed in the hall, close by while she checked out the crime scene.

What happened next?

She shut her eyes.

When Ruth had finished with the body and gone back to Gabriella's sitting room, she'd checked out the balcony, and that was the moment Colonel Tom had appeared. He'd asked her if she was okay. He then sat on the sofa next to Ruth, and they'd watched the video.

However, the time she'd spent between last seeing him in the hallway and that moment on the balcony was plenty enough for Colonel Tom to grab the bag and stash it somewhere.

Ruth opened her eyes and frowned.

Did he spot *it when I opened the door?*

Colonel Tom certainly had been the closest to the bag, and it was unlikely anyone else knew where Ruth had dropped it, but that didn't automatically mean he'd been the one to take it.

Assumptions could be dangerous.

Besides, Laura would have seen him do it, wouldn't she?

And if she or Jeremy hadn't taken the bag when Colonel Tom came into Gabriella's suite, which Ruth thought also unlikely because she and the colonel would have spotted them dart past the door and back again, that left another possibility: the killer, roaming the ship, had seen Ruth take the bag, followed her, and seized the opportunity to snatch it back.

Ruth let out a slow breath and cursed herself for being stupid enough to leave it behind, but she'd been caught off guard. A mistake she vowed not to make again.

Ruth chuckled at that. Up until now, her life had been riddled with mistakes and clumsy accidents. "Why break a habit?" Anyway, blunders were not only the best way to learn but a whole lot of fun. Well, as long as nobody got hurt.

Colonel Tom left Laura's suite and strode over to Ruth. "I think the current arrangement isn't working." He thrust a thumb over his shoulder. "We need to revisit our first idea—stay in one room, all together, where we can sleep in shifts. That way, we'll keep an eye on one another."

Ruth nodded in reply, not meeting his gaze, her expression vacant.

"Are you all right, madam?" Colonel Tom asked. "Is it the shock of—"

"Did you take the duffle bag?" Her eyes rose to meet his.

"Duffle bag? I'm not sure what you mean."

Ruth motioned for Colonel Tom to follow her, opened the door at the end of the hallway, and pointed at the floor outside. "I left a bag right there." She watched his reaction.

Colonel Tom's expression turned to that of confusion. "I'm afraid I didn't see a bag. When did you leave it there? What was in it?"

Ruth shook her head. "You know what, it doesn't matter. Forget I said anything." She wasn't sure she believed his answer, but he was hardly going to admit taking it if he had. Even so, she'd pay closer attention to his actions from now on.

Ruth closed the door, took a deep breath, and got a grip of herself. "It's a good plan. The whole being in one room idea." Ruth forced half a tremulous smile. "We'll set up camp in the dining room, like we originally thought."

"Somewhere with plenty of light," Colonel Tom suggested with a bob of his head.

"We can stay close together, but not too close." Ruth looked at the time on her phone: 8:19 a.m. That meant almost thirty-four hours to wait out until Greg cottoned on. An eternity. But she consoled herself with the fact they were more than halfway through this ordeal.

Laura appeared at her suite door, dressed in jeans and a baggy T-shirt, her hair dishevelled, face pale and drawn.

"How are you feeling?" Ruth asked in a soft tone.

Laura sniffed. "Better." She walked over to them and lowered her voice. "The rest of the lemonade." She looked like she might cry again. "The bottles will be evidence, right? Could be poisoned too?"

"Good point." Ruth cursed herself for not thinking of that yet. She really needed to get a hold of the situation and focus. "Can you show me where they are? Those other bottles? We must lock them away somewhere safe for the police."

"I'll come with you," Colonel Tom said.

Ruth held up a hand. "Tell the other two we're moving, and start packing anything you need." She pointed to the rooms. "Meanwhile, we'll grab those bottles of lemonade, lock them up, and come back here to help. Don't leave until we return. We'll all move together as a group." Before Colonel Tom could question her orders, she marched into her suite. "Back in a minute," she called over her shoulder to Laura.

"Wait." The girl hurried over. "I'm staying close to you." She slipped inside the room.

Ruth hesitated, glanced at Colonel Tom, and then closed the door.

Inside her suite, Ruth guided Laura to the sofa. "Sit." Determination coursed through her, and now fully out of her daze, Ruth marched to her bedroom. "Give me a couple of minutes," she said, and closed the door.

Ruth changed out of her nightclothes and into her usual all-black attire, including an overcoat.

She checked on Merlin, who sat out on the balcony. "Getting some fresh air?"

He let out a low meow.

Merlin wasn't the type of cat to go wondering.

"Hungry?" Ruth fetched a pouch of food, emptied it into his bowl, and put down some clean water. "I won't be long. You'll have to come with us." For now, he was safest where he was.

After a glance in the mirror, Ruth stepped back into the sitting room.

Laura wrung her hands and stared at the floor.

Ruth felt sorry for her. Murder, no matter how sugar-coated, was always a traumatic experience, and you never truly hardened to the sight of it. "Ready?"

Laura looked up. "I don't trust him."

Ruth cocked an eyebrow. "Who?"

"That guy in the suit." She shuddered. "Something's off with him. He's weird."

"Logan?" Ruth sat next to her. "Why do you say that?"

"I don't know. He gives me the creeps."

"Way to be specific," Ruth murmured.

Laura's gaze moved to the door, and she kept her voice low. "Gabriella told me that other guy, the one with the tattoo on his elbow, he's a criminal."

"Did she know him?"

"I don't think so," Laura said. "She might have done. Told me to stay away from him. Said he was bad news."

"But she didn't say anything specific to you?"

Laura shook her head.

"Okay." Ruth stood and held out a hand. "Let's go get those other lemonade bottles, shall we?"

Back in the hall, Ruth led Laura through the door at the end. She put it on the latch, and as it clicked shut, Ruth faced her again. "When I came back earlier, I left something here." She pointed at the floor by the wall. "Did you see anyone take it? A black duffle bag?" She indicated the dimensions with her hands.

"No," Laura said, "but I wasn't really paying any attention. Not after what happened. I was a bit, you know, out there. Sorry."

Ruth rested a hand on her shoulder, sympathy swelled within her for the poor girl. "We'll get through this." She half smiled, although it was the last thing she felt like doing. "Let's keep moving."

As they strode toward the stairs, Laura said, "So, you

found something? When you went to check out that door? You discovered a bag?"

Ruth hesitated, and then nodded.

"What was it?"

Ruth stopped at the stairs. "I don't know," she lied. "I didn't get a chance to look inside." She lied again. "I heard you scream and came running." Ruth decided now was not the time to reveal the bag held a uniform that could well have belonged to the colonel.

Ruth pushed the door open, and they headed on down the stairs. A wave of guilt washed over her, and heat rose up her neck and into her cheeks, but she wasn't ready to share the truth about the bag until she understood its meaning.

As they hurried down the stairs, she said, "You were the first person to discover Gabriella's body, right?"

"While I was waiting for you to come back, I noticed her door was ajar." Laura sighed. "I knew something was wrong."

Ruth pursed her lips. *The door was ajar?* Which meant the killer had left it that way. Rather careless of them. After all, they'd gone to the trouble of poisoning the lemonade, to do it stealthily and remain undetected, only to leave Gabriella's door open as they left the scene.

Did Logan do that during his sneaky visit? He could have left the door ajar by mistake as he left her suite.

Ruth frowned. That couldn't be right. The killer had not needed to be in Gabriella's suite.

The poison could have been planted at any time, maybe days in advance. Had Gabriella fallen ill and tried to get help? No. Her body was in the bathroom.

"Are you okay?" Laura asked as they headed down the next flight.

Ruth snapped out of her thoughts. "I'm fine."

But something didn't add up.

On the next floor down, as they strode from the stair-well and finally made it to the dining room, Laura pointed at a door on the other side of the buffet carousel. "The bar is through there. That's where we got the vodka and lemonade." She went to walk toward it but froze midstride.

Startled, Ruth looked about. "What's wrong?"

Wide-eyed, Laura stared across the room.

With trepidation, Ruth followed her gaze.

The painting at the far end of the table where they'd sat together the first night, the one with a view of Bonmouth in its heyday, had inexplicably disappeared, and on the wall behind, someone had painted a new image: the silhouette of a black cat.

Laura looked at the cat painting, and then at Ruth's cat pendant and her black clothes.

"I didn't do this." Struggling to believe her own eyes, Ruth muttered, "Stay here," and hurried to the wall. She stared at the black cat for a full minute, and then leaned in for a closer look. The paint seemed dry, so no way to tell whether it had been done last night or days ago. *Was it always there, only covered by the painting of Bonmouth?* Under-neath the cat's paws were two parallel vertical lines.

Ruth returned to Laura, who now kept her distance. "Let's grab those bottles of lemonade and get out of here."

As Laura led the way across the dining hall, she kept glancing back at Ruth, almost as if she expected her to pounce when her back was turned.

They entered a sports-themed bar area with a horse-shoe-shaped bar top, the floor crammed with tables and chairs. Signed photos of various sports personalities hung on the walls, none of whom Ruth recognised. Sports was not her thing. Several TVs suspended from the ceiling sat dark, all switched off, and the place was eerily quiet.

Laura lifted a shaking finger. "The bottles of lemonade are in the middle fridge."

Ruth scooted behind the bar and went to grab them, but the fridge lay empty. She checked the other fridges on either side to be sure, but they didn't have any bottles of lemonade either. Ruth then scanned the shelves before turning back. "Are you sure they were here?"

"What do you mean?" Laura leaned over the bar. "Where have they gone? The bottles were right there. Another four. I saw them myself."

"The killer cleaned up after themselves." Ruth pursed her lips. *What's their motive? Why would they kill Captain Pipe and then Gabriella? Where's the link?* She thought back to the cat painting on the wall, and the fact she always dressed head-to-toe in black. *Are they targeting me next?* Ruth's face fell. "Wait a minute."

10

Ruth marched along the suites' hallway and banged her clenched fists on the door to the right of hers.

After a few moments, Logan opened it. He glared at her. "What do you want?"

"To speak to you," Ruth said in a firm tone. "Now."

"Is everything all right?" Colonel Tom asked as he strode over.

Ruth kept her focus on Logan. "I suggest everyone else lock themselves in their rooms until I've dealt with this."

Colonel Tom looked between them. "Dealt with what? Has something happened?"

There was something in the way he said it that made him seem like he knew more than he was letting on, which was out of character. Logan, on the other hand, had looked nothing but disingenuous and snide since they'd arrived.

He smirked and stepped out of the way. "Make yourself at home, why don't you?"

Ruth stormed into his suite.

Colonel Tom went to follow, but Logan slammed the door in his face.

Ruth threw a few scatter cushions from the L-shaped sofa, then a few more for good measure, and plonked herself down.

"Would you like a drink?" Logan asked in a breezy tone as he headed to the bar. "Or a sedative?"

Ruth considered this, and then asked in a sarcastic voice of her own, "Do you have any lemonade?"

His step faltered. "I have wine."

"No thank you." Ruth picked lint from her trousers.

Logan poured himself a giant glass of red wine, and then sat in the armchair opposite. "You think I killed her? That's why you're here with that attitude."

Ruth didn't rise to the bait. Truth was, she didn't know, and although she needed to watch her back with him, she wasn't afraid. She'd dealt with nastier people in her life and wasn't about to be frightened off by the likes of him.

"Yesterday," she said in a level tone, "you had black paint on your finger." She watched his reaction, but Logan didn't flinch. He was either a good actor or ready for the question.

"That wasn't paint." He sipped his wine.

Okay, I'll bite. "What was it then?"

Logan sighed. "If you really must know, it was makeup."

Ruth's eyes narrowed in disbelief. "Yours?"

"No, Gabriella's."

Ruth sat back, sizing him up. "Okay, so let's start with the so-called makeup on your fingers." She'd been sure it was paint. "How did it get there?"

Logan sat back. "The night before last, Gabriella and I were talking."

"Is that all you were doing?" Ruth asked. When he didn't respond, she said, "What time was this?"

"You know what time." Logan took another sip of his wine.

Ruth considered him for a moment. "How did you know Gabriella before this trip?"

"I didn't," Logan said. "Met her for the first time a couple of days ago, along with everyone else."

There was no doubt about it, this lawyer guy wasn't a fool. Snarky, maybe, but not stupid. He wasn't going to slip up easily, and his poker face combined with that stupid smirk gave nothing away.

"Go on," Ruth said, trying not to let her irritation show.

"I told Gabriella I recognised her from magazines back in the day. She said I had a familiar face too. That's when I told her about my acting past."

Ruth's eyebrows lifted. "You're an actor?"

"Not recently, but I was in a famous pirate movie franchise. Which is probably why you recognised me too."

"I do?"

Logan took another sip of wine and set the glass on the coffee table. "Gabriella didn't think it was really me. Or she pretended not to." He lifted his chin. "I told her I could prove it if she let me use some of her makeup." He smirked at Ruth. "The black paint you spotted on my finger was eyeshadow."

"You expect me to believe that?" Ruth said.

"I put the eyeliner on first, and then smeared some eyeshadow across my eyelids. And then, to complete the effect . . ." Logan slumped in his chair, lifted his right shoulder, and opened one eye wider than the other. "Ar, Cap'n. It be over there." He pointed to an imaginary horizon, and then straightened and smiled at Ruth.

She gave him her best blank stare in return.

"You have no idea what I'm talking about, do you?"

Ruth shook her head.

He deflated. "Haven't seen the pirate movies?"

"I might have seen them." Feeling momentarily sorry for him, Ruth offered Logan a small shrug in apology. "My grandson still likes kids' films." But she had no recollection of watching them. She cleared her throat. "Let me get this straight: you washed the makeup from your face but not your fingers?"

"I was drunk." Logan snatched his wineglass back up, almost spilling it. "Gabriella gave me some wipes. Go check. They'll be in her bin." He took a dramatic gulp of the wine.

Ruth remembered seeing the used makeup wipes, so she waved his suggestion away. Besides, the police would send them to a lab and have the DNA tested to corroborate his story. "Doesn't mean you didn't kill her."

Logan inclined his head. "Why would I kill her?"

Ruth and Logan sat in sober silence for a minute as she considered possible motives for him to murder Gabriella.

Perhaps, contrary to what he said, Logan knew Gabriella from way before, had a grudge, and had killed the poor woman by slipping poison into her lemonade. But that didn't explain why he'd offed Captain Pipe.

What links the two victims?

If Ruth could find the answer to that, a way to cut through the fog, she'd soon realise a motive, and a suspect would be sure to follow.

She studied Logan's passive expression. For a guy who'd gotten on so well with the last victim, he didn't seem at all cut up about it.

Ruth pressed on. "How long were you in Gabriella's suite?"

"A couple of hours."

"What about last night?" Ruth asked. "Your second visit?"

"I didn't see Gabriella last night."

Ruth blinked at him. "Yes, you did. I saw you."

Logan set his wine down. "I don't care what you think you saw, and you've already accused me of this, but I did not visit Gabriella last night." His eyes hardened. "You saw me go to her room before and thought I did the same last night?" He shook his head. "I've already told you that had nothing to do with her murder."

"Why are you here?" Ruth kept her tone neutral. "What's your job? What have the ship's owners tasked you to do?" She held up a hand. "My guess is you're a lawyer?"

He stared at her for a few seconds as he seemed to consider answering, and then he said, "Why do you say that?"

Ruth lifted her chin. "A guess." It wasn't luck, though. She had a knack for reading people. Well, some people at least. Everyone apart from expert liars. Okay, Ruth knew she was far from fallible, but she was more often right than wrong. Mostly.

"Why are *you* here?" Logan asked.

"You mean apart from bad fortune?" Ruth huffed out a breath. "Anyway, we're talking about you. What are you doing on this ship? Apart from sneaking into other guests' suites. Why do they require the services of a lawyer?"

"I work for an insurance company," he said. "Only joined the firm a few months ago, so I don't know a whole lot about their clients, but I'm tasked with checking this ship out." He shrugged. "A lot of money invested."

"Wait." Ruth's face fell. "Not a lawyer?"

"Not a lawyer."

Ruth frowned and muttered, "Damn it." She'd been so sure. "What about Jeremy?"

"What about him?"

"You argued. Had the poor guy by the throat. What was that about?"

"You saw that?" Logan tugged at the collar of his polo-neck. "I'm not proud of what I did. I lost my temper. If you'd eavesdropped for long enough, you would have caught my apology."

As far as Ruth could tell, he was sincere. With this part at least. "What were you arguing over?"

Logan reached into his back pocket and pulled out a gold key card.

Ruth's eyes went wide. "Where did you get that?"

"It's not the one the girls found. This is a different card."

"Okay," Ruth said. "But where did you get it?"

"Jeremy." Logan edged forward in his chair and said in a low voice, "He says the ship manager handed it to him."

"He gave Jeremy a key card?" Ruth frowned. "Why would he do that?" She studied Logan. "And while we're on the subject, why are you so pally with him?"

"Keep your enemies close," Logan said. "I don't trust him. There's something odd about the man."

"Why did Jeremy relent and give you the card?" Ruth said. "He seemed pretty determined you shouldn't have it, if that's really what you were arguing over."

Logan kept his gaze level. "When I apologised, he had a change of heart."

Ruth wasn't sure she believed that either. A thought struck her. "Wait a minute. Let's back this up a second." Ruth's brain worked to piece together the timeline. "When did you find out about this other key card?"

"When we fetched all that furniture from the atrium. That's when he dropped it. I spotted him picking the card up and stuffing it back in his pocket. He denied it at first."

"Right, so what about later last night? You said you didn't

meet with Gabriella in her room. So, where did you go? What did you do?" She couldn't understand why he was sharing all this.

Logan stared at Ruth for a few seconds, and then he stood. "It's easier to just show you."

Ruth gave him an incredulous look. "I'm not going anywhere with you." She could be stupid at times, but she wasn't crazy.

"It's important you believe me."

"Why do you care what I think?"

"Because I'm not a killer," he said. "And I don't think Jeremy is either."

Ruth glowered back at him, but he seemed sincere. *Or is he acting?* She had no way to know for sure. "I'll ask the colonel—"

Logan shook his head. "I only trust you. We go alone. And once you see it, you'll understand."

Although the danger was apparent, Ruth had to admit curiosity gnawed at her insides. She couldn't ignore it. What she should have done was lock this guy in his suite, have Colonel Tom guard the door, and wait until the nightmare was over. Instead, Ruth found herself saying, "Fine." She stood and waggled a finger in his face. "But don't try anything funny. I know king fu."

Logan hesitated. "I wouldn't dream of putting your martial arts prowess to the test." He gestured to the door. "After you."

Ruth stormed past him. Trust was such a nebulous, constantly shifting thing. There were so many shades and levels. It could take years for someone to earn your trust, and seconds for them to lose it again.

As far as Logan was concerned, Ruth leaned firmly toward not trusting the guy because they'd only just met, and, so far, he seemed temperamental and shifty, not to mention the fact there was a strong chance he was the killer.

However, if Logan's plan was to murder her next, there were easier ways. If someone really wanted her dead, there wasn't much she could do about it. Poisoned tea would be their best option. Even so, her curiosity outweighed most of the danger.

Not all, but a fair proportion.

Plus, there were better ways of tricking her than saying, *Hey, lady. I've got something to show you. Now follow me to the basement . . . heh, heh, heh.*

Mind you, Logan might have figured Ruth a sucker for a mystery, hence all this creeping about; and on the outside, someone might consider it a reckless act to sneak off without telling anyone else, including Colonel Tom, and then head into the bowels of the ship with a potential lunatic.

Logan used Jeremy's key card to open various doors, and they hurried along a hallway, down a flight of stairs, and across a metal walkway above the engine room. Screaming for attention would no longer do Ruth any good all the way down here.

A twinge of regret fluttered in her stomach. Perhaps she should have insisted on Colonel Tom escorting them after all—or taken Greg's advice from a few months' back and bought an extra-large can of pepper spray.

Oops. Too late.

Ruth pictured Greg's face if he later found out about her recklessness—all screwed up with deep frown lines that shouldn't be possible on a teenager, and with a tilted head, like a disapproving bulldog.

Logan pressed the key card to a lock, opened another

door, and stepped into a room filled with racks of computer servers.

He motioned to a terminal and pulled up two chairs.

Ruth sat in one of them, ready to give him a swift karate chop to the throat should he make the wrong move.

Logan took a breath and faced her. "Yesterday, when we thought the killer might still be on board the ship, I asked Jeremy if there was another way to track people. You know, seeing as someone has tampered with the CCTV recordings, I—"

"The locks." Ruth glanced at the terminal, and then at the key card in his hand. "The doors on this ship have electronic locks, and they're logged." She may have been a bit backward when it came to technology, but Ruth still grasped basic principles of anything security related. That and kitchen appliances. Although one time she did destroy a microwave. Blew the door clean off. That was when she'd opted to take a course on health and safety.

"So, this terminal was password protected," Logan continued. "Which is where I insisted Jeremy step in to help."

Ruth nodded. "You could have shared it with the rest of us, but it makes sense." Especially if they really didn't know who the killer was either.

Logan shrugged. "It took him fifteen minutes to bypass the login, and now we have full access."

Ruth kept a level gaze, and her lips pressed together. She turned her attention to the screen. "Let's see what we have."

Logan clicked on the trackpad and brought up the security logs. "This is the day we got here." Alongside it was a corresponding part of the ship's map, detailing each location.

Ruth leaned forward. Each log entry had a timestamp, a

door location, and the card number used. She pointed. "This is my suite. The ship manager set the palm scanner using his gold key card." The key card number ended in 050. "These other codes must be the ones assigned to our palm prints." Next to each of the six numbers listed as ending in 050 were random letters and door locations, also time-stamped. The ship's manager had accessed each suite door with the same key card.

Logan flipped his card over to reveal a number stamped on the back that ended 098.

Ruth's gaze moved down the list. The logs showed the guests leaving their rooms at various times around 8 p.m. on the first day, and then returning using their palm codes later that evening. "That's all six of us accounted for."

"And these are other places the ship manager went that night." Logan scrolled down the list and pointed out all the 050 logs. "He stuck mainly around the kitchen and dining areas, along with these crew members." There were five other sets of numbers, all logged in the same locations. "And these here," Logan said, pointing to a list of other card numbers, "I guess are the rest of the crew. They worked in various parts of the ship, and then went to their quarters around eleven. After that, everything was quiet until . . . right here."

Ruth's eyebrows lifted. "Hmm."

11

In the security room, the logs showed a burst of activity during the small hours of the morning: various card numbers opening doors, right after the time someone threw Captain Pipe overboard.

Ruth ran her finger up the list. "Scroll back a bit."

"What are you looking for?" Logan asked.

Ruth pointed at the first burst of activity. "This is the ship manager, right? Card ends 050. He seems to be waking everyone up. Going to each of their rooms. Twenty crew members."

Logan nodded. "Looks that way."

Ruth scratched her chin and sat back. "How did he know?"

"How did he know what?"

"The crew quarters must be on the lower decks," Ruth said, thinking it through. "How did the ship manager know someone had murdered Captain Pipe? That happened on the promenade. Upper deck. And then a few minutes later, the ship manager wakes everyone up?" She cocked an eyebrow. "Does he have X-ray vision?"

Logan pointed to a log higher up the list. "Someone left the bridge right before."

Ruth sat forward and tapped the screen. "I bet that's Captain Pipe's card. It doesn't appear again on the logs. He's going for a puff." She pursed her lips. "So, he leaves the bridge, and someone heaves him overboard soon after." Ruth squinted at the screen as she tried to figure it out. "There's no other recorded movement at that time. No doors opening. All we have is the CCTV to prove what happened." She looked at Logan. "We've come full circle, back to the same question: how did the ship manager know what had happened to Captain Pipe?"

"Someone else saw and called him?" Logan asked. "Woke him up?"

"I'm not so sure." Ruth tapped the screen again. "According to these logs, the ship manager was in his quarters. He went to bed at the same time as everyone else, and he didn't stir until the murder. Like, right as it happened. Not after, but the same time. That can't be a coincidence."

Logan frowned at the display. "I don't know how to explain it. You're right: there's no other activity."

"Someone could have tampered with these," Ruth said. "The same way they deleted the CCTV files."

"I already thought about that." Logan lowered his voice. "Jeremy told me they're encrypted and protected. There's no way to mess with them." He scrolled up the list. "Anyway, that's not what I wanted to show you. This is."

Ruth leaned in. "What am I looking at?"

"The night we arrived. After dinner. You can see my door opens here." He pointed. "Then Gabriella's door opens right here." Logan glanced at Ruth. "A couple of hours later, this is me leaving her suite and going back to mine." He sat back. "It proves I didn't go anywhere else, and I didn't kill the captain. I was with Gabriella, and then I went back to my suite. Used my palm print on the door."

Ruth let out a slow breath. "I concede it wasn't you who shoved Captain Pipe overboard." Although Logan's alibi had died with Gabriella.

Also, who's to say Logan didn't tie knotted bedsheets together, shimmy over the balcony, and go on that way? There were no CCTV recordings to back up this theory, or his claims either. It was a stalemate.

"It's my palm print on my door," Logan repeated. "Only a gold key card can override them. Jeremy had one, but he hadn't used it until I asked, and the girls didn't find the other one until last night. You took it."

Ruth held up a hand. "Yeah, so, what about last night? Poor Gabriella. I watched you sneak off. That's when someone murdered her." She scanned the logs. Logan had opened his door, but there was no record of Gabriella's opening at that time. Ruth frowned.

"I've already told you." Logan pointed to another suite door opening soon after his. "This is Jeremy." He then indicated other logs, each with a key card ending in 098. "This is us coming here last night. All the doors to get here. The same ones we used. Then two hours later, we come back. He can corroborate what I'm saying."

Ruth followed the logs closely, but he seemed to be telling the truth. She'd have to speak to Jeremy in order to back up Logan's alibi, and it didn't rule out the pair working in cahoots and coming up with some elaborate plan to fool everyone.

Ruth scanned the door logs for any hint of when the killer may have gotten to Gabriella. "What's this?" She pointed at a log with no key card or palm print attached. "That's Gabriella's door opening from the inside?"

"Right. Because you don't need a card to do that." He pointed at the logs that showed him and Jeremy leaving their suites. "Same."

"That happened earlier." Ruth blew out a puff of air. Judging by the times, Gabriella's door opened before Jeremy and Logan returned to their suites, and that in turn happened before Laura came to see Ruth. "Did you notice if her door was open when you got back?" Ruth cursed herself for not seeing it when she'd left.

Logan shook his head.

"So, Gabriella opened her door from the inside and left it ajar? Why? She knew there was a killer on the loose." Ruth pursed her lips. "This makes no sense." Laura had spotted the door was open while she waited for Ruth to return. "I was hoping coming here with Jeremy last night, and looking at these logs, would clear up who murdered Captain Pipe," Logan said. "But it made things worse. It's odd. And then when someone killed Gabriella . . ." He sighed. "Still doesn't explain how the killer is moving about this ship without triggering doors."

"Well," Ruth said, "we're dealing with a phantom, then. Someone who can walk through them."

Or, the more likely scenario is there really isn't anyone else on board, the killer is still among us, and they've figured out how to bypass the locks.

"Whoever we're dealing with," Logan said, "they clearly have a grasp of security and tech."

Ruth stared at him for a few seconds, and then understood. "The lack of internet? No phone signals?"

Logan nodded.

Ruth sighed. "Let's look at last night again." She flapped a hand at the screen. "Scroll back up."

Logan did as she asked, and then moved slowly down

the list, one log at a time. "Everyone goes to bed. Jeremy and I come down here, we return to our suites two hours later, and all the other doors apart from Gabriella's stay locked until . . . What's this?"

"Laura leaves her suite," Ruth said, reading the time-stamps and locations. "She came to mine. I opened my door and let her in."

Logan carried on reading the logs. "Ten minutes later you leave your suite and use the gold key card ending in 050 to open the hallway door. That's when you say you went down to the promenade, but there's no log of any other doors being opened."

"It was ajar," Ruth said. "Anyone could have opened it at any point and left it that way."

"About that," Logan asked. "What did you find?"

"Nothing," Ruth lied. "No one there." That part was true. "By the time I got back, Gabriella had—" She swallowed and thought about Logan and Jeremy. *Were they out of their suites at the same time Laura heard a noise?* "Let's see when that promenade door first opened."

"Wait." Logan gaped. "Lemonade."

Ruth frowned, and then her eyes went wide. "You think Laura took the poisoned lemonade in to Gabriella? When I was outside?"

Logan balled his fists. "She poisoned her."

"Hold on," Ruth said. "We don't know that."

Logan's face twisted with anger, and he leapt to his feet, sending the office chair flying into a server rack. "She murdered Gabriella."

Ruth stood with her hands raised, palms facing out, while Logan paced back and forth like a lion.

"I told Gabriella that girl was no good," he snarled. "I could see she was jealous. It was obvious in the way she kept fawning over her, but I saw through the facade. I know her true nature."

"You're jumping to conclusions," Ruth said. "Someone could have slipped poison into the lemonade at any point." Maybe before they arrived. It might have happened days ago.

For a moment, Ruth considered the possibility that one of the other guests had poisoned the lemonade when they all ate dinner in the suites' hallway. However, she dismissed that idea because they'd been seated in such close proximity to one another; someone would have likely spotted that happening. It would have been a huge risk for the killer to take.

Undeterred, Logan waved a finger at the screen. "It's her. I know it is." He then waved the same finger at Ruth. "She came to you with some made-up story about someone on the promenade deck, and you fell for it. This got you out of the way, so she could have a reason to be in the corridor and sneak into Gabriella's suite." His expression intensified. "That's what she'd planned."

Ruth stared at him. "That doesn't make much sense." She shrugged. "I agree that if Laura wanted to kill Gabriella, she could have slipped the poison into the lemonade and given it to her." Ruth sighed and shook her head. "But why go to all the trouble to get the key card from me when Gabriella's door was already open?"

"Maybe Laura didn't know her door was open," Logan said.

Ruth shook her head. "Why not simply hand her the lemonade earlier, and then leave it to later this morning, when everyone is up, to find the body? One of us would have discovered Gabriella eventually." She took a breath. "And can I point out that the poison would have likely taken time to work. Is it plausible Laura convinced Gabriella to drink vodka and lemonade in the small hours of the morning? Could have happened earlier."

Logan continued to pace the room, head bowed, and then he spun to face Ruth. "I've got it; she wanted to be the first to find Gabriella's body. Don't you see? Doing that makes her look innocent. She screamed, didn't she? *'Oh, she's dead, she's dead,'*" he said in a high-pitched imitation of Laura. "*'Someone's murdered her. It's terrible. Boo-hoo.'*" Logan's upper lip curled. "If she had waited until later this morning, one of us would have found the body instead. Probably you."

Ruth took a deep breath, let it out slowly. "Are you now suggesting that wee girl also murdered the captain?"

"Why not? You yourself said the killer could have been a man or a woman. I'll prove it." Logan lifted his chin. "We'll confront her about it. Give me five minutes. Let's see what she's got to say for herself." He marched to the door, threw it open, and stormed out.

Ruth followed him.

Can things get any worse?

Ten minutes later, things had gotten a whole lot worse.

Ruth and Logan made it back to the suites' hallway without incident, only to find everyone missing.

They'd first knocked on each of the doors and called, but when not a single one of them had answered, Ruth suggested Logan use his magical gold key card to check in on them.

For a few seconds, as he pulled the card from his pocket and selected a door he said belonged to Jeremy, Ruth pictured all the other guests dead in their suites, each of their faces contorted in agony, eyes grey and lifeless, skin mottled and pale.

However, she needn't have worried because Logan opened Jeremy's door, and after a quick search of his suite, they found him not to be there.

Logan insisted they check another suite to be sure, so they picked one they assumed to be Colonel Tom's.

As it turned out, they were correct. Although identical to all the other suites, on the bar top sat a brown leather pouch, the size and shape of a wash bag, with a black union jack sewn on the largest face.

Next to the bag sat a silver photo frame of Colonel Tom in his younger days—Ruth guessed somewhere in his late forties—dressed in a fine officer's uniform, chest swelled with pride and bursting with medals, his right arm linked with a striking brunette of a similar age. This had to be Colonel Tom's wife or girlfriend. He'd not mentioned her, but then again, they were supposed to keep their private lives to themselves.

Ruth frowned.

Come to think of it, why can't we share?

At first, she'd thought nothing of that request. However, now it was a downright inconvenience. How could they hope to stay ahead of the killer if they knew nothing about each other or what linked them regarding motives?

Ruth vowed to rectify that mistake once they caught up with the other guests. After all, to hell with their remaining payments. If they made it off the boat alive, they had grounds to sue the company. The sabotaged lifeboats alone screamed gross negligence.

Logan stood at the end of the suites' hallway with an

expression somewhere between anger and confusion, hands on his hips. "So where is everyone?"

A few scenarios ran through Ruth's mind: maybe they'd spotted a ship and were on the upper deck, trying to signal it. Or perhaps one of them had come up with a brilliant idea of how to call ashore for help, and they'd all gone together. Safety in numbers. Or, probably most likely, they'd found out Logan and Ruth had gone AWOL and were now looking for them.

Ruth winced and considered their next move.

Logically, she should remain with Logan in the suites' hallway and wait for the others to return. However, if there had been some type of emergency, they needed to know about it.

"Perhaps we should check the upper deck?" Ruth suggested.

That would kill several seagulls with one anchor: they could see if the others were signalling passing ships, or whether the boat was in fact sinking, and if they'd managed to locate life jackets.

Clearly coming to similar conclusions, Logan agreed, and they headed on up to the promenade deck via the stairs. Once there, the pair of them searched to no avail and were about to give up and go back inside when Ruth stopped at the bottom of the metal steps.

She pointed to the bridge. "Shall we see if they're trying to fix the radio?" Rather than waiting for a reply, Ruth climbed the stairs. At the top, she stepped onto the bridge, but all seemed quiet here too: all the controls were still dark, the radio dead.

Logan stared out the window, squinting toward the horizon. "Do you think the crew made it ashore?"

"I hope so," Ruth said.

He faced her. "Why haven't they sent people to help us? They must know we're still on board."

Ruth shook her head. "I don't know, but there has to be a logical explanation." For one horrifying moment, she wondered if the killer had also sabotaged their lifeboat and it had sunk.

Is that why someone damaged all the other launching devices? she wondered. Did *the killer make sure the crew climbed on board only one lifeboat? Were the guests supposed to be on that lifeboat too? And are the crew really so innocent in all this?*

Shaking off the macabre thoughts, Ruth faced the back of the bridge, and then she smiled. "Of course." She opened the door. "This way."

"Where are we going?" Logan asked as he followed her.

A little way down the corridor, Ruth pointed at the sign on the door. "CCTV," she said. "Why search the ship when we can look on the monitors?"

"Good thinking."

Ruth beamed at him. "I know." She opened the door, stepped inside, and groaned.

All the CCTV displays stood dark, and not only that, but someone had smashed each screen. A metal bar lay on the floor.

Logan went to pick it up, but Ruth held out an arm. "Fingerprints."

He swore. "This is ridiculous. We need to get off this damn ship."

Ruth stared at the damage. "How?"

"We make a raft." Logan spoke through a clenched jaw. "We break up a load of tables and chairs, lash them together, and paddle ashore."

Ruth considered this for a moment.

During her time in the Girl Guides, she'd failed all the outdoorsy tasks. She'd attempted an Explore badge but had wound up lost in the wilderness, and they'd had to call mountain rescue. Ruth's first and last time in a helicopter.

She'd also failed her Camp badge in spectacular fashion: Ruth had burned her tent to the ground, along with two others, and her mother had been forced to come pick her up.

No, after several years in the guides, all Ruth had to show for her time were Confectionary, Crafting, and Meditation badges. Although, that last one had been a fluke because she'd fallen asleep, and Brown Owl took pity on her.

"I think I'll steer clear of building a raft." She turned back to Logan. "I'll leave that to you and the colonel. When we find the others." She motioned to the door.

12

Ruth and Logan spent the next thirty minutes searching the upper decks before finally coming across Colonel Tom in the theatre.

Ruth had to privately admit she was glad to see him, but there was no way she'd show that on the outside.

He hurried down the steps at the front of the stage and raced up the middle aisle. "Thank goodness you're okay." He halted and looked between them. "Where were you? We were so worried."

Logan folded his arms and scowled. "We should ask you the same thing. Where's everyone else?"

"We were checking out the doors' security logs," Ruth said. "Looking for any signs the killer's been moving about the ship."

"What did you discover?" Colonel Tom asked.

Ruth sighed. "Not a lot."

At that moment, Jeremy sauntered onto the stage. When Colonel Tom looked back at him, Jeremy shrugged and scratched his beard.

"Damn." Colonel Tom faced Ruth again. "When we

realised you'd gone, all three of us came looking for you." He took a breath and gestured over his shoulder. "We were supposed to stay together, but Laura has gone missing."

"What is it with everyone vanishing on this damn boat?" Logan glanced over at Jeremy and back again. "She's not a set of car keys. You don't misplace a person. Where was she last?"

"Here." Colonel Tom motioned around them. "We were checking the place out, looking backstage, and under it, in the dressing rooms . . . She was right behind me one minute and gone the next."

"Show us where you were," Ruth said. "We'll retrace your steps. She probably hasn't gone far."

"We've already tried that," Colonel Tom said. "That's what we'd done when you arrived. She's not here."

Ruth pointed to the stage. "Let's look again."

Colonel Tom nodded. "Very well."

They followed him back onto the stage, and then the four of them headed through the wings, down a flight of steps, and along a corridor that ran across the back of the theatre. Rows of doors stood open on either side.

Ruth glanced inside each as they passed: several dressing rooms, a cupboard of cleaning supplies, and another filled with racks of costumes.

"This is where we'd gotten to." Colonel Tom waved into a room with various sound equipment. He went to leave.

"Where are you going?" Ruth asked.

"I thought it prudent I try to bust open the ship manager's filing cabinet and get that emergency radio."

Ruth shook her head. "First, I need to know exactly where you last saw her."

Jeremy stepped inside while Colonel Tom remained by the door, peering in.

"She searched all these rooms with us." Colonel Tom pointed at the master dressing room. "There, I think."

"Wait here a minute." Three doors down, Ruth glanced into the room with a dressing table, a mirror surrounded by lights, and a wardrobe. A door on the right stood open, which led to a bathroom.

She pulled back and eyed an emergency exit at the end of the corridor, but to reach it, Laura would've had to walk straight past Colonel Tom, and he would have heard her push down on the bar.

Ruth faced the dressing room again. "Interesting," she whispered.

Logan went to step inside, but she held up a hand, stopping him, and then pressed a finger to her lips.

Ruth edged into the room, scanning the walls, floor, and the ceiling. She tiptoed to the wardrobe, grabbed the handles, and threw it open.

Empty.

Ruth huffed out a breath and turned back to the door to leave, but someone had pulled a curtain to one side, revealing another door. This one was closed, with a computer-controlled security lock.

A sign on the door read:

PRIVATE
SHIP PERSONNEL ONLY

Light spilled from under the door. Ruth pressed an ear to it, listened for a moment, and then stepped back. She eyed the lock and smiled.

Logan joined her. "What's going on?" he whispered.

Ruth nodded at the lock. "She has the key card. The one

ending in 050." Ruth took a breath, knocked, and called, "Hello? Are you in there? It's us."

Logan pulled a key card from his pocket and went to unlock the door, but Ruth stopped him.

"She's scared." The last thing Ruth wanted to do was send Laura into a panic. She'd obviously locked herself in there because that was where she currently felt safest, and Ruth couldn't blame her.

Logan frowned. "We're all scared."

Colonel Tom and Jeremy stepped into the room.

"What's going on?" Colonel Tom glanced about with suspicion. "What are you up to in here?"

Ruth pointed at the door and put a finger to her lips.

Colonel Tom's eyebrows lifted. "She's in there?" he whispered.

Ruth nodded.

However, Jeremy didn't look remotely interested in what was going on. He dropped into a chair and stared at the floor, as though he were a bored teenager forced to listen to his parents argue, his long hair hanging low, shielding his face.

Although she empathised with him, talking things out and asking questions was the only way they could figure what was happening. Right now, Ruth felt like they were not making much progress. In a way, she envied Laura and considered running back to her suite, locking herself in with Merlin, and refusing to come out.

Colonel Tom nodded at the closed door. "How do you suggest we coax her out of there?"

Ruth blamed herself. In some ways, it was her fault Laura had locked herself in a room and now refused to come out. She'd started to trust Ruth, and Ruth had undone that faith by acting suspiciously. If Ruth had gotten a better handle on the situation, not run off with Logan, and explained what they were doing, Laura may have trusted her.

Ruth scratched her chin. The best course of action was not to force the situation. "Let's not," she muttered, and stepped into the hallway.

"Not?" Colonel Tom asked as he followed her.

"Coax her out." Ruth shook her head. "She's locked herself in there so she can feel safe, right? Like us, the girl has no idea who the murderer is. She doesn't know who to trust apart from herself. Let's leave her in there. She's secure. There's a bathroom next door should we need it, so we'll all wait in the dressing room. Keep Laura company." Ruth consulted her phone. "It's coming up to lunchtime." It was a Sunday, and she would normally be preparing a nice roast for Greg and herself. "We have a little under thirty hours remaining before my grandson realizes something's up. In a while, we can go grab more supplies from the galley and lock ourselves in the dressing room together."

Colonel Tom gave a slow, weary nod.

Ruth took a step, and then halted. "Wait a minute." She remembered the gold key card, the one ending in 050. Ruth turned back to Colonel Tom. "This morning, it was you who opened the door to me. Which means you had the key card at that point?"

"Yes, I did," Colonel Tom said. "When you knocked, she gave it to me so I could open the door."

That tallied with Logan's version of events.

"Hearing the commotion," Colonel Tom continued, "the other two came rushing out. Logan and I sat the girl down and comforted her. You returned a minute or two later, and she handed me the card to let you in."

"Where's the card now?" Ruth asked.

It still didn't make sense. *How had Laura opened the door in the dressing room?*

Colonel Tom reached into his pocket and frowned. "Hold on." He checked his other pockets, and his face fell. "It's gone." Colonel Tom scanned the floor around him.

"No point," Ruth said. "That explains it—you dropped the card, and Laura must have snatched it up. Then she ran in there." Ruth waved. "Come on."

She and Colonel Tom hurried back into the dressing room. Ruth explained their plan to stay put, loud enough for Laura to hear them.

Then she sat on the floor by the dressing room door, back pressed against the wall. She let out a slow breath. It was nice to relax for a moment, even though her frayed nerves refused to ease up.

"Why don't you speak?" Colonel Tom asked Jeremy as he dropped into a chair. "Not even so much as an acknowledgement?"

Jeremy didn't meet his gaze and mumbled something unintelligible.

Colonel Tom leaned forward. "Louder, man."

"He said he doesn't have anything to add," Logan snapped. "Unlike you, whose mouth is always flapping. You know the ones who speak the most have the least to say?"

Colonel Tom's cheeks flushed. "How dare you."

"Enough." Ruth sighed and attempted to keep her own temper and exasperation in check. "It's high time we explain what each of us is doing here. Build some trust. Under the circumstances, I think that's more than fair. We've earned the right." She glanced at the closed door and hoped Laura could hear them. "I'll go first."

"Let me guess." Logan scanned Ruth up and down. "Retired police officer?"

Colonel Tom's eyes widened. "You were a cop?"

"Yes, but not retired," Ruth said. "Sacked."

"Really?" Colonel Tom hitched an eyebrow. "How interesting."

Even Jeremy looked over at her.

"I wasn't a very good officer," Ruth said, and that was an understatement. "My parents wanted me to follow in their footsteps and join the force."

"What did you do wrong?" Logan asked. "Must have been pretty bad to get booted out."

Ruth waved the question away. "A story for later." Besides, it was a long time ago. She looked round at the others in turn and gauged their reactions. "I'm a freelance food consultant now."

"What's that?" Logan said with a confused expression.

"I travel the country, visiting various restaurants, hotels . . ." Ruth gestured around them. "This is my first cruise ship, though."

"And how are you finding it so far?" Colonel Tom asked.

"Pretty terrible." Ruth shuffled her weight and crossed her legs. "I get asked to evaluate everything to do with food: from problem-solving recipes to health and safety in the kitchen. I was here to assess their galley, preparation, the variety of meals, and recipes. In their letter, the owners expressed they were eager to make sure it's all world class." Ruth looked over at Colonel Tom. "So, what about you? Why are you here?"

He hesitated, and then obviously realising all hope of receiving his last payment had evaporated, he drew a breath. "I run a website for retired travellers." He glanced at Ruth. "A bit like you, I suppose; I visit various hotels and cruise ships around the world and rate them. I then publish my reviews and recommendations to my online blog."

Ruth had to admit his reason for being there caught her off guard. She'd expected the colonel to have something to do with onboard security.

"A travel blogger." Logan rolled his eyes. "Great. So, you're a freeloading influencer for elderly people?" His gaze wandered to the closed door and then back to Colonel Tom. "Have many followers?"

"Half a million on the mailing list," Colonel Tom said, "and a further six million on social media."

Ruth blinked. That sounded like a lot.

Logan jerked a thumb in the direction of Jeremy. "You already know why we're here."

"Well, I don't." Colonel Tom crossed his arms. "Enlighten me."

"He's here on behalf of an insurance company," Ruth said.

"Great." Colonel Tom shook his head. "And what about you, my mute friend?" He looked over at Jeremy. "Still don't have anything to contribute?"

Jeremy shrank away.

"Really?" Colonel Tom persisted. "Despite everything that's happened, you're refusing to share with us what exactly it is you're doing here?"

"I told you to leave him alone." Logan shot him a furious glare. "They invited Jeremy as a security expert."

Ruth half smiled. In her mind, their appearances would have suggested the colonel and Jeremy's roles were reversed. She really needed to stick to her own advice and not judge people by the way they looked.

Colonel Tom tipped his head back and laughed. "You can't be serious. Security?" He wiped his eyes and focussed on Jeremy. "Okay, Mr Expert, and how would you rate the security so far?"

Jeremy let out a juddering breath, swept hair from his face, and then glanced at Ruth and mumbled, "Pretty terrible."

"Amen to that." It was the first time Ruth had heard him speak. He had a surprisingly deep voice. He really was an enigma. She checked the time on her phone. "We have twenty-nine hours left to sit out, so I suggest we stop bickering and focus on the job at hand." With effort and a lot of willpower, she got to her feet and dusted herself off. "Let's go grab some supplies. It's going to be a long night."

The others stood too.

Jeremy squeezed past them into the corridor.

Logan went to leave, but Colonel Tom held up a hand. "One of us needs to stay here." He nodded at the closed door. "Keep an eye on her."

"Why me?" Logan frowned at him. "You stay behind, and I'll go. What gives you the right to throw around orders?"

Colonel Tom opened his mouth to respond but demurred under Ruth's hard stare. The situation was tense enough without all this pointless bickering. They didn't need extra conflict.

"We'll be back as quickly as we can," she said to Logan. "See if you can get her to talk."

The three of them marched away, while Logan swore and protested, but they kept walking.

"Charming fellow," Colonel Tom said as they hurried back onto the theatre stage. "Forget the killer, I can't wait to get away from him."

Ruth wasn't sure what to make of Logan, or any of them for that matter. Although, his bark seemed worse than his bite. A bit like Colonel Tom in that regard. She put his behaviour down to either too much testosterone or a spoilt life, always getting his own way. Perhaps both. Whereas Colonel Tom had spent a large portion of his working career barking orders, while taking others without question.

The three of them raced up the middle aisle of the auditorium, and as they made their way to the dining room, Ruth said to Colonel Tom, "I meant to tell you we went back to the CCTV room earlier, Logan and I. We hoped to spot you on the cameras, figure out where you'd gone, but someone had smashed the screens. All the monitors in the room."

Colonel Tom's eyebrows arched in surprise. "Who had the opportunity to do that?" He glanced at Jeremy, who strode ahead of them.

"I don't know," Ruth muttered. Truth was, it could have been any one of the guests. Then her thoughts turned back to the possibility of there being someone else on board. That seemed the most logical answer, given the events, but she had no direct evidence of that.

A few minutes later, the three of them strode into the dining room and headed to the kitchen, but as they passed the wall where the painting of Bonmouth had once hung, Colonel Tom stopped dead.

"What the hell?" He stared at the black cat painted on the wall.

So did Jeremy.

Ruth winced. "I was going to tell you about that." Her gaze moved to the marks underneath. However, now there were three straight lines beneath the cat's paws.

Ruth stared at them for a couple of seconds, and then she gasped.

13

With her heart hammering in her chest like a broken egg timer, Ruth ran into the dressing room, with the colonel and Jeremy close behind.

Logan got to his feet and looked between them. "What's happened?"

Ruth bent double, panting hard, and thrust out a hand. "Card."

His forehead wrinkled. "Why?"

"Give me the key card." Ruth straightened. "Now. Hurry."

"Okay, okay. Keep your hair on." Logan handed it over. "Is someone going to explain what's happened?"

Colonel Tom shrugged.

Ruth unlocked the door and peered into a long store cupboard lined with shelves, packed with stage props. Some items had toppled to the floor. "Oh no." She let out a slow, agonising breath.

At the far end of the room, next to an air vent, Laura lay supine on the floor, surrounded by fallen items, her eyes wide and lifeless.

Ruth hurried to her, knelt, and placed a couple of fingers to the girl's neck. Then she took her wrist.

Nothing.

Ruth slumped. "She's dead."

Colonel Tom rushed in. His eyes filled with tears, and he dropped to his knees. He reached out to touch her face.

Ruth stopped him. "It's a crime scene. I'm sorry." She felt terrible, and the pain in his face was all too apparent, but both of them should have left as soon as Ruth ascertained the poor girl was dead.

Colonel Tom pulled back, shaking his head as though he struggled to believe it. "What happened? Who could do this to her?"

Ruth pointed at a set of red marks on Laura's neck. "Strangled." She judged by the size of the bruises and the force needed, most likely by a man.

"Strangled?" Colonel Tom said with a blank expression. "How did someone get in here?" His face dropped in realisation, and then it twisted with rage. "The key card." He stood, pulled a revolver from his waistband, and marched from the storeroom.

Aghast, Ruth leapt to her feet and hurried after him.

Colonel Tom levelled the gun at Logan. "What have you done?" he roared as he marched across the dressing room toward him.

Logan threw his hands up and staggered back, almost tripping over his own feet. "W-Where did you get that?" His eyes bulged from their sockets as he stared down the barrel.

"I'd like to know the answer to that too," Ruth said.

"I belong to a rifle club," Colonel Tom said without breaking gaze with Logan. "Rest assured, I have a certificate. It's muzzle-loading. Perfectly legal in the UK."

"To use for target shooting," Ruth said, incredulous. "Not to carry about and threaten people with."

Colonel Tom's finger tightened on the trigger. He took another measured step toward Logan and snarled, "You murdered her."

"What? She's dead?" Logan glanced in the direction of the storeroom and then at Ruth. "No." He shook his head. "No, I did nothing wrong." He looked back at Colonel Tom, hands still held high. "What are you talking about? I would never."

Ruth checked the back of the keycard: 098. She then held it up for Jeremy to see. "Is this the same one you had originally?" Of course, she knew it was.

He studied it for a second, and then nodded.

Ruth sighed. They should never have left Logan alone. *How could I have been so stupid?* She blamed herself. It was a foolish mistake. The whole point was for them to stick together.

Colonel Tom growled at Logan, "Now, what to do with you?" Jeremy whispered in his ear, and he smirked. "Good idea," he said, and nodded toward the door. "Move."

Logan's hands shook. "Where are you taking me? This is ridiculous."

"We have just the place for you." Colonel Tom's upper lip curled. "Somewhere we can put you and all feel safe."

"What's that supposed to mean?" Logan looked at Ruth, his expression pleading. "Tell him I didn't do it. I'm innocent. You know I am."

"Shut up," Colonel Tom snapped. "I said go." He motioned with the pistol. "Now."

Logan hesitated and then stepped through the door.

Outside, Colonel Tom pressed the gun to his back. "Any sudden moves, I'll put a bullet in you, understand?"

Logan swallowed and nodded.

In a daze, Ruth glanced at Jeremy, and then followed them along the corridor and up the steps. "I don't think this is a good idea. We're jumping to conclusions." She had an image of him making Logan walk the plank. "You need to calm down. Think this through." She wanted to discuss what had happened in a calm and rational manner.

When tempers ran high, mistakes could easily occur.

"Nothing to discuss," Colonel Tom said as they crossed the stage. "This monster murdered three people."

"I-I've not murdered anyone," Logan said in a shaky voice. "Why won't you believe me?"

Colonel Tom jabbed the gun into his back again. "You're a liar. Keep moving."

As the four of them headed down the steps and up the central aisle, Ruth ran through the sequence of events that had led them to this moment.

The first night, she'd spotted Logan sneak out of his suite and slip into Gabriella's. The logs had reflected this. *And yet, despite that, he'd snuck out again and murdered Captain Pipe?* She couldn't rule it out, no matter what the logs said. Perhaps she'd been right with an earlier thought, and he had climbed down from his balcony. It certainly wasn't impossible.

The next night, Ruth caught Logan creeping out again, but this time he'd said it was to check the door logs with Jeremy. Ruth made a mental note to ask Jeremy about that alibi. What with all that had happened, the chaos, she'd not yet had the chance. Logan could have gone to Gabriella's suite for a second night in a row, and poisoned her, but so could anyone else. Ruth couldn't rule out any scenario.

And then, just now, they'd left Logan alone with Laura. He had a key card and could have easily gained access to the storeroom while Jeremy used the toilet. Right at that moment, it was the only thing that made sense, unless Laura had died earlier. The problem with that scenario was that Colonel Tom and the geek were feet away from her when she locked herself in the room. *Surely they would have heard a struggle?* After all, several items had toppled from the shelves.

Ruth sighed. Something felt off. Logan could well have had the opportunity to kill—plenty of times if he'd been sneaky enough—but she couldn't yet figure any motives. *Why did he murder them?* He'd admitted to recognising Gabriella but had then shown Ruth the door logs to prove his innocence. *Why would a killer do that?* Unless he'd somehow tampered with the logs and they weren't reliable evidence.

Once everyone had calmed down, especially Colonel Tom, Ruth would need to speak to Logan again. He still had a lot to answer for. *But a killer?* She wasn't so sure.

Colonel Tom marched Logan through the ship, and down flights of stairs, with Ruth and Jeremy still following. Finally, they stopped in one of the cargo holds, and Colonel Tom nodded Ruth to a caged lockup. Other than a few stacks of boxes, it was empty.

Getting the silent command, she used a key card to open the door, and Colonel Tom ushered Logan inside.

He waved the gun in the man's face. "You stay right here. You understand? Not a peep from you. Any funny stuff, and a loud bang will be the last thing you hear. Got it?"

Logan glared at him.

Once Colonel Tom had made his point and stepped from the cage, Ruth locked the door.

Logan lowered his hands and glared at her now. "You

know I didn't do it. Why are you letting him treat me like this?"

"Don't listen to this murderer." Colonel Tom strode away, with Jeremy hard on his heels.

Ruth gave Logan an apologetic look. "I'll be back soon. We'll talk." And then she hurried after the others, determined to get things back on an even keel.

"Look at the door logs," Logan shouted after her. "They'll prove I'm innocent."

Back in the main atrium of the ship, Colonel Tom pressed the call button for an elevator, but Ruth stepped in front of him.

She nodded at the gun. "Why do you have that here?"

Colonel Tom lifted his shirt and tucked the gun back into his waistband. "I never travel without it." He sniffed. "And now I'm glad I don't." The elevator doors opened, and he went to step round her, but Ruth mirrored his movements, blocking his path.

"You can't keep it on you. It's too dangerous." She glanced over at Jeremy, but he kept a safe distance, gaze averted, hair covering his face. She returned her attention to Colonel Tom. "You could get into a lot of trouble having that here. We need to lock it away."

"With a killer on board?" Colonel Tom lifted his chin. "Not a chance. How can we defend ourselves?"

Ruth stood her ground. "According to you, we've now locked the killer up. There's no need to defend ourselves." She softened her pose. "Please. I'm sure you're very proficient and trained in its use, but it makes me very nervous." Even though she really wasn't sure Logan was the killer, Ruth didn't want anyone having a gun. The best way they could defend themselves was by sticking together.

Colonel Tom hesitated, and then his shoulders relaxed.

"What do you suggest?"

Ruth looked about.

Jeremy pointed across the atrium.

Ruth stared for a moment, and then understood his meaning. She marched over to the reception desk and walked behind it to a door marked Purser's Office. Inside, an open cabinet held an assortment of lockboxes. She selected one she deemed the appropriate size and returned to the reception desk. Ruth set the lockbox on the counter.

The number on the lid read 072b.

Colonel Tom hesitated and then set the pistol inside. "I don't think this is wise."

Ruth locked the box and handed him the key. She returned the lockbox to the cabinet, shut the doors, and then left the room. Back in the atrium, Ruth said, "Follow me, please," and strode to the stairs.

Colonel Tom followed with a bemused expression, and Jeremy looked equally confused.

On the upper deck, Ruth pushed through a set of double doors and stepped onto the promenade.

She pointed at the ocean.

Colonel Tom frowned. "What?"

"Throw the key," she said.

His eyebrows lifted. "Why not have me throw the gun?"

"Because I assume it's sentimental, and if it is, and you really want the gun back, you can explain it to the police. They'll have someone pick the lock for you." She shrugged. "Perhaps you can have it decommissioned or whatever it's called." She gestured. "Go on."

Colonel Tom shook his head, and then pulled his arm back and threw the key.

"Great." Ruth rubbed her hands together. "Now that's taken care of," she said, facing Jeremy, "would you come to the computer room with me? I'd like to check the door logs and see if Logan is telling the truth."

"He isn't," Colonel Tom said.

Jeremy nodded.

Ruth forced a smile. "Thank you." She went to head back inside but turned back to Colonel Tom. "Oh, wait. Laura must still have that gold card on her. It's how she got into that storeroom. We need to get it first. Then we'll have both cards."

"I'll go," Colonel Tom said in a deflated tone.

Ruth stared at him. "We should stick together." Almost every time they hadn't, it had resulted in trouble.

Colonel Tom nodded in a solemn manner. "I'll be fine. I've seen dead bodies before. I will go to the galley and grab some gloves first." His shoulders hunched. "Let's meet back up in the dining room."

Ruth hesitated. She still wanted them to stick together. After all, two of their gang were dead, and one was locked up, which left only three remaining. However, she also needed some alone time with Jeremy, and was prepared to risk her own safety for answers.

Ruth let out a slow breath. "Okay, but touch nothing else in that storeroom," she warned Colonel Tom. "The killer might have left their fingerprints. The police will need to gather the evidence, and you don't want them to suspect you. Find that card and then lock the room."

"I'll be careful." Colonel Tom squeezed her hand and marched away.

Ruth hurried in the opposite direction with Jeremy and looked at the time on her phone. It was coming up on two o'clock in the afternoon. They'd not had lunch yet, and there were still twenty-eight hours remaining before Greg figured something was up. She sighed. *An eternity.*

~

Down on a lower deck of the *Ocean Odyssey*, Ruth and Jeremy walked into the computer room and sat in front of the terminal.

As before with Logan, Jeremy brought up the logs and scrolled through the timestamps. "This is that girl opening the storeroom door." He pointed at the entry for the card number that ended in 050.

Ruth nodded. "The key card she'd taken." That made sense, and their theory about her spotting Colonel Tom dropping the card also tallied. Sure, he could have killed her and then dropped the card, but Jeremy would have seen that happen. Plus, they had no way to know exactly when Laura swiped the card, but a precise time didn't matter.

Jeremy sat back. "That's it."

Ruth blinked. "Huh? How can that be? Someone must have opened the door to murder her." She imagined a hooded figure sneaking down the corridor when Colonel Tom and the geek's backs were turned, and slipping into the dressing room.

"Look for yourself." Jeremy scratched his beard. "There are zero records of that storeroom door being opened again until you showed up."

Ruth leaned in to the screen. Sure enough, there were no other entries of note, apart from the very last one—the storeroom door opening with card 098, the card she'd taken from Logan—and nothing logged before.

Ruth's eyebrows lifted. "He didn't go in there. It wasn't him." She sat back and let out a long breath as she tried to understand. *Is there another way into that room?* "Logan was telling the truth. He's innocent." She eyed Jeremy. "What can you tell me about him?"

Jeremy rubbed the back of his neck. "Only that he's an insurance guy. Works for a company called Bright & Gauld."

"Logan told you that?"

"I've met him before." Jeremy shuffled in his chair. "I did a job for one of the Bright & Gauld branch offices, and he worked there."

Ruth threw her hands up. "Why does everyone seem to know each other?"

"I don't know anyone else here," Jeremy said in a defensive tone. "Only Logan. And I don't know him well. He's the kind of guy I steer clear of."

Ruth could understand that. "He certainly has an abrasive personality."

"He's afraid," Jeremy said, his voice shrinking to barely a whisper.

Ruth stared at him. "Afraid of what?"

"If investors got wind that people have been murdered on this ship, they'd pull the plug, and his company would lose millions. He'd be out of a job."

"And we couldn't have that, could we?"

Money, or the threat of losing it, could be a good motivation for murder.

"I don't think Logan murdered them." Jeremy glanced at the door and kept his voice low. "Who do you think is doing it, though?"

Ruth scratched her chin. "I don't know."

Colonel Tom didn't seem like the murdering type. *Although, who can tell?*

"You must have some idea," Jeremy persisted. "He was in the army, you know? That tall guy. It was his job to kill people. He's used to it. He has a gun. Who does that unless they intend to use it? Bring a pistol on board a cruise ship?"

When the police found out, Colonel Tom certainly would be in a lot of trouble.

With an uneasy feeling gnawing in the pit of her stomach, Ruth swiveled in her chair and stared at the security logs. "Could someone have tampered with these? Deleted entries?"

"No."

"So, no one else opened that storeroom door," Ruth mused.

"Maybe she left the door open," Jeremy said. "Someone killed her, then closed it as they left."

Ruth murmured, "Perhaps."

Although, that wouldn't make much sense. If Laura had taken the card and run to the storeroom to hide, she would have locked the door behind her straight away.

However, if she'd searched the storeroom with someone else with her, someone she thought she could trust, they may well have murdered her then. But Colonel Tom and the geek supplied each other's alibis.

Ruth's eyes went wide as another thought struck her: *if there's only one log entry for the storeroom, does that mean someone could have murdered Laura somewhere else and then dragged her body in there?* If so, the list of suspects dropped to the only two people near her at the time.

Ruth swore under her breath. If only she'd checked the girl's pockets for the security card, she'd have the answer.

She glanced at Jeremy's pockets but couldn't tell if he had anything in them.

His brow furrowed. "What's wrong?"

Ruth snapped out of her thoughts. "Sorry? Oh, erm, nothing." She forced a smile, took a picture of the computer logs with her phone, and then stood. "We should go." Ruth hurried from the room.

14

Ruth marched back through the ship, wanting to get into an open space as quickly as possible. Suddenly, the corridors seemed to press in on her.

"Are you okay?" Jeremy asked as he rushed to keep up.

"Fine," she said through gritted teeth.

"Well, we know it wasn't you or me," Jeremy said. "It must be him, right? That army guy?"

Ruth opened a door and headed up a flight of stairs. She cursed herself for jumping to conclusions without sufficient evidence. It had been one of the reasons she'd lost her job in the force all those years ago. And here she was again—making assumptions and diving in feetfirst.

None of them had heard Laura speak when they gathered in the dressing room. Ruth had made the vital mistake of assuming she'd locked herself in that storeroom, turned on the light, and refused to talk, but she could have been dying while they wasted time. If Ruth hadn't made an assumption, they might have saved her.

Ruth reached the top of the stairs and then headed down another hallway.

"So," Jeremy panted, "that army guy might have done it?" His gaze dropped. "Actually, I was in the room at the end for at least five minutes. He could have snuck off then."

As they rounded a corner, Ruth recalled the dressing room. There had been no marks on the floor from where someone might have dragged the body, but it was still possible. Without cameras, or a crime scene kit, she had no way to know for sure.

"The police will figure it out." Ruth sighed and glanced back at him. "Without a medical examiner, we have no way to be sure what time she died." Ruth stopped at the doors that led to the dining room and reached for the handle, but Colonel Tom walked through, forcing her back a step.

"There you are." He looked between them. "Any luck with the security logs?"

Ruth shook her head. "Did you find the keycard?"

He held it up and let out a puff of air. "Who's doing this?"

"Well, definitely not Logan," Ruth said. "He didn't go into that storeroom. He was telling the truth. The security logs speak for themselves: no one went in there after Laura."

Jeremy kept his distance, gaze averted.

Colonel Tom glanced over at him, eyes narrowed, and then turned the dubious look on Ruth.

"It's true," she said. "The logs prove it." Ruth held up her phone. "See for yourself."

Colonel Tom crossed his arms. "Someone tampered with them. Laura was a trusting girl. Always was. If she—"

"Wait." Ruth frowned at him. "You knew her before coming here, didn't you?" She inclined her head. "How come?"

Colonel Tom opened his mouth to respond, and then

closed it again. His shoulders slumped, and he perched on the end of a table in the hall, looking deflated. "You're right, I did know her." His eyes filled with tears. "We've met a few times over the years. Fantastic young lady. A lot of fun." Colonel Tom let out a long breath. "Your guess was right— Laura was a travel influencer. My website attracts retirees to hotels and cruises, whereas Laura's social media pulls in the younger crowd."

"What about everyone in between?" Ruth asked.

Colonel Tom cracked a rare smile. "Too busy to go on holiday?"

"We owe Logan an apology." Ruth gave Colonel Tom a hard look. "It's not right what we've done to him."

Colonel Tom straightened. "He won't get one from me, but I agree he should be let out." He held up a finger. "From now on, we all stick together like glue. No one leaves or wanders off." He looked over at Jeremy. "Right?"

Jeremy nodded.

Ruth rolled her eyes because they'd tried that several times and failed. She pointed down the hallway.

As the three of them traipsed off, Ruth's stomach rumbled. She looked at the time on her phone: three o'clock. Way past lunchtime and heading toward dinner. There was no way she'd miss meals. It would have to be a life or death— Ruth cringed and decided not to complete that thought.

Back down on the lower decks of the ship, they marched into the cargo hold. Colonel Tom halted, and Ruth almost slammed into him.

"What's happened?" she said.

Colonel Tom rushed forward. "No." The cage stood open. "Damn it all."

Ruth went to step inside the cage, when Jeremy gasped.

Colonel Tom turned to him. "What?"

"He's going to kill us all." Jeremy's eyes darted about the cargo hold as though he expected Logan to leap out at them.

Colonel Tom wheeled around and marched back to the stairs.

"Where are you going?" Ruth called after him.

"My gun," he shouted.

Ruth and Jeremy hurried after Colonel Tom, up several decks and into the atrium. He stepped behind the desk, threw open the door, and went inside.

"How are you going to open it?" Ruth asked as she followed him into the back room. "We threw away the key." She stepped into the office.

Colonel Tom staring down at a table, slack-jawed. On it sat the lockbox—number 072b—open, and the gun missing.

The dumbstruck colonel reached for the empty lockbox, as if he struggled to believe his own eyes, and as though the gun would suddenly appear.

"Don't touch it," Ruth warned him. She failed to understand how Logan could have known the gun's hiding place. "There could be—"

"Fingerprints." Colonel Tom pulled back and scowled at her. "Care to explain this?"

Ruth's eyebrows shot up. "Me?"

Colonel Tom's nostrils flared. "It was your idea to leave the gun here."

Ruth put her hands on her hips and inclined her head. "What are you suggesting?"

"Rather convenient, wouldn't you say?"

Ruth gaped at him. She couldn't believe the nerve of the guy. *How dare he.* "I was with him the whole time." She waved a hand at Jeremy. "What? You think we're working together? That we came here and took your precious gun?" Talk about a conspiracy theory.

"Not exactly out of the question, is it, madam?" Colonel Tom's narrowed eyes moved to Jeremy and back again. "The first night, where were you when someone shoved the captain overboard?"

"In my suite." Ruth's blood boiled at the accusation. "Asleep. Where were you?" If only Merlin could talk, he'd be a credible witness.

"And the next night?" Colonel Tom asked with a dubious expression. "When someone poisoned Gabriella, where were you that time?" He nodded at Jeremy. "We both know for a fact you left your suite. You never explained what you were up to."

"Yes, I did," Ruth said in a defensive tone. "Laura heard a noise and saw someone on the promenade. She came to tell me, and I went to investigate." At the time, she'd thought she'd done the right thing, but now Ruth regretted her choice to investigate.

"And yet you didn't bother to call me or anyone else?" Colonel Tom persisted in a sarcastic tone. "You decided to go alone? Without an escort?"

"I don't need an escort." Ruth balled her fists. *How dare he accuse me.* She'd done nothing but try to help. And the truth was, Ruth had considered calling for help at the time but decided not to wake everyone.

Colonel Tom's eyebrows lifted. "You wanted no one to accompany you, despite saying we should all stick together and knowing there was a killer on board this ship?"

"I—" Ruth glared at him. "Well, I—"

"And what about Laura?" Colonel Tom asked.

Ruth's face drained of colour. "What about her?"

"Not only did you figure out where she was," Colonel Tom said, "but you simply happened to know someone had murdered her? Can you see through walls? Or do you have divine foresight?"

"I didn't know someone had killed her." Ruth could not believe what she was hearing. She looked over at Jeremy for moral support, but he now stared at a spot on the wall, as was his habit. *Does that mean he thinks the same?* Ruth swallowed a mixture of hurt and anger, faced Colonel Tom again, and tried her best to keep her tone neutral. "I haven't murdered anyone. If you don't want to believe me, then that's your problem. Truth will out."

Colonel Tom lifted his chin. "I don't know what or who to believe."

Ruth threw her hands up. "Exactly."

Colonel Tom glared at her through slitted eyes.

"Oh, get out of my way." Ruth nudged him aside, leaned down, and examined the box. "No signs anyone has forced their way into it. They must have had a key."

"You threw it overboard," Jeremy said to Colonel Tom.

"By jove," Colonel Tom barked. "It's a miracle. He speaks."

"Be nice." Ruth straightened. "All this leaves us with a couple of possibilities: either Logan had a spare key, or he picked the lock without leaving marks." Her brow furrowed. "Which still doesn't explain how he knew we'd put your gun in here. He was in a cage at the time."

"Must have got out and followed us," Jeremy said.

Ruth nodded. "We should have checked he didn't have another key card."

"In that case, it seems like I was right not to trust the scoundrel." Colonel Tom glanced between Ruth and

Jeremy. "I still say you both had the opportunity and the means."

"We were down in the computer room," Jeremy said in an exasperated tone.

"And I only have your word for that," Colonel Tom retorted.

"You could have come back here." Ruth looked Colonel Tom up and down. "Maybe it was you." She considered the possibility that he'd feigned throwing the key overboard. It wasn't out of the question. It wasn't as if she'd seen it leave his hand and hit the ocean.

"A ridiculous accusation," he said with a dismissive wave.

"Then you don't mind us searching you." Ruth took a step toward him.

Colonel Tom edged back, and his upper lip curled. "I most certainly do mind."

"You're right about one thing," Ruth said. "This is ridiculous." All this bickering was getting them nowhere. She looked at the time on her phone: 3:45 in the afternoon. Ruth groaned. "That's the final straw." She stomped from the purser's office.

"Where are you going now?" Colonel Tom called after her.

"Back to my suite," Ruth said over her shoulder. "Where I can be comfortable." She needed to check up on Merlin. Ruth walked across the atrium and headed up the stairs. "I intend to stuff my face full of sausage rolls and cake, drink a gallon of tea, and soak in a bubble bath."

"What about Logan?" Jeremy asked as they followed her.

"If he comes anywhere near me, I'll punch him on the nose. I suggest you do the same." Head held high, Ruth stomped across the next level and up another flight of stairs.

Colonel Tom and Jeremy rushed after her.

"Logan has a gun," Colonel Tom said.

"We don't know that for sure," Ruth said, breathless. Beads of sweat formed on her forehead from the exertion.

"We should go back and try to find a way to open the ship manager's filing cabinet," Colonel Tom said. "There must be an emergency radio in there."

"How do you know?" Jeremy asked.

Colonel Tom shrugged. "A hunch."

Ruth reached the top of the stairs, stomped across the upper walkway, through the hexagonal waiting area, and then down the hallway to her suite.

Like a pair of dutiful puppies, Colonel Tom and the geek followed, as if they were unsure what else to do.

Ruth unlocked the suite door with her palm. "I'm keeping this open," she said to them. "I suggest you two do the same. If someone is hell-bent on killing us, a locked door doesn't seem to put them off. Better be open, and we can shout if there's trouble." She held up a finger. "Apart from my bedroom door. There I draw a line." She motioned to the supplies. "We have plenty of snacks. Help yourselves." Ruth forced a smile. "Good afternoon, gentlemen." She marched into her suite.

She opened her bedroom door and slipped inside.

Merlin paced back and forth, agitated. He made for the door, but Ruth closed it. Merlin let out a low meow of annoyance.

Ruth frowned at him. "What's the matter with you?" It seemed everyone's tempers were running high at that moment, and she was sick of it.

~

Twenty minutes later, Ruth sighed as she sat in the bath, a mound of coloured bubbles heaped over her like a fragrant cloud of pure loveliness.

After she'd filled his food bowl, changed his water, and massaged his ears, Merlin had finally settled down to his normal, if ever-so-slightly grumpy self. Ruth assumed his agitated mood was due to the fact she'd left him alone for so long. Merlin rarely got separation anxiety, but perhaps he sensed trouble. He wasn't fond of strangers either. Whatever the case, he'd finally jumped into his box and was now fast asleep, as per the norm.

In the bath, Ruth tipped her head back and closed her eyes.

An image of her late husband, John, appeared, as so often happened when she missed him the most.

He had a serene expression, almost inquisitive.

Ruth smiled as she returned to her memory of their ill-fated sailboat expedition.

After she'd recovered from the wave and almost drowning, the torrential rain, and having to bail out the boat, they'd finally made it to Poole harbour, only to sail into a heavy bank of fog.

"John . . ." Ruth set a bucket to one side. "Where are we?"

He was about to answer when an almighty grinding shook the boat, and they both fell forward.

John helped Ruth to her feet and then peered over the gunnels to the water below. "Ah."

Ruth sighed. "What now?"

"Run aground. Sand bank." John cleared his throat. "Looks like the tide's out."

"Great." Ruth frowned at him. "Didn't think to check the tide timetable before we left?"

"Nothing else for it." John lowered himself over the side of the boat.

"What are you doing?" Ruth said.

He dropped into the water, which reached his waist. "Walking to shore. Come on." He held up his hands.

Ruth peered down at him. "I can't jump that far."

"I'll catch you."

Ruth shook her head. "No way."

John glanced over his shoulder. "Hold on," He waded into the fog and disappeared.

"Where are you going?" Ruth called after him.

"Won't be long."

Twenty minutes later, John reappeared with a ladder and placed it against the side of the boat.

"Where did you get this?" Ruth asked as she climbed down.

"There's a beach and houses right over there." He waved toward the thick fog.

Ruth lowered herself into the water. "I don't know how I let you persuade me to do these things."

John rested the ladder on his shoulder, and the pair of them waded through the water until they reached the beach.

As they walked from the water, a man with his dog stared at them, open-mouthed. He looked at Ruth, John, and then the ladder.

John tipped his cap. "Afternoon. We're boat window cleaners."

That was more than thirty years ago. Ruth had engaged in several relationships since John, but although they were fun at the time, none really lived up to him. Big shoes to fill. Sure, Ruth had put John on a pedestal in some ways—no one was perfect—and the other men had relieved some of her loneliness over the years, but now being independent was what made her truly happy. After all, relationships and other people didn't define her. And as for the loneliness, Ruth had her daughter, Sara, her grandson, Greg, her grand-daughter, Ellie, and, of course, Merlin, to bring her all the joy she needed.

John's image swam back into view.

Ruth smiled at him and murmured, "I miss you."

15

Two blissful hours later—now doing her best to push all thoughts of murders, crime scenes, and killers from her mind, and after stuffing her face with one of the pastries—Ruth, wrapped in a bathrobe, put her slipper-clad feet up on the coffee table. Then, with Merlin on her lap, a bucket of tea in one hand, and a remote in the other, she flipped through onboard, pre-recorded TV channels, pleased they were working, and hoped for a good programme to distract her from the horrific events of the past couple of days.

However, it all seemed to be real-life docusoaps of youngsters getting up to no good. The type of rubbish Greg enjoyed. Ruth wanted an old-fashioned black-and-white movie, or a comedy series from the seventies. Either would have done nicely, but as she continued to flip through the channels, her hope dwindled.

There came a knock at the door.

Ruth groaned inwardly. *Can I pretend to be out?* No, the door was still open. *Darn it.* She looked over. Colonel Tom stood there. "Yes? How may I help?" *He'd better make it quick; I have at least fifty more channels to go through.*

Colonel Tom stepped inside with the expression of a sheepish schoolboy who'd accidentally thrown a cricket ball through her kitchen window. "Am I disturbing you?"

"Yes." Ruth stared at him for a few seconds, and then let out a slow breath. She set her mug down. "What do you want?"

"A brief word." Colonel Tom went to close the door.

"No," Ruth said. "Leave it open, please." She stroked Merlin's ears, and he let out a low, rumbling purr.

Colonel Tom stared. "You brought a cat on board?"

Ruth gave him a sour look in return. "Seriously?" She couldn't believe the nerve of the guy. "You brought a gun."

"Fair point." Colonel Tom took a few tentative steps into the room. "I wondered whether you'd like to make a deal."

Ruth blinked at him. "What kind of deal?"

This should be good.

"A pact." Colonel Tom cleared his throat. "That we stick together like glue from now on. For real. No deviation. No broken promises. No running off."

Ruth's eyes narrowed to slits. "Not two seconds ago you accused me of being the killer."

"I did not," Colonel Tom said in a defensive tone.

"Yes, you did." Ruth continued to massage Merlin's ears, trying to keep her voice level. "You also suspected me of taking the gun. You implied I had the opportunity to kill the captain, Gabriella, and Laura." As if she could do such a thing.

Colonel Tom sat on the edge of the sofa and rubbed his temples. "It's been a stressful few days. I apologise whole-heartedly." He sighed. "With someone murdering half of us, I—"

"Half?" Ruth frowned.

Colonel Tom blinked. "I mean—" He shook himself. "Well, almost half. I was including the captain in that statement."

Ruth glanced at the open door to her suite. "Where's Jeremy?"

Before Colonel Tom had a chance to respond, Jeremy rushed into the room. "I've done it." He clutched a tablet to his chest, spotted Merlin, and frowned. "Where did that come from?"

"Done what?" Colonel Tom asked.

Jeremy ignored him and sat opposite Ruth. He showed her the tablet display. "I've hacked into the security computer remotely." The screen showed the logs and a detailed map of the ship. "We can get live updates as doors open and close." Jeremy scrolled up the list. "This is the cage door opening in the cargo hold. Logan must have had another key card."

Ruth squinted at the screen. Sure enough, the card ended in 222. She blew out a puff of air. "Another key card. Awesome. Where did he get that from?"

Jeremy scrolled down. "Logan left the lower decks and went here."

"Where is that?" Ruth asked.

Merlin looked up at her, let out a raspy meow, and closed his eyes again when she resumed massaging his ears.

Jeremy zoomed in on the map of the ship and pointed.

Ruth's eyebrows lifted. "We should go see what he's up to."

"Hold on," Colonel Tom said. "Are you suggesting we track a killer through this ship?" He gave them both an incredulous look. "Are you out of your damn minds? My bet is he now has my gun. He's twice as dangerous as before."

Ruth shrugged. "I, for one, am not letting Logan get away. He must answer for what he's done. We can't let him go free or get to one of us."

"Where exactly will he go?" Colonel Tom said. "He's trapped here. We should sit tight and wait for the police."

"By which time, if he is the killer, Logan can get up to all manner of mischief," Ruth said. "He'll have an escape plan too."

As if he agreed with her, Merlin purred.

"You're right that Logan could kill one of us next," Jeremy said. "I think we should go after him. Put Logan on the back foot. He won't be expecting us to do that."

Colonel Tom stared at Ruth.

She pursed her lips as she considered this. On the one hand, they were better off staying put, but on the other, Jeremy was right: who knew what Logan could get up to in the next—she checked her phone—twenty-three hours and thirty-five minutes.

After a long silence, Ruth lifted Merlin from her lap, and with him clutched to her, she stood.

"Where are you going?" Colonel Tom asked.

"To get changed." Ruth padded off to her bedroom. This was probably a bad idea. A *very* bad idea.

Once changed into more suitable attire for hunting down a murderer—sensible shoes and a black cardigan, but minus a blunderbuss, safari hat, and twirly moustache—Ruth checked that Merlin had settled down in his box again, and then closed the bedroom door. She followed Jeremy and Colonel Tom through the ship's hallways, humming to herself.

"I wish I had my gun," Colonel Tom grumbled. He glanced back at her. "Do we have a plan once we've caught up to him?"

Ruth shrugged. "He'll be armed, dangerous, and a little miffed that we locked him up." She smiled. "I guess we'll have to play it by ear." Besides, it was Colonel Tom's fault Logan now had a pistol and an attitude to match, so he could be the first one to confront the guy.

However, if Logan planned to kill them off one by one, Ruth couldn't understand why the murders had been so elaborate in their execution. Plus, she struggled to understand Logan's motives. The person he openly disliked the most seemed to be Colonel Tom, and he was alive and kicking. Well, for now at least.

The three manhunters reached an intersection. To their right stood a row of shuttered shops, but to the left sat the entrance to a casino.

Jeremy double-checked the logs on the tablet, then the map, and finally looked at Ruth and nodded.

Ruth stepped around him and approached the doors with her key card in hand.

"Madam?"

She turned back.

Colonel Tom swallowed. "Be careful."

Ruth stared at him for a few seconds. *He's an army guy and should know how this works. Oh, but he was an officer, used to being way behind his troops, far from the front line.*

She gave him a grin and a double thumbs-up, and then faced the doors again, unlocked them, took a deep breath, and went on through.

The space beyond had a low ceiling with recessed lights, held aloft by ornate pillars.

With Colonel Tom and Jeremy following, Ruth edged

her way past various slot machines, all switched off and eerily quiet.

The space opened to various blackjack, craps, and roulette tables.

Jeremy pointed to a VIP sign at the back of the room.

Ruth walked over to it, and after a glance back to make sure her companions were still following, she nudged open a black door and stepped through.

The room beyond, decked out in an art deco style with gold embellishments, had an oval poker table in the middle.

Ruth gasped and clapped a hand over her mouth; it took a moment to understand what she was seeing.

Eight people sat around the table. No, not people but mannequins dressed like them. The one nearest had a white beard and wore a cap, with a pipe jutting from his mouth.

The captain?

"What twisted nonsense is this?" Colonel Tom stepped into the room with Jeremy, both looking dumbstruck.

Ruth circled the table.

Someone had dressed the players in various outfits, including a female mannequin clothed all in black with a pink hat.

"That's me." Ruth peered at her. "And that's my hat." She couldn't remember the last time she'd seen it. "Wait. I think these are mine too." She indicated the black blouse and trousers.

Jeremy stared at a mannequin representation of himself with jeans and a white T-shirt. "These are my clothes." He looked over at Ruth. "Someone stole them from our rooms."

She nodded. "Remember Gabriella said someone had taken her dress?" She pointed to a mannequin wearing a blue dress with white panels.

"And this is supposed to be me?" Colonel Tom indicated

another mannequin dressed in a military uniform. "He must have also taken these from my room."

Jeremy frowned. "Why did you bring your uniform?"

"Publicity photos," Colonel Tom said. "I have one formal picture taken at each place I go." He shrugged. "It's my gimmick. Look it up on my site, and you'll see."

"No internet." Ruth leaned in and examined the outfit with its medals pinned to the chest. "And this is definitely the same one I found."

Colonel Tom cocked an eyebrow. "Excuse me?"

She straightened. "The duffle bag on the promenade deck I mentioned?" She pointed at the military mannequin. "This uniform was inside."

Colonel Tom glared at her. "The bag you said went missing the night someone murdered Gabriella?"

Ruth stared back at him with what she hoped was a passive expression.

"What?" he said. "I had no idea someone had stolen the uniform from me." Colonel Tom narrowed his eyes. "Why the hell didn't you say something at the time?"

Ruth's attention moved to the other people at the poker table. There was also a representation of Laura with her puffy white jacket, Logan in his suit and black polo-neck, and another person she didn't recognise. The man had a red wig, taped-on moustache, jeans, and a lumberjack shirt.

Her gaze shifted to the table itself.

"Scrabble." Colonel Tom circled it. "There's only four players allowed in the rules. There's eight here."

"I don't think the killer cares," Jeremy muttered.

Sure enough, a Scrabble board sat in the middle of the table, and four of the mannequin players had a selection of letter tiles in front of them.

The killer had already placed four words on the board:

DROWNED going horizontally through the middle square, with the word *CHOKED*—a blank tile in place of the *H*—

intersecting the letter *O* in *DROWNED*. Also intersecting the *E* in DROWNED was the word *SMOTHERED*, with the *H* in that word starting another: *HIT*.

Ruth's attention then moved to objects in front of the mannequins. Laura had a pair of leather driving gloves, whereas in front of Gabriella sat a small brown bottle.

"Poison." Colonel Tom pointed at it.

"Murder weapons," Jeremy breathed.

"Smothered and choked." *Is this a sick game?* It had to be. Someone playing tricks. *Logan?*

Ruth looked at the tiles placed in the rack in front of her mannequin: *B, D, B, S, T, E,* and the Colonel Tom mannequin seated next to hers only had *T, O, H,* but Logan's mannequin had *A, R, N, T, S, E, G, L.*

Colonel Tom waved a finger at it. "Eight letters. Someone's definitely not playing by the rules."

Ruth shook her head. She was never much use at this game, rules or no, and anagrams always perplexed her.

"Who's this supposed to be?" Jeremy indicated the eighth guest with the red hair and moustache. In front of the man lay a wrench with a yellow handle.

Ruth stared at the wrench for a few seconds. "I've seen this before."

"Where?" Colonel Tom asked.

Ruth hesitated while she racked her brains, and then it dawned on her. She rushed past Colonel Tom and Jeremy, back into the main casino.

Colonel Tom followed her across the casino. "Madam?"

Ruth reached the door and looked back. "Where's Jeremy?" She called, "Jeremy?"

The door to the VIP room opened, and he jogged over to them. "Sorry. Almost forgot this." He held up the tablet.

"We must stick together," Colonel Tom reminded him.

Jeremy nodded.

"Let's go." Ruth marched from the casino, fists balled, and a renewed surge of determination coursed through her. When they stepped into the stairwell and started their ascent, she said over her shoulder to Jeremy. "Any movement from our lawyer friend?"

He scanned the logs on the tablet. "Only us."

Ruth muttered, "Where exactly is he?"

Five minutes later, Ruth and Jeremy strode across the dining room, into the galley, and through the back into the storeroom.

Ruth rushed to the end of the shelves and found the yellow tool bag. "Here we go. I knew I'd seen it before." Sure enough, inside were yellow-handled tools. The walk-in freezer drew her attention. She glanced back at Colonel Tom and Jeremy, and then held her breath and opened the door.

Ruth stiffened.

Lying on the floor, on his back, frozen solid, was a dead man with red hair and a moustache, partially naked, only his socks and underpants remaining.

"The clothes on that mannequin." Ruth edged her way into the walk-in freezer. She scanned the shelves and floor, looking for clues or any hints as to what had happened to the poor guy. He appeared to have been in his late thirties.

Colonel Tom stared down at the body. "Who the hell is this?"

"If I were to guess by his tool bag," Ruth said as she focussed on his face, "some kind of maintenance person."

"Doesn't this prove there's someone else on board this ship?" Colonel Tom said. "Another murder?"

"Could have happened at any time," Jeremy said. "Unless you know how long he's been dead?" he asked, keeping his distance and not looking in their direction for more than a brief glance at a time.

Ruth pursed her lips. "He's frozen solid. I have no way to tell. Could be days. Maybe happened before we got here."

"If that's the case," Colonel Tom asked, "why didn't any of the crew find him?"

"We had a buffet dinner," Ruth said. "Nothing from frozen. All fresh and previously cooked." Thankful for that, she knelt and peered under his head. "Hit with that big wrench we found in the poker room." She sat up, looked about, and pointed at a set of parallel scuff marks on the floor, leading from the door to the body. "Someone dragged the body in here, which means they murdered him some-where else." She stood. "And if the killer dragged him, rather than carried . . ."

"The deed took place nearby," Colonel Tom said.

Ruth ushered the boys out of the freezer, and she closed the door. "No one goes back in there." She sighed. "It's another crime scene."

Jeremy pointed to the drag marks crossing the storage room.

"The entire damn ship is a crime scene," Colonel Tom said. "And we're in it up to our necks. The sooner we get out of this living hell, the better."

Ruth followed the drag marks across the floor, careful where she placed her feet, and indicated for the other two to do the same. She walked behind a set of shelves and stopped.

Blood splattered the floor and wall next to an air vent, and a clipboard and pen lay nearby.

Jeremy leaned down and examined the top sheet on the clipboard without touching it. "That guy was a health and safety inspector. David Franks." He pointed at the date. "The day before we arrived."

"Judging by his current state of health," Colonel Tom said, "I'm guessing he rates the safety at a solid zero."

Despite the dire situation, Ruth smirked. It was either that or burst into tears, scream, and run from the room, which were all plausible alternatives.

She looked at the man's notes, and sure enough, the health and safety guy had marked several concerns regarding the ship. The sheet listed twelve issues, but among them were no mention of damaged lifeboat davit controls. The last entry did point out that the air vent grilles were push-fit rather than held with bolts, and the fact kids could crawl inside. Ruth eyed the large nearby vent and had to agree with his damaging assessment.

But why kill him? What did the killer have to gain?

With her heart in her throat, Ruth checked the immediate area for further clues. After finding nothing out of the ordinary, she motioned for them to back away. The sooner they got out of here, the better.

16

Once back in the galley, Ruth closed the door to the storeroom and put on a brave face. "I'm starving. How about I rustle us up something?"

"I'll help," Colonel Tom said.

"How can you eat at a time like this?" Jeremy asked. "I don't want anything."

"Nonsense," Ruth said. "You need to keep up your strength." They all did. She looked at the time on her phone. "Besides, it's almost ten o'clock at night. We've missed lunch and dinner." A single pastry didn't count as a meal. "We need something more substantial to see us through to morning." She waved to the door that led back to the dining room. "Go set up a table for the three of us." Staying busy would be good for all three of them.

Jeremy hesitated. "I'm a vegetarian."

"I've got you covered," Ruth said. "Nut allergy too, right?"

Jeremy nodded.

Colonel Tom rolled his eyes. "What is this generation coming to? Back in my day, we ate everything."

Ruth rolled her eyes too. "Of course you did." She

opened a fridge. "Ah, here we go." Ruth grabbed some steak, marrow, and a few leftovers from the buffet. Then she faced the stove. "Grab me a large pot, would you?"

Jeremy did as she asked.

Ruth cut the steak into chunks, seasoned it, and browned it in a pan before adding chopped onions, a hint of garlic, and balsamic vinegar to two pots. Then she included tomato paste and dumped the beef into one pot, along with lentils, chickpeas, and black beans into the other of water, and sprinkled the beef stew mixture with a liberal amount of flour.

While she stirred, Colonel Tom fetched a full-bodied red wine, thyme, a few bay leaves, and sugar, which Ruth added in exacting amounts to each, along with two cups of broth in with the beef and a tablespoon of Worcestershire sauce.

Finally, she added carrots, chunks of potato, peas, and Italian parsley to both pots, before placing them in the oven.

"That should do it."

"How long?" Jeremy asked.

Ruth wiped her hands on a tea towel. "Two hours."

Colonel Tom's eyes went wide. "Two hours?" He looked at his watch. "It'll be gone midnight before we eat. Couldn't we have a burger instead?"

"No, we most certainly could not." Ruth nodded to the door. "And now"—as she'd planned—"we have the time we need."

"Time for what?" Jeremy asked as he and Colonel Tom followed her out. "Oh, hold on." He jogged into the sports bar, grabbed a bottle of white wine, and hurried back.

Ruth and Colonel Tom sat at a table in the dining room, while Jeremy poured wine.

"I can get red, if you prefer," he said.

"This is fine by me." Ruth held up her glass. "To making it off this tub alive." They chinked glasses, and Ruth lifted the wine to her lips, but hesitated. She looked at Jeremy. He took a big gulp of his wine, so Ruth shrugged and did the same.

Colonel Tom, however, set his glass to one side. He rubbed his hands together and pointed at the cat painting. "Are you going to explain this? You have a black cat, no?"

Ruth stared at the three marks under the cat's paws. *The killer has been back to add another? Do those strikes represent bodies? Is he counting? David Franks not included?* Ruth shuddered and turned her back. "Right, so it's time for us to share the full truth." She took a breath. "I'll go first." Ruth looked between them. "I expect you've been wondering about my past. I already told you I was once a police officer."

"They sacked you," Jeremy said.

"Correct," Ruth said. "Thirty years ago."

"What did you do?" Colonel Tom sat forward with a look of interest.

"Someone murdered my husband."

An uncomfortable silence greeted this.

Ruth steeled herself and pressed on. "It happened while I was training to be a detective. I was never going to solve every crime and set the world on fire, but I enjoyed it. The puzzle solving, I suppose. The bringing bad people to justice. I was a different person back then. Eager to make a mark. Turns out, a little too eager." Ruth took another swig of wine. "I got myself involved in John's case."

Colonel Tom's brow furrowed. "Your husband's death? Surely that's a—"

"Conflict of interest," Ruth finished. "Yeah. The chief told me to back off, as well he should, but I ignored him." She gripped the edge of the table, fighting back the bad memories. "I continued to investigate in my off time, inter-viewed suspects, examined evidence, broke every rule and oath." She clenched her teeth at the painful memories. "I had to know what happened to John. I wanted to under-stand why someone would murder such a nice, unassuming, vibrant guy." She paused. "He was a gentle, kind man. Wouldn't hurt a fly. Loved and respected by everyone he met." Ruth shook her head. "It made no sense why someone would want to kill him. I had to know why."

"Your boss caught you again?" Colonel Tom asked.

Ruth sat back. "Yep. The second time the chief had no alternative but to sack me."

"What did you do next?" Jeremy asked.

"Nothing," Ruth said. "Well, not anything to do with John's murder. That's been a cold case for over three decades." Ruth glanced at the ceiling, then back again. "John's business took care of itself—he was a registered cat breeder and employed a good team. When she was old enough, my daughter, Sara, took over." Ruth sighed. "So, it wasn't about money, but I wanted to do something with my life, you know? I'd always enjoyed cooking." Ruth smiled. "I started with this clapped-out sandwich van. I travelled around industrial estates, selling homemade pies and cakes. Pretty soon that expanded with more vans, employees, a few shops." She shook her head. "A few years of that and it turned into a little empire. I was very proud to be part of it. Had a great team of people."

Colonel Tom tipped his head in appreciation. "Good for you, madam."

"Yeah." Ruth took another swig of wine. "I sold it."

Jeremy topped up her glass. "Why did you do that?"

Ruth shrugged. "It all got to be too much. I still followed my culinary passion, only in a different direction from then on. I studied hard, got a degree in food management and culinary arts, acquired a food handler's licence, and the rest you know."

"What about your grandson?" Colonel Tom asked. "Is he assisting you with your latest venture?"

"Greg?" Ruth smiled again. "He does help out, but that's not why he asked to tag along." She focussed on Jeremy. "I guess we should address the elephant in the room: Why were you in prison?" She cringed at her forwardness, but these were desperate times.

Jeremy recoiled. "How did you know that?"

Colonel Tom shot him a furious glance but kept his mouth shut for a change.

"The cobweb tattoo on your elbow," Ruth said to Jeremy. "It has a few different meanings, some more odious than others, but I figured yours likely commemorates a stretch you served at Her Majesty's pleasure." She took a breath and pressed on. "The tattoo is clean, neat, and therefore it's unlikely you had it done during your time there, but after. When you came out?"

Jeremy hesitated and then nodded.

"How long were you inside?" Ruth asked.

"Nine years. I was eighteen when I went in." His jaw muscles flexed.

"What were you in for?" Colonel Tom asked.

"Does it matter?" Jeremy mumbled.

"Yes." Colonel Tom faced him. "It matters a lot."

Jeremy hung his head. "Hacking a government website."

Ruth studied him. Now was not the time for them to press the issue. Just because someone had been in prison before, it didn't automatically make them a criminal now. Certainly not a killer. She was a firm believer in rehabilitation. Well, for most criminals. The ones who didn't kill people, that is. She hadn't quite made up her mind if Jeremy was capable of murder. "And you're a security advisor? You're here to assess this ship?"

Jeremy nodded and looked away.

"What about you?" Ruth asked Colonel Tom. "What's your story?"

"No story to tell." He tugged at his cuffs and stared at the table. "Joined the army fresh from school. Attended officer college, worked my way up through the ranks, did my fair share of tours of duty, and retired at fifty-five." His eyes rose to meet Ruth's. "Like you, madam, I followed my passion. Started a website, a blog only at first, and travelled. It grew from there." He glanced at the painted cat.

Ruth decided that Colonel Tom, unlike Jeremy, was capable of murdering someone. There was a chance he'd killed during his time in the army, so it wasn't a stretch to imagine he could do it again, given the right circumstances and motivation.

She sat back, knowing there were whole swathes of personal history the boys had left out, and chose to sip her wine at a more leisurely pace as she mulled over their brief backstories.

～

The next few hours passed in a blur as Ruth, Colonel Tom, and Jeremy chatted and ate stew.

Finally, Colonel Tom yawned and stretched. "Are we staying up all night? It's almost one o'clock in the morning."

Ruth stood. "I need a few minutes."

"Not alone. We'll come with you." The colonel went to get to his feet, but Ruth held up a hand, stopping him.

She then pointed to the windows. "I'll be right there.

Won't get out of sight." She marched from the dining room —glanced at the painting of the cat as she strode past—then along the hallway and outside.

Once on the promenade deck, Ruth paced back and forth, taking deep breaths, trying to get a grip of the situation and sober up.

The killer had murdered four people, that they knew of, and he, or she, didn't look like they were about to let up.

Questions chased each other round Ruth's brain.

What's the deal with the painted cat? And why are there only three marks underneath, instead of four? Has the killer left out the health and safety guy? If so, why? Was he an unplanned murder? After all, an extra mannequin taken from one of the shops and placed at the poker table would not have been much trouble to set up.

And what about the cat itself? Ruth mused. *Is it a dig at me somehow or a coincidence?*

Then she thought about Logan and muttered, "Where are you hiding, and what do you have planned? How do you fit in?"

Also, the killer had an uncanny way of keeping one step ahead of them, almost as if they knew— Ruth stopped dead in her tracks, and her eyes bulged from their sockets. "Of course."

She rushed back into the ship and found her companions tidying up in the galley. Ruth hurried over to Jeremy as he loaded a dishwasher. "Can you deactivate the logs from here?"

"No." He frowned. "Why?"

She glanced between them. "Don't you find it strange the killer has been able to avoid us all this time? That he's been one step ahead of us the whole way? We're running from one thing to another but not getting there in time."

Ruth's heart rate increased. "The killer has a knack of sneaking up and murdering someone with such ease. How? It's like they know where the victims are at any given moment of the day, and then strike at the right opportunity."

Jeremy stared at her. "You think the killer is using these to track us?" He held up the tablet and the security logs.

"Precisely." Ruth lifted her chin. "The very thing we're using now, he's used against us this whole time." She cursed herself for making another mistake, and a wave of guilt gnawed at her stomach for not realising it sooner.

"But that's precisely it," Colonel Tom said. "We found that VIP room. We know where he's been. We've tracked him."

"Did we?" Ruth ground her teeth. "Don't you also find it odd that the only logs on there led us straight to those weird mannequins?" Her stomach tightened. "He wanted us to see that room. Part of the game. He deliberately guided us to it."

"Why would he do that?" Jeremy asked.

Ruth paced. "Every step has been under his control. We're like rats in a maze, and he's the scientist controlling it all." She shook her head. "Isolated on this ship? No way to call for help? Phone signals blocked. Killed off one by one in such elaborate ways?" Ruth stopped pacing and nodded at Jeremy. "It's time we turned the tables."

Jeremy frowned. "How?"

"We deactivate the computers, so he has no way to track us." Ruth huffed out a breath. "What do you think? That'll put a stop to his game."

Jeremy shook his head. "Then we'll be blind too."

"I think it's a superb idea, madam," Colonel Tom said. "The killer clearly has a way of avoiding the security. That was apparent the moment he threw the poor captain overboard."

"Then it's settled." Ruth gestured to the door.

Back in the computer room on the lower deck of the *Ocean Odyssey*, Ruth and Jeremy sat at the security terminal, while Colonel Tom watched over their shoulders.

"Can you deactivate this without damaging it in any way?" Ruth asked. "We mustn't destroy evidence."

"It's simple enough," Jeremy said in a low voice. "I can leave it running but restrict access with a password, in effect locking anyone other than us out of the system."

"And what will you set the password to?" Colonel Tom asked.

Jeremy reached for the keyboard, but Ruth stopped him.

"Hold on." She scrolled up the logs and checked the time and location of each as she went. She stopped on a few. "Look at this."

Colonel Tom leaned in. "What have you found?"

Ruth pointed at one of the entries. "This is when we locked the cargo cage door, right? With Logan inside?"

Jeremy nodded. "The card ending in 098."

"And these next entries are us moving about the ship," Ruth said. "And then comes the other card, 222, showing up when the cage door opened again but not before that moment. That's the first occurrence."

"What's your point?" Colonel Tom asked.

Ruth's finger moved down the list, and she muttered under her breath as she went through the sequence of events. "Next entries appear at the casino. Nothing in between." She sat back as her blood ran cold in sudden realisation. They'd made a mistake. More to the point: she'd made the error herself, and it was a stupid one. "We need to check something out." Ruth motioned for Jeremy to work. "Hurry."

In a few minutes he had the system locked with a password. The second he'd completed the task, Ruth leapt to her feet and marched from the room.

"Are you going to explain what's going on?" Colonel Tom asked as he and Jeremy raced after her. "Or are we to develop the skills required to read your mind at every turn?"

"It's better I show you," Ruth said over her shoulder. "And I hope I'm wrong." She prayed she was, but her gut told her otherwise.

Once down in the cargo hold, Ruth marched to the cage with the open door, and with her heart in her throat, she peered inside.

"What are you searching for?" Colonel Tom asked as he and Jeremy caught up. "There's nothing here. He's gone."

Ruth stepped into the cage, edged behind the stacks of boxes, and winced.

Colonel Tom and Jeremy joined her.

Slumped on his side in the corner of the cage, his head rested on a crumpled box, knees pulled up to his chest, lay Logan, his eyes wide and lifeless.

"He was in here this whole time?" Colonel Tom said with an incredulous shriek to his voice.

A shiver ran along Ruth's spine. With trepidation, she knelt beside Logan and felt his wrist for a pulse. "Nothing." He was cold to the touch. "Been here a while." She let out a juddering breath and sat back. "We can rule him out as the killer."

"Which leaves us with very few suspects remaining."

Colonel Tom looked between them. "Or we're back to the theory that there's someone else on board."

"I think there must be," Jeremy murmured.

"Not necessarily." Colonel Tom's eyes narrowed. "Either one of you had ample opportunities to sneak down here and perform the deed." He took a step back toward the door. "Perhaps you're working together. In cahoots, as it were. Would explain why my gun is now missing."

Ruth scanned the body, but there was no sign of it.

Jeremy shook his head and muttered, "You can't be serious."

"I'm deadly serious, young man."

"How do we know it wasn't you?" Jeremy said. "You also had time to come down here. You make your dislike for people very clear."

Ruth stared at him, surprised he'd finally decided to stand up to Colonel Tom.

"What killer in their right mind announces their dislike for a person before murdering them?" Colonel Tom said with a flick of his wrist. "Preposterous. Such behaviour makes me the least likely culprit."

"Or it makes you an idiot," Jeremy muttered.

Colonel Tom stepped toward him. "How dare you."

While they bickered, Ruth took the opportunity to gather her wits and examine the body. There was no blood or obvious marks, other than a slight redness showing on Logan's neck, poking from underneath his polo-neck, and there were also two small cuts to his right knuckles. They looked fresh.

Did he punch his assailant?

Ruth glanced at Colonel Tom and Jeremy, but neither had any visible bruises. She then scanned the rest of the body and Logan's clothes. Ruth leaned in. Several pink fibres clung to his polo-neck, beneath Logan's chin.

Are they from my hat and scarf? Does that mean he was the one who stole my clothes and put them on the mannequin? The same with the others?

Ruth was about to turn away when something else caught her eye: something square in Logan's pocket.

17

In the storage cage, Ruth leaned forward for a closer look at Logan's pocket. The square object within looked about two centimetres in size and flat.

Ruth glanced at the men again, but they were still squabbling and not paying her any mind, so she slipped a handkerchief from her pocket, and in turn slid her fingers into Logan's pocket and pulled out a . . . Scrabble tile.

Ruth flipped it over in her hand. It had a letter *T*. She checked Logan's pocket again, and pulled out more Scrabble tiles: *R*, *A*, *O*, *I*, *R*, and another *T*.

"If it was you all along," she breathed, "then how come you're dead?" Her brow furrowed. "What went wrong?" She turned to show the tiles to Colonel Tom and Jeremy, but instinct told her to hold off.

She hesitated for a moment, wrestling with her conscience. She'd keep the evidence to herself for the time being.

Ruth wrapped the tiles in her handkerchief, pocketed them, and stood. "Enough." She squeezed around the boxes and between the men. "We can't do any more for him here."

She stepped from the cage, momentarily tempted to lock them in, and waited for them to join her.

As soon as Jeremy and the colonel left the cage, Ruth shut the door. Then she glanced at the time on her phone. "It's almost two o'clock in the morning. I've had more than enough." She spun on her heel and went to march away when Jeremy called after her.

"What about breakfast?"

Ruth stopped and turned back.

Colonel Tom scoffed. "A little early for breakfast, wouldn't you say?"

"No, he's right." She glanced between them. "If I make us a spot of breakfast now, we can have it later, and there's no need to leave our suites for the rest of the day. We have enough supplies left up there for lunch." Hopefully, they wouldn't need to worry about dinner because Greg would have arrived by then. "Come on." Ruth hurried to the stairs.

In the galley, Ruth busied herself with pots and pans, trying not to focus on the fact a dead body was still mere feet away. Now she came to think of it, *should we have put all the bodies in the freezer? No, that's a terrible idea.* After all, they'd already contaminated the crime scenes, and on top of that, when the police found out Ruth had once been a member of the force, they'd have more questions for her, along with a mountain of criticism for both her past and present actions.

Jeremy opened a fridge. "Well, this saves you a lot of bother."

Ruth stepped to him and peered inside. Serving cartons packed the shelves labelled *Room Service Breakfast, Room Service Lunch*, and *Room Service Dinner*. She opened one of the breakfast packets. Inside were poached eggs, bacon, hash browns, and half a tomato. "Not great, but good enough." She found one marked Vegetarian and handed it to Jeremy. "Okay?"

He opened it and nodded.

"Excellent." Ruth marched from the kitchen.

"Where are you going now?" Colonel Tom called after her.

"To bed," Ruth said as she headed across the dining salon. "I'm tired."

"Can I make a suggestion, madam?"

She sighed and turned back. "What?"

Colonel Tom took a breath. "I think we should sleep together."

Ruth's eyebrows shot up. "Excuse me?"

Colonel Tom's cheeks flushed. "I mean, I think we should spend the remainder of the night in the same suite." He gestured. "All three of us. Together. Clothed."

Ruth pondered this intriguing offer for a moment, and then shrugged. "Suit yourself, but I'm going back to my bed, in my suite. You two can fight it out for the sofa." As she headed on up the stairs, Colonel Tom and Jeremy bickered about who was to spend the night on the floor.

"Play rock, paper, scissors for it," Ruth said.

An hour later, after completing her late-night ablutions and checking Merlin had everything he needed, Ruth stood at her bedroom door and yawned. She peered down at Jeremy on the floor. He lay on a makeshift bed formed of scatter cushions. He'd gone with paper, while Colonel Tom had hit him with scissors. "Comfortable?" she asked.

Jeremy glared at her as if it were her fault. He rolled over and closed his eyes.

Colonel Tom lay sprawled across the widest part of her sofa, hands behind his head, looking supremely comfortable. "Good night, madam."

She closed the bedroom door and pressed her back against it. "Gift us with one quiet night, please?"

Merlin leapt onto the bed and gave her a look as if to say, *And what bloody time do you call this?*

Ruth climbed under the sheets and hoped that if one of those guys turned out to be the murderer, she'd hear them trying to kill the other one before they came for her.

Another few hours later, Ruth lay in bed, with Mrs Beeton and her book of household management tossed to one side —there were only a finite number of obscure recipes she could absorb in one sitting—and stared at the ceiling, unable to sleep.

She flipped over the Scrabble tiles within the handkerchief as her mind replayed the previous days' events over and over.

What Ruth should do was stay in that bedroom, warm, safe, wait out the next twelve hours, and refuse to open the door, even for the boys. Considering what they'd all been through, twelve hours was nothing. She'd clear her mind of all the events, switch off, and hold out for the police . . .

So, was it Logan who set up those mannequins? No, that wouldn't make much sense considering he was a victim. Was he working with someone? If so, who?

"Stop," Ruth grumbled to herself, and she laid the handkerchief and Scrabble tiles on the bedside table. "Leave it alone. Go to sleep." She rolled over and closed her eyes.

Someone else has to be on board.

She knew that for sure.

Ruth's eyes opened. "How to prove it, though?"

What is their next move?

Who is their next intended victim?

Ruth huffed, rolled onto her other side, and gazed at the Scrabble tiles. "Why were they in his pocket?" she murmured.

A deliberate clue left by the killer?

But there weren't any Scrabble tiles on the other victims, otherwise—

Ruth jerked up in bed.

Merlin opened one eye and let out a low meow-growl of annoyance.

"There were tiles on the other bodies?" Ruth hadn't thought to look at the time. "Why would I?" After all, she'd been trying not to disturb the crime scenes.

She glanced at the door, threw off the sheets, and swung her legs out of bed. *And while we're on the subject of doors:* "How is the killer getting about the ship without triggering them?" That was a mystery she needed to solve. *It's almost as if—*

Ruth gasped and clapped a hand over her mouth as a sudden epiphany hit her. "I've been so stupid."

No change there, then.

Ruth swore, leapt out of bed, hurried to the walk-in closet, grabbed a few extra handkerchiefs, and threw on a pair of black trousers, matching shirt, and her sensible shoes.

She then raced back to the bedroom, folded the

Scrabble tiles into the handkerchief, and slipped them into her pocket.

Ruth paused for a second as she considered telling the colonel and Jeremy but opted to keep what she'd discovered to herself for the time being. After all, she still wasn't convinced which, if any, of them she could trust.

After another glance at the door, Ruth snatched up her phone, gave Merlin a quick rub on his neck, and then hurried into the bathroom.

Ruth knelt and examined the air vent. She could make out light on the other side, coming from the sitting room. She'd have to be as quiet as possible.

Using the torch function on her phone, she examined the outer edge of the air vent. "No screws." She slipped the phone back into her pocket and ran her fingers around the frame, and then gripped it on either side and gave it a tug.

Ruth almost fell backward as the air vent cover came away with ease. "This is how he's getting around the ship without triggering doors." She cursed herself for over-looking something so blinkin' obvious.

Ruth peered inside. Although a small space, there seemed enough room to crawl about. It didn't look too bad. *Only one way to find out . . .*

She took a few deep breaths, and then crawled on all fours and backed into the air duct.

Ruth shot out again. "Can't do it." She shook her head and pulled in big lungfuls of air. "Really can't."

A few months prior, the bathroom door in the motorhome had jammed with Ruth inside. This had sent her into a panic until Greg had heard her muffled cries and busted the door open.

It was almost as if life knew what upset her and kept throwing challenging situations and tight spaces her way.

Ruth went to stand, hesitated, and dropped back to the floor. "This is ridiculous." She gritted her teeth. "Have to. No choice. Must know." Swearing under her breath, every muscle tensed and screaming for her not to do it, Ruth backed into the air duct again and pulled the vent grille closed.

Her body shook as she continued to back down the ventilation duct. Ruth stopped at the grille that opened to her sitting room, held her breath, and peered out.

Colonel Tom and Jeremy both appeared asleep, but even so, Ruth moved as slowly as she could, backing away with as little sound as possible while trying not to imagine the walls and ceiling of the duct pressing in on her.

A few feet along, she reached an intersection. This would be a good place to turn around so she faced the direction of travel.

It wasn't.

First, Ruth stayed on all fours and attempted to pivot. *Nope.* Nowhere near enough room.

She shuddered and tried to remain focussed as sweat blossomed from every pore of her skin, soaking her shirt, stinging her eyes.

Next, Ruth clawed her way into a seated position, but her feet still pointed down the tunnel, heading back the way she'd come. Ruth placed her hands on either wall and tried to roll forward. In her youth, she could manage at least ten sit-ups in a row, and almost touch her feet; now she struggled to reach her shins.

With her head bent to her chest, knees pulled close, Ruth endeavoured to scooch round, using her butt as a makeshift lazy Susan. This only resulted in her becoming wedged sideways in the tunnel: her back pressed against one wall, knees and feet squished against the other.

She let out a muffled cry. "No, no, no." Panic gnawed at her insides. Next came the uncontrollable shaking and the urge to scream.

The trembling increased as she tried to get a grip of herself. Ruth went to turn back, only to find she could no longer move. And that was when the panic turned to sheer terror.

Wedged in the tunnel, Ruth opened her mouth to shout, to alert the boys, but stopped herself by shoving a clenched fist between her teeth.

"Stop it, stop it." Ruth took deep breaths, and forced herself to relax, if only slightly. After all, if she'd gotten into this position, she sure as hell could get out of it.

Now in a detached state, Ruth rotated back in the direction she'd come, a millimetre at a time, and finally her legs sprang free.

With a huge sigh of relief, she lay down in the tunnel, on her back.

Ruth's chest rose and fell as she reevaluated her life choices. *Whose idea was it to come onto this cruise ship?* "Well, mine," she muttered. *Right, but whose stupid notion was it to crawl into this tunnel?* "Mine again. Darn it."

Then a sudden revelation struck Ruth. Her head now pointed the right way down the tunnel, so she rolled onto her front and lifted herself back onto all fours. "Yes." She congratulated herself for finally figuring it out but vowed never to make the same mistake again.

Ruth crawled along the tunnel and peered through grilles every time she passed: into lounge suites and bathrooms, until she reached one near the end.

Ruth stared into Gabriella's bathroom.

Gabriella's body lay on the floor exactly the way she'd last seen it: wearing her silk pyjamas, in the foetal position, face pale and turned to one side, signs of lividity now well and truly visible in her limbs.

Ruth sighed. "Poor girl." She nudged the grille open, and it screeched in protest.

Ruth winced and held her breath.

No other sounds came, no running footfalls, no shouts from the colonel or Jeremy, so Ruth gave the grille another shove, and it popped from its mount.

She grabbed it before the metal-framed grate hit the floor and leaned it to one side. Then she crawled from the air duct.

Once in the bathroom, Ruth sat up, and a groan escaped her lips as her joints creaked. "Should have brought kneepads." Although, she didn't own any.

With effort, using the vanity basin for support, Ruth clambered to her feet and stretched, breathing hard, wiping sweat from her brow with her sleeve.

Once she'd recovered sufficiently, Ruth's gaze fell back to the body.

She knelt beside it and scanned Gabriella from head to toe. "No pockets." She then checked her hands: sure enough, in the right one, despite her twisted fingers, lay another set of Scrabble tiles where there had been none before.

Ruth shuddered, removed one of the other handkerchiefs, and used it to take the tiles from Gabriella's hand. She sat back and examined them: *B*, *N*, *O*, and *S*. Ruth folded them inside the handkerchief, slipped it into her other pocket, and then scanned the body and surrounding area again for any more clues.

Finding none, Ruth's attention moved to the bathroom door. For a moment, she considered leaving that way, but she wasn't ready to share her discoveries with Colonel Tom and Jeremy yet. She couldn't risk them hearing. Which meant . . .

Ruth grumbled under her breath as she crawled back into the air duct. "Keep calm. You're fine. You did it before." She pulled the grille closed and paused for a moment, composing herself.

Ruth looked to her left. The duct ended in a grille, and through it she could make out the hexagonal seating area.

If she went that way, she could sneak about the ship without the colonel and the geek knowing, but she'd risk bumping into a murderer, alone, and then most likely dying in some horrific manner. Or, at the very least, getting into a serious amount of trouble.

She thought about the Scrabble tiles she had so far, really wanting to know if there were others on the remaining bodies. But it wasn't worth risking her young —*cough*—life.

However, if Ruth went right, she could make it back to the safety of her suite, block the air vent with something, and no one would know she'd snuck out.

She'd then force herself to sleep—because that was the number one cure for insomnia: sheer willpower—and she'd stick to the sensible plan of waiting it out until the police arrived. Going right was the safe, logical thing to do, and all intelligent people would go with that option . . .

Ruth went left.

18

After ten more feet of crawling through the air duct, with her knees now screaming at her—God had not designed them for hard surfaces—she peered through a grille into the hexagonal seating area.

Spotting no axe-wielding, chainsaw-swinging masked murderers on the other side, she popped open the vent and crawled out. "Sweet freedom." Ruth sat on the floor for a minute, breathing hard, and stretching each leg in turn, grimacing with the effort. "I knew I should have watched that *Yoga for Seniors* DVD Greg bought me for Christmas."

Ruth also now had a small amount of admiration for the killer—not because he or she murdered people, that was nothing to venerate, but for their ability to use the ship's air ducts to sneak about unseen. It was no small feat, and the killer clearly had stronger knees than her. Probably made of titanium. Ruth pictured the murderer as a sprightly young acrobat with evil red eyes and horns.

Using a nearby table for support, she clambered to her feet and stretched out the soreness some more.

She eyed the elevator and let out a breath. "You and me,

buddy boy." She reached for the call button but stopped herself. "Nope. Still can't do it." Ruth spun and jogged toward the stairs.

～

Ten minutes later, Ruth strode down the middle aisle of the theatre, up the steps, and then backstage to the dressing rooms.

She hesitated at the door to the store cupboard, steeled herself, and then went to swipe her card over the lock but stopped short.

Ruth stood there for a full minute, weighing her options. *What if the killer has reactivated the security computer? Would Jeremy know instantly via his app? If so, do I want to keep it a secret that I've been down here on my own?*

However, the thought of finding the right air duct and crawling inside did not exactly fill her with joyful excitement.

Also, seeing as the killer used that route to murder Laura, Ruth climbing in there would obliterate all the evidence. She'd done enough of that for one day.

That settles it—Ruth unlocked the door with the card.

Despite Ruth knowing what was in there, her heart skipped a beat at the sight of the dead body of another woman taken before her time.

Ruth knelt, wrapped her fingers in another handkerchief, and slipped them into Laura's pocket.

Instead of Scrabble tiles, Ruth pulled out a piece of torn paper with directions to a lower deck level, along with a room number scrawled across it.

Ruth frowned, set the paper aside, and tried Laura's left pocket. Sure enough, she removed more Scrabble tiles.

These ones comprised the letters *T*, *H*, *B*, *C*, and *I*. She wrapped them up, slipped them into her own pocket with the others, and picked up the paper again. "What was she doing with this?"

Ruth flipped it over to reveal part of the *Ocean Odyssey*'s logo. The room number suggested a crew member's quarters. She muttered under her breath as she got to her feet and left the storeroom.

Back in the hallway, Ruth stared at the paper. There was nothing else for it: she had to check it out.

Another ten minutes later, after three wrong turns despite the note's directions, Ruth found her way to a lower deck and stood outside the room number indicated. She looked left and right. The hallway was plain and narrow, with a single CCTV camera at one end.

Using the gold security card, Ruth opened the door and went inside.

Beyond lay a room with a single bed, a desk, and a TV on the wall. The bathroom door stood open. There was a wardrobe, but that was empty too.

Ruth was about to leave when a glint of light caught her eye. By the bed lay a gold cuff link. She snatched it up. Engraved initials read *DD*.

"The ship manager." Ruth glanced around the room. "He stayed here, which means . . ." She stepped back into the hallway and stared at the CCTV camera. However, the recordings up in the security room had long since been deleted.

"Why did Laura have a note with his room number?" Ruth pursed her lips. *Did he give it to her in the hopes of a late-*

night tryst? A youthful dalliance? Although plausible, Ruth wasn't so sure.

She went to leave but hesitated because she didn't recall seeing any views of this hallway, meaning there was a chance this camera was on a separate system.

She hurried over and peered up at it. Then Ruth followed the wire from the back of the camera. It ran along the top edge of the wall near the ceiling and disappeared through a hole above a black door.

Without hesitation, Ruth opened the door. On the other side was a compact storeroom with a couple of metal cabinets. The one on the right stood open, and inside was a monitor, keyboard, and mouse.

Ruth shook the latter, and the screen sprang to life, showing a view of the hallway. "Bingo."

Obviously, this was an isolated system here for the staff's safety and security without them feeling like they were being spied on by the ship owners.

After a few minutes mucking about with menus, and several colourful swear words later, Ruth found the playback section and keyed in the time when someone had thrown Captain Pipe overboard.

She waited as the minutes ticked by, and then the ship manager's cabin door finally opened, and he stepped out.

Ruth's brow furrowed. "No one came to warn him." Well, not unless they'd called. However, he wasn't holding a mobile phone or a radio. "Maybe it's in his pocket," she mused.

Her frown deepened as the ship manager wheeled a suitcase behind him. He looked anything but agitated or in a panic.

He put his suitcase in another room with a yellow door, and then knocked on the other doors in turn, unlocked them with his card, and peered inside. After a few moments, the crew members stepped out with their own bags and suitcases. They too loaded them into the room. Not a single one of them appeared perturbed or frightened in any way. In fact, several chatted and had smiles on their faces.

Once they were finished stowing their belongings, the crew left in a calm and orderly manner, with the ship manager closing the hallway door behind them.

Ruth blinked at the screen. "What the—?" She played the video again to make sure her eyes weren't deceiving her, while also recording the screen with her phone.

In a daze, Ruth left the storeroom and opened the yellow door opposite. Sure enough, the crew had stacked their suitcases inside.

She stepped back, shaking her head as she tried to piece together the events, and then spun on her heel and hurried from the hallway.

Ruth made her way back up through the ship, found the casino, and marched into the VIP section.

Sure enough, the creepy mannequins were still there.

Ruth opened the handkerchiefs and placed the sets of Scrabble tiles on the poker table. She was about to try and make sense of them when three things caught her eye: one was the appearance of her pink scarf, now neatly folded in front of Logan's mannequin, another murder weapon; two was the fact his tile rack now lay empty; and three, on the board, intersecting the *D* in *CHOKED* was a new word, *STRANGLED*.

Ruth stared at her scarf, and then the image of Logan's body popped into her head. More specifically, the red mark peeking above his polo-neck sweater and the pink fibres.

She swallowed. "Someone is trying to set me up." Ruth's gaze moved over the other mannequins, the murder weapons, the Scrabble board, and finally the tiles she'd recovered from the bodies.

First up were Gabriella's; it took only a moment to spell out the word *SNOB*. Ruth set the tiles in front of the mannequin representing Gabriella.

She then turned her attention to the tiles she'd gathered from Laura's body: *C, T, B, H, I*.

"Okay. So, we've got *B, I, T* . . . Oh." It didn't take a rocket scientist to figure out that word either. "Charming." Ruth placed them in front of Laura's mannequin.

Last, she examined Logan's tiles. She laid out the seven she'd recovered from his pocket, and they read *R, I, T, A, T, R, O*.

Ruth rearranged the tiles into *RAT, RATIO*, and *TAROT*. She inclined her head. "Use all the letters," she said, and then it hit her: "Traitor." She shuffled the letters around and placed them in front of Logan's mannequin.

"Wow." Ruth shook her head. The tiles in front of the bodies represented motives, along with the murder weapons, followed by method of death spelled out on the Scrabble board.

Someone had a macabre, twisted personality. A theatrical type. Grandiose. Narcissistic, perhaps. They could have not bothered with any of this nonsense. *So why are they taking the risk?* "What are they trying to say?" Their DNA must have been all over these items—no matter how careful they'd been, there would be a print or a hair fibre.

Ruth's gaze moved to Colonel Tom's mannequin in his military uniform, and then to Jeremy, and then back to the tiles in front of each.

Hers comprised *B, B, S, T, E,* D, followed by Colonel Tom, who only had three letters in his rack, *T, O, H,* and then Jeremy's, *A, C, N, I, E, R, T.*

If this were a real game of Scrabble—despite the eight players instead of four—given that the health and safety guy was seated first, Captain Pipe second, and then round the table to Gabriella and Laura, followed by Logan. That would make Jeremy next in line, then Colonel Tom, and finally Ruth.

She slid Jeremy's tile rack over and set to work, mumbling under her breath as she rearranged the letters. "Trance, erm. Hmm. Nectar? Hmm. How about recant?" Ruth frowned. "Recant for what?" She carried on. "Retain, retina, enact, cater. No, wait." She glanced at the board. "Will use all the letters." Ruth groaned. And that also meant using one of the letters on the board, so the words intersected. So, she had to hunt for an eight-letter word. She huffed out a breath. "Eight letters." Her gaze moved to the various words. There were limited places to set down all the tiles. Easiest of which fit across the top and intersected with the word *SMOTHERED*.

"*S, M, O, T* . . ." Ruth glanced between the letters and the board, and then her eyes widened. "Hold on . . . *O*? Reaction?" Her face fell. "Oh no." Ruth straightened, and looked at her watch: 7:15 a.m.

She ran full pelt from the VIP room and across the casino hall. Ruth pressed the gold card to the lock, but the red light remained solid. Her brow furrowed. She examined the card and tried again. The door still wouldn't unlock. She eyed a laundry cart set to one side of the door. "Was that here earlier?" Ruth swore and turned around. "Back way out." There had to be one. She rushed across the casino hall and into a corridor with a door at the far end. This also had an electronic lock.

Ruth held her breath and pressed the security card to it. *Nothing.*

Shocked, she staggered back as panic washed through her insides. "You have to be kidding me." Ruth spun back. "I'm trapped? No." She shook her head. "I've got to get out."

Ruth raced back into the casino hall and hunted for air vents. She found only one at ground level, partly obscured by a dormant slot machine. She frowned at it.

Has someone deliberately tried to block an alternative escape route?

It certainly looked that way considering the slot machine sat out of place compared to the others in the row: a bigger gap between it and its neighbour, along with the fact it sat proud by an inch or so.

Or perhaps she was being paranoid.

Either way, Ruth shoved on the side of the machine, putting her shoulder to it and pressing the ground with her feet, finally moving it enough to get at the air vent grille.

She dropped to her knees, popped the grille from its mount, and set it to one side.

Then, with a heavy sigh, she crawled in.

Once she reached a T-junction, Ruth tried to get her bearings and prohibit her cleithrophobia from taking hold. She looked left and right, picturing the ship's layout, and decided on left.

Sure enough, twenty feet of crawling later, she reached another grille, shoved it open and slid out.

Panting from the exertion, Ruth clambered to her feet and glanced about. She stood a little way down from the main parade of shops, around the corner from the casino.

Wasting no more time, she jogged down the hallway, shoved a door open, and raced into the stairwell.

Ruth had three floors to climb, divided into six flights, and she'd made it up the first and turned to the second when the lights snapped off, plunging her into darkness.

With blood pounding in her ears, Ruth stood in the blackness. Now she knew someone was trying to stop her. She gritted her teeth. "It'll take a lot more than that to stop me." She reached out for the handrail, grabbed hold, and edged forward until she found the second flight of stairs with her toes.

Careful to keep a tight grip on the railing, Ruth headed on up, crossed the landing to the third flight, same again with the fourth, and up the fifth set of stairs.

It was only when she reached the sixth and final flight of stairs that she realised something.

Feeling stupid, she pulled her phone from her pocket, activated the torch function, and hurried up to the next floor.

Ruth burst into the hallway and raced back to the door at the end of the suites. Predictably, the lock remained red, despite using her now-not-so-magical card, and Ruth swore at it. "Stupid thing." She raised her clenched fist to bang on the door but thought better of it. *What if the killer is in one of the suites?* She hurried to the air vent.

Ruth pulled away the grille and crawled inside. A few minutes later, she emerged in her bathroom, raced into the bedroom, and threw open the door to her sitting room.

Both Colonel Tom and Jeremy sat at the bar, breakfast packets open.

"There you are," Colonel Tom said. "When we knocked just now and you didn't answer, we assumed you were in the bath or—"

Ruth sprinted across the sitting room and knocked the fork from Jeremy's hand. She looked into the container. "How much have you eaten?"

He stood. "What?"

"How much?" Ruth shouted.

Jeremy frowned at her. "A couple of bites."

"Do you have epinephrine?"

His eyes went wide, and he looked down at his breakfast.

Ruth grabbed Jeremy's arms. "Where is it?"

"I-In my suite." Jeremy stepped back a few paces, his face drained of colour.

Ruth thrust a finger at the door. "Go. Now. Hurry."

Jeremy clutched at his throat and hurried from the suite.

Ruth leaned down to the bar and sniffed the tomato. She then picked up the fork, split it open, and pushed around its contents before moving on to the other items.

Colonel Tom stood. "What is going on, madam?"

"Reaction," Ruth said. "Allergic reaction."

"Someone put nuts in his breakfast?"

"Excuse me for a minute." Ruth entered her bedroom. Merlin let out a raspy meow. She scooped him up, opened the French doors, and stepped onto the balcony. Ruth then held Merlin in her arms, closed her eyes, and pulled in big lungfuls of sea air.

After a few minutes, she composed herself and returned to the bedroom. She lowered Merlin to the floor, and after a drink, he slinked off to his box.

"Are you going to explain what's going on?" Colonel Tom asked from the doorway.

Jeremy stepped beside him, his skin pale, and glistening sweat sticking hair to his forehead.

"Are you okay?" Ruth asked.

He nodded.

"No trouble breathing?"

He leaned against the doorframe and shook his head. "I got to the pen in time."

Ruth sighed and dropped into a chair.

"Well?" Colonel Tom asked. "What's going on?"

Ruth massaged her temples. "Someone tried to kill him."

"Yes," Colonel Tom said. "I figured as much, but how did you know?"

Ruth sat forward, trying to gather her wits and clear her head. "We have to turn the tables."

Colonel Tom stared at her. "And do what?"

Ruth looked at Jeremy. "Pretend he died."

19

Colonel Tom and Jeremy stared at Ruth as though she were mad. True, sometimes she appeared that way with her randomness and general haphazard behaviour, but she wasn't all crazy. Well, mostly not. Okay, maybe a little, but as far as she was concerned, that added extra spice to an already hot dish.

Ruth grinned.

Colonel Tom and Jeremy frowned back at her.

"Okay, fine," she said. "I'll explain. Do you know what has been bothering me?"

They both shrugged.

"How do you get twenty crew members to abandon a ship?"

Colonel Tom leaned against the bedroom doorframe. "The killer—"

Ruth held up a hand. "No." Then she stood, fists balled.

"Then how?" Colonel Tom asked. "Some kind of emergency?"

"If there had been a real emergency, they would have called for help," Ruth said. "The crew abandoned ship in an orderly manner, in the middle of the night. As far as we can safely gather, they reached land. Or at least we hope they did." She held up a finger. "And yet not a single one of them called the police or told anyone else what had happened."

"Maybe they drowned," Colonel Tom said.

Ruth shook her head. "Those modern lifeboats can withstand anything but a hurricane. As far as I know, there haven't been any hurricanes in the last few days."

"Are you suggesting they're all in on it?" Colonel Tom folded his arms. "The entire crew? The idea is preposterous."

"I agree," Ruth said. "That many people trying to keep a secret? One of them would slip up."

"Well, damn it all, madam," Colonel Tom said with a look of exasperation. "What's the answer?"

Ruth took a breath and stared out the French doors to the horizon. "When we first got on board, the ship manager said they were only the short-term crew, that another team would be along to relieve them." She looked back at the men and raised her eyebrows. "So, what if it was an exercise?"

"Exercise?" Jeremy swept strands of long hair from his face. "What do you mean?"

"What if the crew were informed there would be a fire drill? They were instructed to abandon ship and make it ashore to test the lifeboat system." Ruth turned back. "They thought they would be relieved of duty. They knew their time on the cruise ship would come to an end with a drill. It had been prearranged, which explains why they didn't call for help, why they left in such a calm, organised manner, and why they didn't come to help us. No crew would abandon their passengers in a time of crisis. That's because there was no crisis at all."

And it also explains why there were no signs of panic on the crew quarters' security video, Ruth thought. And why they'd stowed their luggage in that storeroom: because they followed prearranged instructions. They knew they couldn't take luggage on board the lifeboat, as in a real emergency. The crew must have been assured the luggage would be collected and returned to them later.

"Wait a moment." Colonel Tom's eyes narrowed to slits. "Wouldn't your grandson have seen all the commotion back in Bonmouth?"

Ruth frowned. "That's true." Then she groaned. "The deckhand, Steven was his name?" She shook her head, and her shoulders slumped. "He took Greg clubbing."

"What about earlier?" Colonel Tom gestured over his shoulder. "How did you know about the nuts in Jeremy's breakfast?"

Ruth yawned. "I figured out the killer's been using the air vents to get about this ship. I tried it for myself." She shuddered at the memory of the confined space, and the three of them stood in sober silence for a minute.

Finally, Jeremy said in a small voice, "You want to set a trap, don't you?"

"For whom?" Colonel Tom asked. Then his eyes widened. "The killer?"

"As I said, by pretending he's dead." Ruth lifted her chin. "We lure the killer back here, where we can corner him."

"Why would he come back here?" Colonel Tom asked with a furrowed brow.

"Scrabble tiles," Ruth said. "The first time I examined Gabriella's body, I'm sure there were no Scrabble tiles in her hand. This time, there were."

Colonel Tom stiffened. "You checked again? When you

crawled about the air vents? Why not let us in on what you were doing?"

"I didn't want to wake you," Ruth lied.

"I say." Colonel Tom waved a finger at her. "That's not on. We're supposed to stick together."

With exhaustion now catching up with her, Ruth squeezed past Colonel Tom and Jeremy. She headed to the bar, and they followed.

"And what about that?" Colonel Tom persisted. "How did you know the killer's next target would be our friend here?" He thrust a thumb over his shoulder at Jeremy. "How did you also know the killer had tampered with his breakfast?"

Ruth let out a long breath as she poured three glasses of water. "I went back to the VIP room. There were more clues." Ruth looked at Jeremy. "The letters spelled *REAC-TION*, and I figured out you were next."

Jeremy nodded. "Thank you. I'd be dead if you hadn't."

"So, let me get this straight," Colonel Tom scratched his chin. "The killer knew his dietary requirements and that he'd have one of those breakfast packs?" he said in an indignant tone. "That he would have a reaction to it? Well, I find that a little hard to believe."

Ruth didn't have an immediate answer to that. She thought back. "The killer returned to Gabriella's body to plant those letter tiles. I know that now." She looked between them and slid a glass to each. "With the others, I thought maybe I could have missed the tiles the first time around, and now I think that's exactly what happened." She leaned against the bar. "The killer couldn't plant Scrabble tiles on Gabriella at the time, like the others, because he didn't kill her with his bare hands. He used poison."

"Like with me," Jeremy murmured.

"Exactly. He's been using the air vents all this time," Ruth said. "Whoever is doing this snuck past us and avoided doors. The only times the killer has used a key card is to lead us to the casino and the VIP room."

"Must have used it on that storage cage too." Colonel Tom balled his fists.

"How are we going to catch him?"

Ruth sipped her water and eyed Jeremy. "As I said: you'll make-believe you're dead."

He shuffled from foot to foot.

Ruth pointed to the floor. "Lie down there." She pointed to her bedroom—"I'll wait in there"—and tried not to picture her bed calling to her.

"And me?" Colonel Tom asked.

"You'll need to use this card." She set it on the bar in front of him. "Open doors and be somewhere else. Far away from here. The killer has clearly been following us using the security system. He thinks we'll stick together from now on."

Colonel Tom's eyebrows shot up. "You expect me to leave you both here alone?"

"Be ready on the promenade deck below." Ruth stepped to the French doors. "Once I hear the killer, I'll sneak out of my bedroom, onto the balcony, and put a towel over the railing. This will be a sign. You'll rush back here, and we'll corner the killer between us."

Colonel Tom looked away and murmured, "I wish I had my gun."

Jeremy scratched his beard. "The killer has it."

Colonel Tom threw his hands up. "Then how can we hope to capture him?"

Ruth took another sip, set her glass down, and steeled herself. "I don't think he'll use it." *Evidenced by the creepy mannequins in the VIP room.* "He has a plan he's following."

"Or her," Jeremy said.

Ruth blinked at him and wondered if he knew something she didn't. Either way, male or female, the killer's murder streak stopped here. She pointed at the floor. "Lie down. We've wasted enough time."

Jeremy hesitated, and then did as he was told.

"Can we go through the plan one more time?" Colonel Tom asked as she escorted him to the door. "I want to make sure I understand."

She forced a half-hearted smile. "You'll be fine."

"I'll go to the bow of the ship," Colonel Tom said, "opening as many doors as I can, and then circle back via the promenade. I'll watch for your signal." He then leaned in and whispered, "Please be careful, madam," and pecked her on the cheek.

Ruth blushed as he left, and then got a grip of herself, checked Jeremy was still in position, and stepped into her bedroom and closed the door.

She leaned against it, closed her eyes, and took a few deep breaths. "We've got this." Steeling herself, she opened the French doors fully and hurried into the bathroom.

An hour later, Ruth sat on the floor by the air vent in her suite's bathroom, back pressed against the tiled wall, fighting off exhaustion.

The sitting room vent was further down the air duct, with the bathroom's one at the end, so the killer wouldn't need to pass by. Even so, Ruth made sure to stay out of sight.

Her chest rose and fell in slow rhythm as she waited, listening for movement, and her eyes drifted closed. An image of her late husband swam into view, only to be replaced by Ruth's police chief during her time on the force.

Ruth screwed up her face as she recalled that moment standing in his office, the two of them shouting at each other, Ruth demanding to know every detail about John's murder, and the chief saying he had no choice but to let her go.

But she'd never understood that choice. He could have kept her unofficially off the case while she still worked behind the scenes. She would have been useful. Ruth knew everything about John, his history, his life. She was the perfect person to liaise with during the investigation.

Conflict of interest?

What a load of tosh.

If he'd so desired, the chief could have bent the rules for one of his hardest-working officers, the same person he'd only commended a few months prior for her diligence.

"You had a choice," she mumbled.

A scraping made Ruth's eyes snap open, and she looked over at the air vent grille.

Another scraping, followed by a metallic clink.

Ruth got to her feet and backed to the bathroom door. The killer would be slipping into the sitting room at any moment.

With her heart in her mouth, Ruth lifted a towel from the rack, slipped out of the bathroom, and hurried across the bedroom. Once on the balcony, she placed the towel over the railing and glanced down at the promenade below but couldn't make out Colonel Tom anywhere nearby.

Praying he'd spotted the signal and would come running, Ruth tiptoed to her bedroom door, opened it a crack, and peered into the sitting room.

From her vantage point, she didn't have a direct line of

sight to Jeremy, but the killer would have to cross the room directly in front of her to reach him.

Ruth's pulse pounded in her ears as she waited, but as the minutes ticked by, her anxiety grew. She opened the door by a few more millimetres and looked to her left. She couldn't tell if the killer was there or not. *What is he waiting for?*

The door to the suite burst open, and Colonel Tom rushed into the room.

Ruth stepped out of the bedroom.

Colonel Tom looked about. "Where is he?" His gaze moved to the closed air vent.

Ruth edged her way over to Jeremy and peered down at him.

He wasn't moving, and she could detect no signs he was breathing.

Ruth dropped to his side and gripped his shoulder.

Jeremy opened his eyes and looked up at her. "What happened? I fell asleep." He yawned. "Sorry. Must have been the epinephrine. Makes me drowsy." He screwed up his face. "And queasy."

Ruth sighed and slumped back on the floor, shaking her head. "It didn't work." She pinched the bridge of her nose.

"But you heard him?" Colonel Tom asked. "You gave the signal. Was he in the air duct?" He glanced back.

"I think so," Ruth murmured. "Something must have spooked him."

Colonel Tom's eyes narrowed. "How do you know it was the killer?"

With effort, Ruth got to her feet. "It would have been a big rat otherwise." She groaned inwardly. They'd failed. *She'd* failed. Her plan had been a stupid one. Clearly, the killer had seen through it. *So now what?* She checked the time on her phone. It was almost midday. All she wanted to do was go to bed and sleep for a week.

Jeremy stood too and faced Colonel Tom. "Is it worth breaking open that filing cabinet in the ship manager's office? The one you mentioned earlier. You really think there could be a radio inside?"

"I don't know," Colonel Tom said. "I'll go down to the office and see if I can open it."

"We shouldn't split up," Ruth said. "It's too dangerous. I'll come with you."

"I'll be fine. The killer will back off now he knows we're onto his tricks." Colonel Tom gave her a hard look and stormed from the suite.

Ruth couldn't blame him for being angry.

"I need a shower." Jeremy scratched his beard. "Meet you back here in thirty minutes?"

"Sure," Ruth murmured. "You're welcome to use my shower if you want to stay close."

"It's okay," Jeremy said as he swept hair from his face and traipsed into the hallway. "I'll leave my door open."

"When you're both done, we'll go to the kitchen together," Ruth called after him. "I'll make us dinner. Fresh," she added. "No prepacked meals. No nuts." Ruth yawned and shuffled into her bedroom, dejected.

Merlin let out a low, raspy meow.

Ruth found him in the bathroom. "What's the matter with—" She froze.

Merlin sniffed around the air vent, and Ruth pictured the killer in there, staring back at her right at that very moment.

Time came to a screeching halt as she remained rooted to the spot, eyes wide, heart hammering in her chest.

Finally, Ruth got a grip of herself and knelt next to

Merlin. She activated the torch on her phone and shone it through the grille. The air duct was empty.

Ruth let out a slow breath. "Come on." She stroked Merlin and stood, but he didn't follow. Merlin kept sniffing around the grille. Ruth hesitated for a few seconds more, scooped Merlin up, and set him on the chair in the bedroom. She returned to the bathroom and closed the door behind her.

Ruth removed the grille, held her breath, and peered into the vent.

Something lay a few feet inside.

She slipped her phone back from her pocket and shone the torch at a leather pouch with a strap, a black union jack sewn on the side, recognising it from Colonel Tom's suite.

Ruth considered leaving it exactly where it was, but curiosity got the better of her. She removed a hand towel from the rack and used it to retrieve the bag. Ruth set it on the side by the sink, and with trembling hands, unzipped it and peered inside.

Between thumb and forefinger, Ruth slid out a photograph by its corner and gasped. It was a printed image of her late husband in the back garden of the same house where someone had murdered him, along with a clear view of his killer.

Ruth clapped a hand over her mouth.

Colonel Tom, decades younger but clearly the same man, stood behind John, large kitchen knife held high.

20

R uth stared at the photograph of her late husband, and a tear rolled down her cheek. "Oh, John."

She'd not seen this image before. It showed an angle as if taken from a neighbour's house, aimed over the fence at the garden in East London. No one had figured out what John had been doing there. The building, abandoned several years prior, stood empty and derelict.

After an anonymous call, the police had discovered John's body in the kitchen, and those crime scene images would be forever burned into Ruth's memory. And now here was another one, even more horrifying.

Her emotions overrun with sadness and guilt, Ruth struggled to maintain a grip on reality, and her attention moved back to the part of the photograph with Colonel Tom and the raised kitchen knife.

Anger pushed aside the hurt.

Ruth paced the bathroom, fists balled, teeth clenched, trying to focus but losing miserably. She wanted to kick and scream, wanted him to pay for what he'd done.

Why did he bring this photo? Ruth stopped pacing and

stared into space. *To taunt me? Has it been Colonel Tom this whole time? He set all this up?*

Her gaze drifted back to the open vent and the leather bag. So, the colonel had climbed through the duct and dropped it. *When? Was he watching me at some point? Had the colonel planned something else but then changed his mind? If Jeremy had been his next intended victim, the colonel was in the room with him, so it couldn't be that.*

However, there was another item inside the bag: Colonel Tom's pistol. *Was the gun a backup plan in case Jeremy survived? Or was I the next intended victim? A bullet with my name on it? The final victim?*

The gun's presence meant the colonel had been the one to retrieve it after all. He'd appeared to throw the key into the ocean, but Colonel Tom was no stranger to sleight of hand. He could have easily palmed it, and Ruth cursed herself for being so trusting.

Anger threatened to boil over into rage as she stuffed the photograph into her back pocket. Her vision tunnelled as Ruth lifted the pistol from the bag, checked it was loaded, and slipped it into her belt.

She then stormed from the bathroom, and her face dropped. "Merlin?" Ruth looked about.

He was no longer on the chair where she'd left him.

"Merlin, I don't have time for this." Ruth hurried to his box, peered inside, and let out a slow breath. The silly cat had curled up on his cushion. "There you are."

Merlin opened an eye and let out one of his customary raspy meows before going back to sleep.

"I need you to stay put." Ruth grabbed his water bowl and set it inside the box. "Won't be for long," she muttered. "When I come back, I'll give you breakfast." She closed the front of the box.

Ruth straightened and stormed into the hallway, closed her suite door, and marched over to Jeremy's room. His door stood open, and the patter of a shower running came from inside.

She hesitated for a moment, wanting to tell him, wanting to explain, but at the same time Ruth did not want anyone else involved. This was her problem to deal with, and it had been a long time coming.

Ruth marched to the atrium and down the stairs.

On the deck below, with Colonel Tom's pistol now in hand, she jogged along the upper atrium balcony, down a short corridor, and into the ship manager's office.

Colonel Tom, kneeling in front of the filing cabinet, worked the lock with a screwdriver. He looked up at her. "Ah, madam, I'm glad you're here. Would you mind helping me with—" His eyes went as wide as dinner plates when he spotted the gun. "Where on earth did you find that?"

Ruth's hand shook as she aimed it at his chest; she cupped her other hand around the first, attempting to steady her aim.

Colonel Tom's face drained of colour, and he raised his hands.

He had to pay for what he'd done. The decades of hurt, the unbearable grief, the career taken from her . . . not to mention he'd lied to Ruth this whole time.

"W-What are you doing?" Colonel Tom asked. "Whatever it is you think I've done—"

"Get on the floor." Ruth's voice sounded detached and cold, yet strangely calm given the fact her thoughts raged. "And not another word." She nodded at the ground. "Do it."

Colonel Tom hesitated but obliged.

"All the way," Ruth said.

He lay flat on the floor, put his hands over his head, and interlaced his fingers.

As she stared at his back, Ruth's breath caught in her throat, and the fog of rage lifted in an instant, as though she'd woken from a nightmare; clarity returned. With the gun still aimed at the colonel, she pulled the photograph from her back pocket and studied it.

Colonel Tom turned his head to one side in an attempt to look up at her. "Madam?"

Tears streamed down her face. "Of course. I've been so stupid." She took a breath and refocussed on the colonel. "I'm sorry. Now hold still. Don't move."

"Please. I—"

Ruth screamed, pulled the trigger, and the gun went off: a deafening explosion sending a bolt of pain through her eardrums. She winced and dropped the pistol, and then spun on her heel and raced from the office.

With her heart hammering in her chest, Ruth threw open a random door in the hallway and entered another office. This one smaller, with two desks crammed between its walls.

Ruth pushed the door closed, bent double, put her hands on her knees, and fought the urge to throw up. She took in deep breaths, trying to calm herself, to avoid hyperventilating, but her whole body shook.

She only hoped she'd done the right thing.

Footfalls thudded from the other end of the hallway, and she straightened. Ruth opened the door of the cramped office by a few millimetres, held her breath, and pressed her eye to the crack.

A moment later, a figure in a parka, hood up, stepped past her door and approached the ship manager's office.

Ruth couldn't tell if they were a man or a woman, but given her newfound lucidity, she had a pretty good idea.

As the person drew near the office, Ruth slipped into the hallway and tiptoed after them. The hooded figure reached the doorway, stepped through, and then threw their hands up.

Ruth raced down the hallway and stopped outside, panting, heart thumping.

Her improvised plan had worked. *Thank goodness.* She shuddered at the thought of how close she'd come to making a life-changing mistake in a moment of blind anger. But she guessed that had been the whole point.

Colonel Tom aimed his pistol at the hooded figure. "I suggest you make no sudden moves." He looked over their shoulder at Ruth. "That was an interesting turn of events."

She cringed. "I'm so, so sorry." Ruth was glad he was uninjured. "I had to pretend I'd killed you."

Colonel Tom snarled and gestured to the hooded figure. "Out."

They stepped into the hallway, and Ruth yanked their hood down to reveal Captain Pipe.

She let out a slow breath. Ten minutes ago, Ruth would've felt surprised at seeing him still alive, but things clicked into place. Of course there had been someone crawling about the ship and killing people, and of course the captain had faked his own death. Seeing him here, some of what had happened over the past few days now made sense.

Ruth balled her fists, fighting back anger.

Captain Pipe had played them all from the start. The only thing that remained was for her to find out why, and more selfishly, *why me? What have I done?* Ruth couldn't yet understand his motives. *Why has he murdered people, and why did he try and have me kill the colonel?*

She shuddered at the idea she'd let her rage almost force her to make the biggest mistake of her life, and she vowed to never make the same error of judgement again.

The captain's face looked a lot paler than the last time she'd seen him, with dark bags under each eye, as though he hadn't slept in days. He'd torn his jeans and bloodied his knees—no doubt from all the crawling about the ship—and he stared at them both with the deepest look of contempt.

"Atrium." Colonel Tom waved the gun. "Move."

With his hands still raised, Captain Pipe led the way along the corridor.

Ruth got a grip of herself and held up the photograph to Colonel Tom. "I thought this was real. It almost had me."

The colonel's eyes widened. "Your husband?"

"A doctored photograph." Ruth gnashed her teeth as frustration at almost falling for the trick washed through her. *How can I have been so stupid?*

In fact, even exhausted and with her emotions running high, if Ruth had taken a moment to calm down, she would have realised much sooner.

"I'm glad you figured it out," Colonel Tom said as they stepped onto the balcony and circled the atrium. "You could have explained your idea, though, madam. Damn near gave me a heart attack." He winced. "Not to mention burst eardrums. Going to have this damn ringing for weeks."

"Couldn't risk it," Ruth said. "Once I realised, I knew I had to act fast, and assumed we were being watched."

They headed down a flight of stairs to the main atrium.

Colonel Tom motioned to a chair. "Sit."

Captain Pipe did as ordered, his expression still cold, showing nothing but loathing for the pair of them.

Ruth and Colonel Tom sat opposite.

Colonel Tom let out a long breath and looked at her. "Care to explain this, madam? Let's start with that photograph. How did you figure out it was a fake?"

In her anger and hurt, Ruth had not asked herself a basic question: Who'd taken the picture of John and Colonel Tom? The neighbours at the time didn't have CCTV, and if someone else had snapped the photograph, Ruth had wondered why they hadn't handed it in to the police, and why Colonel Tom now had it in his possession.

Ruth studied the photograph. "First of all, John was stabbed in the chest, not the back. This is staged. A composite of several images." She glanced at Captain Pipe. "Although it's the same back garden from the scene of the crime, the poor quality suggests the image was a photograph released to the public, during the investigation." She shook her head. "And now I'm looking closely at it, I can spot more problems." Ruth held it up so the colonel could see too. "The figure used here, the one with the knife, he's not as tall as you. Someone has pasted an image of your face onto their body. No doubt took a portrait from your website."

Colonel Tom nodded. "Indeed."

"As for John," Ruth said, "I can't be sure without checking, but they've taken an image of him from my daughter's social media and pasted that too." Her gaze moved to Captain Pipe. "You hoped I'd not look close enough. You'd bet on the fact I'd be tired and not thinking clearly." Now they'd caught up with the killer, she felt both relief and guilt for not figuring it out sooner.

"Why did you do it?" Colonel Tom asked.

Captain Pipe remained tight-lipped.

The colonel snarled, leaned forward, and aimed the gun

at the captain's forehead. "Don't think for a second I won't do it."

Ruth motioned for Colonel Tom to stand down. "Please, don't do anything rash."

Colonel Tom let out a mock laugh. "This monster murdered four people. The fact he's still breathing grates on my sensibilities." However, he lowered the gun and sat back.

"Tell us what this has all been about," Ruth said to the captain. "What could these sweet people possibly have done to you?"

"Sweet?" Captain Pipe snarled. "They're scum." He shuffled in the chair. "My family 'ave been part of Bonmouth fer over a 'undred years." His mouth twisted with anger. "And in my lifetime, I watched it be destroyed by the likes of yer type."

Colonel Tom screwed up his face. "I visited Bonmouth a few years ago. Run-down hole of a place."

Captain Pipe looked like he wanted to leap at the colonel and strangle him. "I invested all our family's money into opening a new 'otel. Everything I 'ad, both personally and financially, went into that place. Gave it my all." He waved a fist at the colonel. "These scumbags ruined everything."

"What did they do that was so bad?" Ruth asked before the colonel could respond.

Captain Pipe's eyes narrowed. "During the 'otel's renovation, we aimed to secure more financing fer the rest, but then the investment manager visited, took one look around, and 'alted the deal."

"Let me guess," Ruth said. "Logan was the investment manager?"

"My son persuaded 'im to come back in a couple of months and reconsider." Captain Pipe shook his head.

"Logan wanted to see more improvement with the 'otel, along with some positive, third-party reviews about what was to come. So we started by hiring an interior designer."

Ruth remained calm. "Let me guess, Gabriella?"

Captain Pipe spoke through a clenched jaw. "She stayed at the 'otel and loathed every minute of it. Kept bangin' on about 'ow it would take a miracle to save it, and how it would damage her reputation. She made all these outrageous demands that would have cost us tens of thousands. She wouldn't see sense, or meet us halfway, and wanted to walk out on our deal. We begged her to stay and help us, but Gabriella refused. Then when we didn't pay, she sued."

Ruth let out a slow breath. "Laura?"

Captain Pipe's eyes darkened. "She was a parasite. We covered everything—travel, accommodation, all 'er meals, and even a bar bill for 'er and three friends. What did she do then?" Captain Pipe spat. "Despite us repeatedly telling 'er the hotel was far from finished, and even though we showed that girl drawings of our vision, she slated the 'otel on social media. No more advanced bookings after that. Again, my son pleaded with her to reconsider, but she refused, despite everything we'd done for 'er."

Ruth's heart sank. "And what about him?" She pointed to the colonel.

"I think I can answer that question, madam," Colonel Tom said in a low voice. "I must confess my review was no less complimentary."

Captain Pipe glared at him. "Yer moaned that the only entertainment we 'ad was a battered game of Scrabble, and even that 'ad missing letters."

"And you tried to have me kill him for that?" Ruth asked, incredulous.

"That's not all he did." Captain Pipe leaned forward and snarled. "We lied for you."

"Lied about what?" Colonel Tom asked. "That's utter rubbish." Then his face fell. "Wait. Do you mean—" He put his head in his hand.

"What happened?" An image of the Scrabble board and tiles popped into Ruth's thoughts. Colonel Tom's tiles consisted of three letters: *T, O, H*. She pondered this for a moment. The obvious word made out of those would be *HOT*, but the word needed to use another letter off the board. It only took a second to piece it together. "Shot," she breathed. "Was it something to do with the gun?"

Colonel Tom took a few deep breaths and looked up again.

Captain Pipe glared at him. "He had the nerve to bring it to the 'otel with 'im. Can yer imagine? Maid found it. Shock nearly killed 'er." His lip curled. "We covered for yer though, didn't we? When the police came, we lied. We stopped yer from going to prison. And, despite all we did, yer still left that nasty review. Everyone saw it." Captain Pipe balled his fists. "That was the final straw as far as Logan was concerned. Told his bosses and it was deal off. Hundreds of thousands lost. Lives ended."

"What lives ended?" Ruth asked. "Apart from the ones *you* took."

Rage filled Captain Pipes eyes. "My son's."

Colonel Tom looked flabbergasted. "How? What on earth happened?"

Ruth recalled the bearded guy in the painting, and now assumed that's who it represented.

"My son tried to put it right," Captain Pipe said. "He visited Logan and begged 'im to change 'is mind about financing. Logan promised 'e would give us one more "chance, if we showed enough improvements within a month." Captain Pipe sat back. "My son spent weeks, working on his own, day and night, to the point of exhaustion, doin' everything 'e could to save us."

Ruth's stomach tensed. "What went wrong?"

"He—" Captain Pipe swallowed. "He slipped off a ladder and fell twenty feet to concrete steps. Broke his back. Fractured skull."

Colonel Tom winced. "I'm so sorry."

"He didn't die right away," Captain pipe said in a low voice. "Took 'im another two weeks."

After a few moments of silence, Ruth said, "And you murdered David Franks, the health and safety guy, the day before because he threatened to ban guests from coming on board this ship? You'd lose your chance to get revenge."

"You son of a b—" Colonel Tom lifted the gun. "He didn't deserve to die for that."

"You might have gotten away with it," Ruth said in a calm voice, wanting to bring the temperature down a notch or two, "except you made a mistake targeting me."

Colonel Tom looked at her askance. "He targeted you? What do you mean?"

"The Scrabble tile clues. The elaborate setup. Not to mention the cat painting on the wall." Ruth kept her focus on Captain Pipe. "You knew about my past and wanted to make it a case I couldn't refuse investigating. You deliberately coaxed me." She looked at Colonel Tom. "I was supposed to kill you, and then no doubt I'd come to my own sticky end, or I'd be arrested for the murders."

Perhaps he intended on planting evidence at each crime scene. Then she remembered the pink fibres on Logan's neck and her scarf.

She studied the captain again and his anger-filled reaction. "You pushed it too far with the photograph. Picking my beloved John?" She lifted her chin. "I may not be tech savvy, but I'm not stupid either." She glanced at the photograph again and spotted yet another obvious error: John had been stabbed with a kitchen knife, but it wasn't a chef's knife, it was a utility knife. Similar shapes, but the latter was slimmer and smaller in size. She tossed the photograph onto a nearby table and leaned forward in her chair, locking eyes with the killer. "What have I done?" she asked with genuine bewilderment. Ruth had never visited Bonmouth before, let alone spoken ill of it.

The captain looked away.

"What about the health and safety guy?" Colonel Tom asked. "Did you really kill him because he stood in the way of your plan?"

"David Franks had the power to ban guests from the ship until the problems he'd pointed out were rectified," Ruth said when the captain didn't respond. One of the issues had been with the air vents: big enough for people to crawl through, and push-fit instead of bolts holding the grilles in place. "All this started for us when someone threw him overboard." Ruth pointed at the captain, and gasped. "Wait." Her heart sank. "Oh no. Someone threw him overboard." Ruth's sluggish brain worked to piece together the details. "We've been led the entire way. Every step engineered." Her eyes went wide. "Of course." She slapped her forehead.

Colonel Tom's face dropped. "Jeremy?"

Ruth stood. "He's either directly involved or helping him." *Whatever the case, they're working together.* She only wished she'd twigged it sooner.

"Let's pay our friend a visit." Colonel Tom got to his feet and motioned with the gun. "Get up."

As they followed Captain Pipe to the stairs, Ruth said, "You couldn't have done it without help. You wanted people in the right place at the right time, which is where Jeremy came in. He steered us like sheep. How did you communicate? Through the tablet?"

Captain Pipe remained stoic as they headed up the stairs.

"You poisoned bottles of lemonade," Ruth said. "And Jeremy saw to it that Laura got them, but what you didn't bank on was poor Gabriella winding up dead first. You had to act quickly and shift your plan."

Colonel Tom's eyes narrowed, and he snarled, "He wanted to kill Laura first?"

"I guess in the end it didn't matter to them," Ruth said as they reached the top of the stairs. "It was Jeremy's suggestion you search the theatre?"

Colonel Tom nodded and gestured along the landing.

"Jeremy must have pointed out the secure room to Laura when your back was turned," Ruth murmured to the colonel. "Perhaps he spotted you'd dropped the card and seized his opportunity."

"Or he picked it from my pocket."

They entered the hexagonal room.

Ruth shrugged. "Whatever the case, Laura wound up exactly where they wanted her." She cleared her throat and turned her attention to Captain Pipe. "You used the air ducts to get to her." Ruth pointed at his torn trousers and bloody knees. "Next up was Logan," Ruth continued, thinking it through. "Jeremy suggested we lock him in the cargo hold, and we did. Where you once again got to him." She nodded. "You took my scarf and used that to strangle him."

Colonel Tom opened the door and ushered the captain into the suites' hallway.

"Wait here," Ruth whispered. She hurried to Jeremy's suite before the colonel could protest. At the open door, she took a calming breath, determined to look casual. Ruth knocked. "Jeremy?" When no answer came, she stepped inside. The sitting room was identical to hers. The bedroom door stood open. "Jeremy?" Ruth called as she walked through the bedroom, finding it empty too, and then into the bathroom.

Jeremy wasn't there either.

Ruth hurried back out of the suite and faced Captain Pipe. "Where is he?"

The captain folded his arms. "How would I know?"

"We have to find him," Ruth said to the colonel.

"I know." Colonel Tom considered their captive for several seconds. "What are we going to do with you while we search for your partner in crime?" Then he smirked. "Actually, I have just the place."

21

"Yer can't do this," Captain Pipe said as he backed into the galley's walk-in freezer. "I'll die in 'ere."

"Not with that lovely warm coat you're wearing." Colonel Tom patted him down and removed a phone and key card from his pockets. "Besides, it's only for a few hours. As long as you keep your core body temperature up, you'll be fine. Jog on the spot. And while you do that, reflect on what you've done." He pointed to the body of David Franks, and then slammed the door and locked it. The colonel faced Ruth. "Right." He tossed the phone onto a nearby shelf. "Where do you think our snivelling friend Jeremy is hiding?"

"Not hiding." Ruth pursed her lips. "Their plan has failed, meaning he'll likely—"

"Try to escape."

"Exactly." Ruth picked up the health and safety report. "There's nothing on here about lifeboats. This was the day before. Meaning, someone likely sabotaged them once we were on board and after the crew abandoned ship."

"Another reason they deleted the security footage."

Colonel Tom tucked the gun into his belt. "They didn't want us to see them tampering with the lifeboat controls."

"And the captain lied to the crew that another team were on their way to replace them." Ruth set down the clipboard and composed herself. "I think there's a good chance we'll find Jeremy on the promenade deck." She went to leave and then stopped dead in her tracks.

"What's wrong?"

Ruth looked about. "David Franks's tool bag is missing. The yellow one."

"Then we have a good idea who has it." Colonel Tom waved to the door, and they strode through the dining hall. "If Jeremy pushed the captain overboard, how did he get back onto the ship? I saw no evidence of a rope ladder, and even if there was, that's a hell of a climb." As they headed up the steps, the colonel added, "And why did they want us to conceal our identities and private information from one another?"

"To keep us secretive," Ruth said. "Making sure we wouldn't find a common link between us and figure out what was happening." Although she still couldn't understand why they'd targeted her. She'd never left a hotel review in her life and wasn't about to start.

Colonel Tom glanced back. "And that?" He pointed at the cat painting.

"Arousing my curiosity," Ruth said. "Making sure I'd take it personally and investigate." Although she didn't enjoy making something about her, it seemed the logical explanation. The killers somehow knew about Ruth's police past. "Also, to create some suspicion in our group." Not to mention evidence left for the authorities, so they'd pin the murders on her.

They pushed through the doors and headed along the hallway.

And the same with the note on Laura's body. The one with the ship manager's room number. Another clue deliberately left for her to follow.

At the end of the corridor, they turned right.

"What about my gun?" Colonel Tom asked. "How did they get it? We locked the damn thing away."

"The captain must have had a spare key." Ruth stopped at the door that led to the promenade deck and lowered her voice. "If you remember, it was Jeremy's idea to stash it in the purser's office. Once we did, he relayed the information to the captain, who retrieved it."

Colonel Tom nudged open the door and peered out. "Clear."

They stepped onto the promenade deck. Ruth looked left and right. "We don't know what side of the ship he'll be on." She gestured toward the aft section of the boat.

As they hurried along the deck, Ruth cursed herself. She should have realised all this much sooner. "Do you know how hard it is to lift someone over a railing?"

Colonel Tom shrugged.

"Neither do I," Ruth said. "But what I do know is it would have taken someone with a lot of upper body strength."

"Jeremy," he said with a nod.

"That, and the fact the captain didn't put up a fight," Ruth said. "He didn't grab the rail as he went over. The captain let it happen. He expected it." She shook her head. "I should have noticed all of that."

On the aft deck of the *Ocean Odyssey*, Ruth stood on the port side, Colonel Tom starboard, giving them both a clear view of the full length of the ship.

Ten cold and breezy minutes later, at the point where Ruth considered running back to her suite and grabbing a coat, her breath caught as a door at midship opened.

Coincidentally, the very door she'd checked out a couple of nights ago.

Ruth beckoned Colonel Tom over. He joined her in time to see Jeremy step onto the promenade deck, a yellow tool bag in hand.

Colonel Tom went to rush forward, but Ruth stopped him. "Let me handle this." She still had plenty more questions she wanted answered. "Be cool." Ruth took a calming breath and sauntered along the promenade deck like she didn't have a care in the world.

When Jeremy spotted them approaching, he stiffened. "There you are. I-I've been searching everywhere for you." He looked between them. "W-What's going on?"

"You know very well what's going on," Colonel Tom snapped.

"Way to be cool," Ruth murmured. She nodded at the tool bag. "What are you up to, Jeremy?"

"Oh, I, err, I found some parts of the lifeboat controls." He opened the bag to show them. "Was going to see if I could get one working."

"Bet you were," Colonel Tom snarled.

Jeremy recoiled.

Ruth held up a hand. "We know what you've done. That you've been working with the captain. He's told us what happened."

Colonel Tom waved a fist at Jeremy. "You murdered them."

Jeremy glanced between Ruth and the colonel, dropped the tool bag, and straightened. His shoulders rolled back, chin lifted, stance transformed from meek to confident.

"Well, no, actually." His voice now sounded clear, well spoken, but with a strong hint of a London accent. "I haven't murdered anyone. The captain did all the dirty work. My hands are clean. I'm not a killer."

"You're still an accessory to murder," Ruth said, stunned by the transformation in his demeanour. It was like a completely different person now possessed Jeremy's body.

"Which makes you as bad in my book," Colonel Tom added.

"Then you don't understand the law," Jeremy said in a bored tone. His eyebrows lifted. "And where's the proof I had anything to do with it?"

"Locked up," Colonel Tom said. "When the police get hold of him, he'll spill the beans."

Jeremy cocked his head to one side. "I don't think he will. The captain is a raving lunatic."

"He works for you," Ruth said in a quiet voice. "You're the mastermind behind all this, aren't you?"

"I merely threw the dear captain a lifeline," Jeremy said. "He'd lost everything. I told him that it wasn't over, and I would help him to find investors. They would rejuvenate Bonmouth and open a new port for the *Ocean Odyssey*. That in turn would bring in a flood of tourists and staff. All the family money he'd lost would be repaid tenfold."

"Any of that true?" Colonel Tom asked.

Jeremy smirked and gestured around the ship. "Logan represented the investors. I merely played a small part in steering him and them toward an outcome that would be to the captain's advantage. They were free to pull the plug at any time."

Ruth's stomach twisted. "You manipulate people."

"I wouldn't say so." Jeremy shook his head. "No, not at all." He leaned against the railing with a smug expression. "I only suggested a way for the captain to have his revenge on the people who ruined him. Those very people who caused him to lose everything he and his family had worked for. That after those nasty individuals had gone, his path to a bright future would be secured. If he happened to get caught, then the captain had my word Bonmouth would flourish in his absence."

"You egged him on," Ruth said. "Goaded him. Made his issues seem a thousand times worse, and then offered solutions. All to twist the situation to your favour."

Jeremy gave a dismissive flick of his wrist. "I didn't force him to do anything. It was all his choice. He was upset and bitter from the start. I'm surprised he hadn't yet killed them all."

"No one tried to ruin him," Colonel Tom snapped. "He's crazy. Lost his mind."

Ruth stared at Jeremy. "Why me? What have I done to deserve this? Why did you try to set me up?"

"And now we come to the fun part." Jeremy pushed off the railing. "Don't you recognise an old friend?" He did a twirl. "I'll admit I will be glad for a shave and a haircut." Jeremy scratched his beard and winked at her. "I grew this especially for you, Ruth Morgan. Didn't want to give the game away, you understand?"

Is this more manipulation? Ruth thought.

She continued to stare at him but still couldn't identify the man.

Jeremy put his hands in his pockets and gazed at the horizon. "Over thirty years ago, when you were a police officer, you caught me in a pawnshop."

"Sabian?" Ruth's blood ran cold. "You're Marcus Sabian?" She couldn't believe it, after all these years . . .

He looked back at her, eyes now dark and cold. "You

recall how we were trapped in there? Together? How you panicked?" Sabian glared at her. "I helped you, Ruth Morgan. I calmed you down, looked after you, and how did you repay me?"

Ruth thought back to the teenage boy with the shaven head, and she now recognised his deep brown eyes. "We had to turn you in," she breathed as reality fell away.

"*We?*" Sabian shouted. "It was *you*." He stabbed a finger at her. "You're the one who saw to it that I was put in cuffs. *You* gave evidence at my hearing. *You* made sure I went to prison."

"And you broke the law." Ruth said. "You can't blame me for your actions. Besides, I put in a good word with—"

"You did nothing for me." Sabian's expression darkened further. "Your actions that day set off a series of events that changed the course of my life for the worse, along with others caught in my orbit. You have no idea the damage you caused." He ground his teeth. "If only you'd bothered to check up on me."

"I'm sorry for what happened to you," Ruth said. "I really am, but—"

Sabian shook his head. "You don't get off that easily. Do you know how long I've waited?"

"Why not kill her?" Colonel Tom asked. "Why play these elaborate games?"

"Not helping," Ruth murmured through the corner of her mouth.

Sabian's smirk returned. "I want Ruth Morgan to suffer. I want her to feel everything I did. Go through everything I endured. To know what it's like to be locked up for years. To have everything you cared about snatched from you."

"You had a long criminal record leading up to that day in the pawnshop." Ruth sighed. "You would've gotten caught eventually, and something else you did later would have instead been the last straw. Blaming me for the inevitable is unfair."

Sabian stepped toward her; face twisted.

Colonel Tom pulled the gun from his belt.

Sabian's lip curled.

Ruth took a deep breath and gathered her thoughts. "That's why you told the captain to move about the ship via the tunnels." She shuddered at the memory of the confined pawnshop and the darkness. "You thought that even if I figured it out, I wouldn't follow. How many other things over the last few days did you manipulate?" She thought back to all the times he'd suggested a course of action to people, and now understood that was part of his plan. He was controlling almost everything.

Ruth had met some obsessive people in her life and work, but this took it to a whole new level.

Sabian crossed his arms, his focus only on her. "When I saw you'd become a freelance food consultant, it was a sign. An opportunity to hire you and bring you close. I only needed to find a bitter and twisted old fool to make that happen. Someone willing to murder people for his own petty reasons, so you couldn't resist the urge to investigate, and stick your beak where it didn't belong."

"And then pin the murders on me." Ruth shook her head.

"Why did you try to fake your own death?" Colonel Tom asked with a look of puzzlement.

"Part of his plan," Ruth said. "It would leave him free to escape while I killed you. Then I'd be responsible for one murder, and likely framed for the others."

"You woke me up early for breakfast," Colonel Tom said to Sabian, his eyes wide. "Why? Because your scheme changed? Ridiculous. Anyway, how could you fake your own death? I know CPR."

Sabian gave him a dismissive wave. "I was to go to my bathroom and take a shower. Once there, I would pretend to choke, collapse, and block the glass door, preventing your ability to check for a pulse, and making it appear as though I'd died." He looked back at Ruth. "You weren't supposed to sneak out. I thought you would stay in your bedroom. The captain spotted you in the casino. He panicked and locked you in."

"But I escaped via the air duct and rushed back to you," Ruth said, piecing it together. The pair must have been communicating with one another the whole time. *Through the tablet computer?* "There was a laundry cart in the casino. He was there to clean up? Remove evidence?"

Sabian stared at her with cold eyes.

Ruth's stomach tightened as she pictured the final set of Scrabble tiles in front of her own mannequin: *B, D, B, S, T, E.* Rearranging the letters and adding another letter *A* from the board gave her the word: *STABBED.*

Stabbed like my husband, John?

Did *Jeremy or the captain plan to carry out that last murder? Or did they expect me to inflict that final act on myself in a fit of grief and remorse for killing Colonel Tom?*

Ruth shuddered at the idea.

"I've heard enough." Colonel Tom waved Sabian back a couple of steps. "Turn around," he said, and motioned Ruth to the tool bag.

She removed a thick cable tie, and as she bound Sabian's wrists, she whispered, "I really am sorry. It didn't have to come to this."

They led Sabian through the ship and into the manager's office. There were two vents, but only a few inches high each. No way anyone would crawl through those.

Ruth patted Sabian's pockets, pulled out a gold key card, and then they locked him in the room.

Colonel Tom eyed the door. "Are you positive he's secure in there?"

"He's not going anywhere," Ruth said as relief washed over her.

"In that case," Colonel Tom said, tucking the gun in his belt and checking his watch, "how about a spot of lunch?"

The colonel rustled up an egg and bacon sandwich with fries and a side salad, and then several hours after that, Ruth made them an extra spicy curry for dinner.

By the time eight o'clock in the evening finally came around, they sat in deck chairs on the promenade, blankets over their legs, sipping brandy, trying to stay awake.

It had been the longest three days of Ruth's life.

Despite the cold, it was nice to be outside in the fresh air, rather than the confined ship.

Ruth had also insisted the colonel check up on Captain Pipe several times, which he had begrudgingly done. However, the captain's expletive-laden rants had proven he was far from freezing to death.

Merlin sat curled up on Ruth's lap, and he seemed to appreciate being out in the open too.

"I thought your grandson would have realised something was up a couple of hours ago," Colonel Tom said.

"He probably did." Ruth massaged Merlin's ears. "But allowing an hour past six for him to worry, plus another hour to call for help and travel here, means he should be here soon. He knows what direction we headed but not how far we travelled." Ruth hazarded a guess at northwest from Bonmouth, but directions and maps were Greg's domain. With his uncanny way-finding senses on hand, one rarely needed a sat nav. She offered the colonel a smile. "They'll find us."

"Where are you planning to go next?" he asked.

"Ivywick Island, off the coast of Scotland." Ruth took another sip of brandy. "And it'll be as far from an exciting adventure as I can manage." Although, given the link to Ruth and John's past, she doubted that. But at least she'd finally get to solve a decades' old mystery.

The colonel nodded. "I would love to travel the country. I can work remotely, so perhaps we could team up some day?" He gave her a wry smile. "Besides, I think you've enjoyed it here." Colonel Tom raised a hand before Ruth could respond. "Not the murders, obviously, but the mystery, and the hunt. You seemed energised."

Ruth thought about that. One thing she'd learned over the past few days was that she still had a lot of anger and other emotions she'd thought she'd moved past.

The recent events had taught her that up until now she had avoided anything to do with investigating or the police force in general because of John's death. His murder had obviously been an absolute tragedy, a traumatic time that still weighed heavily on Ruth, but it shouldn't have stopped her from missing her time spent training to become a detective.

From now on, Ruth would be less inclined to run in the opposite direction if a mystery presented itself. After all, the detection and prevention of crime had been her first love.

Ruth snapped out of her thoughts and smiled at the colonel. "Thank you."

"For what?"

"For sticking with me, despite me screwing up on more than one occasion and almost killing you."

"Oh, that?" He gave a dismissive flick of his wrist. "Water under the bridge, madam."

Ruth chuckled.

Colonel Tom leaned over, gave her a tender kiss on the cheek, and then raised his glass. "Here's to more grand adventures."

"I bloody hope not," Ruth muttered.

The faint rumble of an engine drew their attention.

Ruth lifted Merlin from her lap, stood with the colonel, and they both rested on the railing as a police boat sped toward the ship.

"I'd better open the side door for them." Colonel Tom squeezed Ruth's arm and strode off.

As the police boat drew alongside, Ruth squinted down at it and made out a gangly teenager hunched over the gunnel, throwing up.

Despite herself, not to mention the exhaustion, Ruth grinned.

22

Three days later, back in the safety of Bonmouth harbour, Ruth stood outside her motorhome with her hands wrapped around a giant mug of tea. As if sensing Ruth's return to land, the sky had turned overcast, and drizzle hung in the air.

She reflected on the past week, and guilt still gnawed at her insides. If she'd not been so reluctant to investigate, to look more closely at Captain Pipe's murder, or at the very least Gabriella's, then no one else might have died.

Obviously, that in and of itself was a little egotistical of her, to assume she would have figured it out sooner, but at least Ruth could have given it a damn good try.

The door to the brown brick building opened, and the colonel strode out. He caught Ruth's eye and quick-marched over to her.

She beamed as he approached. "The police have finished with your interview?"

"I thought I was done with debriefings years ago." He cracked a smile back at her. "They still haven't found the captain's accomplice, though." The colonel's eyes darkened.

Ruth nodded. Despite her previous confidence, Sabian had somehow escaped his makeshift prison in the ship manager's office, and the police had spent the last few days searching the ship. "They'll find him eventually." She glanced at the sleek motorboat at the end of the pontoon.

"Don't you think he would have had another escape plan?" the colonel asked. "I mean, the lifeboat seems a bit last-minute and clumsy."

"Yeah," Ruth said in a low voice. "That's been bothering me too."

"At least the police have the murderer in custody," Colonel Tom said. "They'll catch up to the mastermind eventually."

Greg stepped from the motorhome and shot the colonel a suspicious look.

Colonel Tom cleared his throat and held out a hand to Ruth.

She shook it. "It was nice meeting you."

"Likewise, madam. May our paths never cross again." He winked at her when Greg wasn't looking.

Ruth chuckled.

As the colonel strode away, Greg hurried over to his grandmother. "Mum called for the billionth time."

Ruth winced. She'd have to face Sara at some point, but her daughter had a habit of overreacting, and Ruth hadn't decided how to break it to her about all the murders. Mind you, Greg had been nowhere near them, which she was glad about.

"Grandma." He held up his phone. "I found all the original source photographs they used to composite that one of Grandad and Colonel Tom in the back garden. Mainly from Mum's social media. I've sent the links to the police."

"Great. Thank you."

"That's not all." Greg flipped to an image. "Recognise this man?"

She squinted at the display. "Oh, sure. He was in that painting of Bonmouth." Ruth couldn't forget his dark brown eyes and black hair.

"His name was Ben Owen," Greg said. "Died in a car crash a few years ago." He flipped to a new picture on his phone. This one showed Ben Owen joined by another man.

"Captain Pipe," Ruth said.

Although decades younger and less dishevelled, it was unmistakably him.

"Ben's father," Greg said. "Ben was set to inherit the hotel."

Ruth sighed. "Tragic." She had originally joined the force to arrest bad people, but never wished them ill, only rehabilitation, and certainly not the death of either them or their loved ones.

Greg pocketed the phone. "Now Ben's son will inherit everything."

"Captain Pipe has a grandson?" Ruth said. "Who?" And then the penny dropped. "Steven? The deckhand?"

"Yeah. Steven." Greg looked away. "Guess the captain can rest assured the hotel will go to him."

Merlin appeared at the door to the motorhome and let out a raspy meow.

Ruth placed a hand on Greg's shoulder. "What say we get out of here and find you one of those MacDoogle's you're so fond of?"

Greg rolled his eyes as he followed her on board. "Okay, but I'm having double of everything." He dropped onto the sofa bench, and Merlin leapt onto his lap.

As Ruth went to climb into the driver's seat, Greg said, "Oh, Grandma?"

She turned back.

Greg hesitated. "Erm. Just in case this comes out at some point, I went to a nightclub with Steven."

Ruth braced herself. "Go on."

"Well . . ." Greg's cheeks flushed. "I might have thrown up after." He waved a hand at the bathroom. "I think I cleaned it all. I'm just saying, you know, in case—"

"What is it with you and throwing up?" Ruth asked with a smirk. "If you ate healthy food once in a while, maybe your body wouldn't feel the need to keep rejecting it."

"It's not that," Greg said. "Steven made me drink fast. I downed a few pints and several shots in a couple of hours. I passed out right after I was sick."

That would explain why he didn't hear any of the crew coming ashore that night.

"Steven wanted to get back to the village by three," Greg continued. "He was really urgent about it."

Ruth stared at Greg, and then her jaw dropped. "Of course. Captain Pipe's grandson."

Steven had taken the motor yacht out to the ship and had been waiting below for him. When the captain fell into the water, Steven hauled him on board.

Ruth slapped her forehead. "They had another accomplice. That's how he got back onto the *Ocean Odyssey*." She ruffled her grandson's hair. "You're a good boy," she said, and raced from the motorhome.

Ruth hurried over to the brick building, went inside, and found the officer in charge—Detective Inspector Jane Worthing—seated at a desk near the door.

DI Worthing looked up, and Ruth caught a flicker of annoyance. "What can I do for you, Mrs Morgan?"

"Steven." Ruth pointed outside at the sleek motorboat. "The deckhand."

"What about him?" DI Worthing said in a bored voice.

"He's in on it," Ruth said. "He went to the *Ocean Odyssey* that night Marcus Sabian pushed the captain overboard. Steven waited below. He pulled him on board."

DI Worthing stared at her. "Your evidence?"

"You need to question the captain again," Ruth said. "And now Steven. My bet is he snuck out in the last couple of days and brought Marcus Sabian back ashore." Before DI Worthing could answer, Ruth wheeled around and marched from the building. "Now it's up to you," she muttered, vowing never to return to this seaside village again.

Ruth climbed back on board the motorhome and rubbed her hands together. "Right, Greg, I think that'll do. What do you say to us getting out of here? After all, we have a two-hundred-mile drive to Scotland."

He groaned and slumped forward in his seat, already turning an alarming shade of green.

Book 2 in the Ruth Morgan series - Murder at Vanmoor Village - is coming October 9th 2023.

Visit peterjayblack.com and join the free VIP list to be notified of future releases in the series.

*Also grab a **FREE** copy of*
DEATH IN BROOKLYN
A Short Story set in the Fast-Paced
Emma & Nightshade Crime Thriller Series

IMPORTANT
Please remember to check your spam folder for any emails. You must confirm your sign-up before being added to the email list.

PETER JAY BLACK
BIBLIOGRAPHY

DEATH IN LONDON
Book One in a Fast-Paced Crime Thriller Series
https://mybook.to/DeathinLondonKindle

Emma leads a quiet life, away from her divorced parents' business interests, but when her father's fiancée turns up dead in her mother's warehouse, she can't ignore the threat of a civil war.

Unable to call the police, Emma's parents ask her to assist an eccentric private detective with the investigation. She reluctantly agrees, on the condition that when she's done they allow her to have her own life in America, away from the turmoil.

The amateur sleuths investigate the murder, and piece together a series of cryptic clues left by the killer, who seems to know the families intimately, but a mistake leads to the slaying of another close relative.

Now dragged into a world she's fought hard to avoid, Emma must do everything she can to help catch the culprit and restore peace. However, with time running out, could her parents be the next victims?

"Pick up Death in London today and start book one in a gripping Crime Thriller Mystery series."

***

DEATH IN MANHATTAN

Book One in a Fast-Paced Crime Thriller Series

https://mybook.to/DeathinManhattanKindle

When someone murders New York's leading crime boss, despite him being surrounded by advanced security, the event throws the underworld into chaos. Before anyone can figure out how the killer did it, he dies under mysterious circumstances and takes his secret to the grave.

Emma's uncle asks her to check out the crime scene, but she's reluctant to get involved, especially after the traumatic events back in London. However, with Nightshade's unique brand of encouragement, they figure out how the killer reached one of the most protected men in the world. Their lives are then complicated further when another member of the Syndicate is murdered, seemingly by the hands of the same deceased perpetrator.

Emma and Nightshade now find themselves in way over their heads, caught up in a race against time, trying to solve clues and expose a web of deception, but will they be quick enough to stop a war?

URBAN OUTLAWS
A High-Octane Middle Grade Action Series
mybook.to/UrbanOutlaws

In a bunker hidden deep beneath London live five extraordinary kids: meet world-famous hacker Jack, gadget geek Charlie, free runner Slink, comms chief Obi, and decoy diva Wren. They're not just friends; they're URBAN OUTLAWS. They outsmart London's crime gangs and hand out their dirty money through Random Acts of Kindness (R.A.K.s).

Others in the series:
URBAN OUTLAWS: BLACKOUT
mybook.to/UOBlackout

Power is out. Security is down. Computers hacked. The world's most destructive computer virus is out of control and the pressure is on for the Urban Outlaws to destroy it. Jack knows that it's not just the world's secrets that could end up in the wrong hands. The secret location of their bunker is at the fingertips of many and the identities of the Urban Outlaws are up for grabs. But capturing the virus feels like an almost impossible mission until they meet Hector. The Urban Outlaws know they need his help, but they have made some dangerous enemies. They could take a risk and win – or lose everything ...

URBAN OUTLAWS: LOCKDOWN
mybook.to/UOLockdown

he Urban Outlaws have been betrayed – and defeated. Or so Hector thought when he stole the world's most advanced computer virus. But Hector will need to try much harder than just crossing the Atlantic if he wants to outsmart Jack and his team ...

URBAN OUTLAWS: COUNTERSTRIKE
mybook.to/UOCounterstrike

The Urban Outlaws face their biggest challenge yet. They have to break into the Facility and find the ultimate weapon – Medusa – before Hector does. But there are five levels of security to crack and a mystery room that has Jack sweating whenever he thinks about it.

URBAN OUTLAWS: SHOCKWAVE
mybook.to/UOShockwave

The Urban Outlaws have been infected! Hector Del Sarto used them to spread the deadly Medusa virus and now the whole of London is in lockdown. Only Hector and his father have the antidote. Can Jack, Charlie, Obi, Slink and Wren work together to bring down the Del Sartos once and for all? The whole city depends on them!

Made in United States
Orlando, FL
06 October 2023

37637707R00152